A PRAYER FOR JUNIE

Fran Clark

ISBN: 978-0-9933381-4-4

A Prayer For Junie
Island Secrets Series Book 2

Also in the series:
Holding Paradise Bk 1
The Long Way Home Bk 3
When Skies Are Grey Bk 4

Also by Fran Clark
Lovers
The Hope Series

Before, during …

I knew everything about the murder. Not only was I a witness, I was complicit. But I kept the truth to myself. The whole truth, that is. Not the things they said afterwards. God knows they talked about it for years to come. The gossipers in the village lived for that kind of scandal, that kind of excitement, because before Junie came, there hadn't been much else to talk about. Her life up on that plain, with that man. Yes, she was news all right.

What was even more painful was that I knew something like this would happen; I'd said it from the beginning. And I could have prevented it. If only I had been more persuasive. Stronger. I shouldn't have given up on Junie. I saw the blood on her clothes and tried to cover up my involvement. It was easy for me, I suppose, because I had somewhere to escape to. I could run away from everything I knew. So, I left all of this behind, the gossip, the accusations and the stories.

Maybe they were all complicit, the villagers. They knew something was wrong. Their faces, brown, hot and shiny in the morning sun. With eyebrows raised and mouths ever open, telling tales and laughing loudly. They could spread their lies and talk their nonsense all day if there wasn't work to be done. Not one of them shed a single tear for her. But they never spoke about her to me. They knew better than to come to me with stories about Junie Williams. Junie was my friend. Once.

1

Moments before the boy and his sick mother arrived, the light changed. Clouds drifted into the clear, topaz sky and dimmed the light that filtered through the tall trees surrounding the flat plain where the two houses were built. Philomena had to tilt her book towards the window to see the tiny black letters on the yellowing pages. From the window seat, she looked up and then across the plain. Opposite the two wooden houses and across a narrow road was a large patch of wild grass, flowers and tall trees. She noticed for the first time since becoming enthralled by the adventures coming to life in her own living room that not only was it peaceful inside the house but that the branches were still and even the birds had stopped singing. It hadn't occurred to Philomena's ten-year-old mind, so caught up in sunken ships and pirates' treasure, that anything had changed in her small corner of bliss or that anything could be wrong. She turned her attention to the page, scanning the paragraphs for her place but shifted her focus back to the window when she heard the creak of wheels and a low grunt from an animal coming up the road.

She couldn't see them at first, she only heard the sound they made as a horse and cart rolled up the hill from the village. A boy of about her age came into view from around the bend in the road. His clothes were small on him, khaki shorts and a matching shirt with rolled-up sleeves. His skin was so much fairer than hers, the colour of straw. His hair, a shade darker than his skin, was thick and tightly curled. A wild mane that made his face look pathetic and small. Philomena had never seen anyone like him. He was carrying a swaying stick that he used, ineffectually, to beat the bushes that over-hung the side of the road. Behind him, driven by a woman who looked far older than her own mother, came a laden cart pulled by a grunting horse. The wheels creaked with each revolution, and the horse, perspiring, made slow progress to-wards Philomena's house.

The old woman's cough rattled in her lungs, and she loos-ened her grip on the rein to rub her chest. The boy stopped outside the house next door to Philomena's. The woman halted the horse, but before she could climb down, she coughed again and shook her head. The boy grimaced at the sound she made and did nothing to help her down. *Is that his mother?* Philomena wondered. She would have left the house to greet them, but her mother had given her strict in-structions to stay inside. If she wasn't well enough to visit her aunt that morning, then she shouldn't go out to play.

The arrival of these new people was a surprise. The house had sat vacant for almost two years. Weeds grew so close to the door and up to the window, Philomena worried that the house would turn into a tree and grow too high for anyone to get in. She was glad that someone would be living there at last. She closed her book and stood up from the window seat. She didn't notice that the dark shadow cast by the clouds just moments before the newcomers arrived had passed. She forgot about her book, the story and that she had actually been reading. The book remained on the seat, her place in it lost. All she felt was excitement at the prospect of having new friends, of people occupying the quiet hilltop other than just her mother and her older brother, Pearson. All they ever did was boss her around, anyway.

On that first day, she wouldn't have known that the new occupants would bring with them a sorrow she had never experienced, lies she would later learn to weave for herself, unimaginable suffering and the death of two people.

Philomena watched for several impatient minutes as the woman and boy looked around the house. They pushed and pulled at the door, eventually settling on shaking the shutters on the window to try to let themselves in. She wished she knew how to help, and she looked eagerly at the bend in the road, hoping to see her tall teenage brother strolling up the hill carrying mother's large basket for her. They would know what to do, they could help her new friends. The sick woman returned to the front door and yanked at the door handle. She pulled and pushed, but the door would not give. She shrugged her shoulders and tried again. Then she began to cough. She coughed loudly and uncontrollably, and her shoulders slumped further down each time her chest tightened. She leaned against the wall of the house with its flaking paintwork and rubbed her chest. The boy began to cry.

'Shh.' His mother tried to soothe him, hand on her throat as though it hurt to speak. 'We'll just rest and think of something.' She looked across at Philomena's house. The girl caught her breath and took a swift step back. Thankfully, they returned, Pearson and her mother. Philomena saw Pearson step into the neighbours' front gate and ran out of the house to catch him up, but her mother grabbed her hand before she could enter next door's front yard.

'Patience,' her mother whispered.

They had been making introductions. The boy's name was Gregory, and his mother was Mrs Evangeline Williams. Philomena waved, unnoticed. Gregory hid behind his mother, peeking from around her stooped frame with his hands in front of his face, regarding Philomena's family through the gaps of his fingers.

'If you can help me, I will be very grateful.' Mrs Williams had managed to stop coughing, but her chest rattled and wheezed, and Philomena saw it rise and fall as she spoke.

Pearson walked to the front door and slid his hand along the side edges. He stepped back, looked up at the door, turned and slammed his back into it so that the door juddered. He did the same again a few times, then added the heel of his boot until the door moved inwards by a fraction of an inch before jamming. Pearson turned sideways on and shoved the door with his shoulder. It opened wide into the living room. With a very proud expression on her face, Philomena looked at Gregory who stood with his mouth open in disbelief. Mrs Williams' face broke into a broad smile. Creases formed under her eyes and around her mouth, her teeth large and white.

'You good, boy!' she exclaimed. 'Thank you so much. I am blessed to have such good neighbours.'

'If you ever need anything,' Philomena's mother called, 'you only have to ask.'

'Thank you Mrs Scott. You are very kind.'

There was a stark contrast between the two houses. While the Williams house was weather beaten and in need of repair, the Scott house had been freshly painted. Light blue walls and fresh white on the window frames. A spindly oleander shrub separated their land, pink blossoms dotted among the thin dark leathery leaves, swaying this way and that.

'Maybe Pearson can help you unload?' Mrs Scott said, now with her arms around Philomena, pinning her to her stomach. Philomena itched to break away. She had so much to tell her new neighbours. About their new chickens. About how the sound of the wind blowing through the trees on the opposite side of the road is like someone sighing. And how she sometimes plays in the wild grass and kicks a ball with Pearson and that he lets her win all the races. She was aching to ask Gregory to play with her, at least a race would be fairer against someone smaller than her.

'Oh my goodness, thank you,' Mrs Williams replied. 'I don't know how I would have managed.' She ushered Gregory out from behind her. 'Go and help.'

Reluctantly, Gregory shuffled towards Pearson. He stood by the cart, watching Pearson unload a small table, two chairs and, eventually, a stack of ancient furniture that looked fit to chop up for fire wood.

Her mother walked Philomena back to the house.

'Can I stay and help?' Philomena looked eagerly up at her mother.

'You told me you were not feeling well. If you feeling better, then come and help me prepare lunch. Those two don't look as though they have eaten in days.'

Philomena kept looking out of the kitchen window as they began making a vegetable soup, wishing she was older, stronger, a boy perhaps. She wondered if Gregory was quiet because he was hungry. She looked forward to when they could walk to school together.

2

It was another six months before Gregory joined Philomena's school. She had already turned eleven, the school year was almost over and she was dreading the two months of summer when she was not permitted to be in the one place she most enjoyed. In the corner where the teacher kept the Readers and the books for the older children she could lose herself in new and different worlds from her own. She loved the stories and read several books twice over, devouring each page, captivated by journeys back in time, countries she would love to visit. Even the ones that did not exist. Lost in a book, she did not have to worry that someone would call on her to carry out a chore: clean out the chicken coop, carry laundry to the river, fetch water for a bath. She was happy to do chores for her sickly neighbour, though. Mrs Williams' cough seemed to be getting worse. The horse and cart she'd arrived in hadn't belonged to her. She had borrowed it from a cousin who came a day after they'd moved and rode it away. He hadn't stayed long, this cousin, and from what Philomena could see, Mrs Williams had no other visitors. Apart from the doctor's visits, but they rarely made house calls. Gregory had to fetch her medicine if Gregory could ever be found. How that woman called her son, and how with every syllable a rattling splutter caught his name in her throat until all she could do was cough again. Her mother had only to look at Philomena for her to know that Philomena must pop over to her neighbour to see if she could help in any way. Mrs Williams accepted the kindness fondly. She never let Philomena leave the house without blessing her and wishing she didn't have to rely on her so much. Philomena often wondered why Gregory would leave his mother alone so often and why on earth he didn't come to school.

On his first day, he wore an old blue shirt with long sleeves. It had been Pearson's. The sleeves were too long, and he wore them rolled to three-quarter length, his freckled arms dangling aimlessly at his sides. His shorts were his own. The too small khaki ones he always wore. He had grown at least an inch taller than Philomena. The extra inch seeming to be in his legs. They had grown longer but hadn't filled out. His whole outfit just made his arms and legs appear twice as thin as they actually were. Philomena was already composing a story in her mind about a boy who was part spider while Gregory stood at the front of the classroom, his eyes not particularly focused but his face moving around the room as though his only sense was that of smell.

'This is our new student,' the teacher said and landed a palm on Gregory's shoulder. Gregory staggered forward, and the class erupted into fits of laughter.

'You're too skinny.'

'Hold yourself up, boy.'

'His skin is too pale, maybe he's a ghost or something.'

Philomena scowled at the other children, even at Pearson who sat at the back with the older students. He of all people should know that we should show more grace than that. She stood up at her desk.

'Teacher Walcott, the new boy can sit here.' She pointed at the empty space to her left.

'Hurry up,' the teacher said, and Gregory shuffled his way to the vacant desk. By morning recess Gregory had gone.

Fled to heaven knows where, and Philomena worried so much about his disappearance, it brought on a headache. No one mentioned the missing boy, not even Teacher Walcott who read from the thick Charles Dickens book until the bell sounded for the end of the school day.

And so, Gregory's erratic attendance at school continued for several years. Apart from Philomena, no one tried to befriend Gregory. His fair skin and light brown hair were a source of constant amusement. The children stared at him, inspected his hair by roughly pulling it and asking him what he thought he looked like.

'Is your daddy white?' A few of the children had asked him. 'Are you half-caste?'

'I don't know my daddy.' Gregory very rarely answered or spoke back to the children with their taunts and questions. Usually he scampered away, the older boys kicking out at him to hurry him out of their sight. He had muttered under his breath about not knowing his daddy, a glassy look in his eyes as he ran away and hid by a large tree in the corner of the yard. Philomena knew he would be behind that tree, wiping tears from his face. She felt sorry for Gregory. Everyone should know their daddy, even if he didn't live with them, like Philomena's father. Gregory had left the school grounds early that day.

Philomena would knock on the Williams' front door each morning to ask if Gregory wanted to walk with her and Pearson. He would often decline or reluctantly leave with them and linger several paces behind. Pearson wouldn't allow his sister to call on Gregory after a while. 'He's making us late,' Pearson would complain. 'Just leave him.'

In the end, that's what everyone did. Left Gregory to his own devices. Even the teacher who had run out of patience when Gregory refused to read aloud, refused to say prayers before lunch, refused to play fair and never once produced a piece of homework. Philomena could see that Gregory was being taunted and bullied at school, but eventually, when the teasing had lost its flavour and the students found better things to do, some of them wanted to include Gregory in their games and conversations. Gregory, who had never once tried to ingratiate himself with any of them, turned his back on their offers. In the end, he became short with anyone who even looked at him and began making up obscene names to taunt some of the smaller children with. He had a way of causing a child physical pain without a soul catching him in the act. But there a crying child would stand rubbing his arm, leg or jaw saying it was Gregory but there not being a single witness to the act.

Once, Philomena cornered him and asked if he had permission to come and go from school because his mother was so unwell.

'Mind your business,' he'd said curtly and walked away. They were teenagers by then. Philomena had endlessly tried to help Gregory to adjust to school, bringing over her books when her mother sent her to take food parcels and Mrs Williams' fresh bed linen. He had never been interested in the homework assignments; the reign of King Henry VIII left him unmoved, he had no time for the Brontë sisters and what did he care about the planets, there isn't a heaven up there and there's nothing else but sky.

Philomena wasn't convinced by his rebuffs, she couldn't believe that Gregory could be so disengaged, so uninterested in science, religion, literature. So she planned to find out what it was that held Gregory's attention and kept him away from school and his own house for hours at a time. She followed him one late afternoon to the river. The overgrown lane leading to the river was rich with dark scrubs and bushes. The roots of old trees spiralled beneath the black earth and tripped her up because she was looking at Gregory's retreating shirt rather than where she was going. At the point where the forest became more dense, Gregory froze. Philomena took in a sharp breath and instinctively hid behind a tree. She held her breath for several seconds until she heard Gregory start up again, noisily hitting at the tall grass with his hand and releasing a breathy, tuneless whistle. Philomena's back, pressed tight against the tree, was prickling with perspiration. She thought about going back home, abandoning the idea of spying on Gregory, but her curious mind got the better of her. She peeled away from the gnarled bark and continued on, not knowing if she was going the right way. The whistling had stopped and so had Gregory's noisy bustle through the wood. It was not long before sunset, and the sky would blacken suddenly. She had no torch and neither had Gregory, as far as she remembered. He had come so deep into the wood, where no one ever came. Philomena wondered if he must know by heart how to navigate his way back. She wasn't sure she could, so maybe this was all a stupid mistake.

Just as she was about to give up on her mission, she heard a noise, not too far from where she stood. She followed the sound, like an animal that had been trapped or was hurt. What if it was wild? Would she know what to do? She looked desperately in all directions. She was alone with whatever was howling and Gregory, out there, somewhere, possibly watching her. It came again, that sound, weak, as though the animal was in pain. The thunder in her chest drove her onwards, stooping low in the grass, quietly, slowly trying to track the wounded animal. Then she stopped, fell to her knees and positioned herself behind a large fallen tree. She saw Gregory lift a cutlass and bring it down hard on the animal he held to the ground by the throat. A goat, the top of its head cracked open and bloody. He hacked off its remaining paw and then slit its abdomen, stepping back to watch the creature struggle into death before it lay still. Philomena realised she had not been breathing and gasped as if she'd been held under water.

Gregory's head whipped round, and Philomena ducked down, motionless, holding her breath intentionally this time. Darkness crept through the wood. Philomena lay on her side until it was numb. Tears rolled from her eyes, across her face and down onto the grass pricking her cheek. She wasn't sure how she found her way home, and when her mother questioned her about her lateness to dinner, the state of her skirt, she lied and said she was reading by the river and fell asleep.

'And you left your book behind?'

'Oh, I must have done.' Philomena looked at her empty hands, dirty from the earth.

On graduation day, no one even asked after Gregory as all the students stood in their gowns. Philomena accepted her certificate with pride. It had been the happiest day of her life. She never spoke to Gregory about school again, where he went, why he left early on the days he did attend. She tried to ignore and avoid him as far as possible. She knew that if she didn't, she might just reveal her discomfort around him, her disgust and the growing feeling of hate she had for him. She was sure to give herself away, and he'd know she followed him, he'd know she'd discovered his secret. There was no telling what he might do to her if he ever found out she'd seen him. As it was, whenever she went to read to Mrs Williams, who was by then housebound, Philomena would find Gregory staring at her, as though he had some plan for her in mind. Pearson had long since left school and had left home. Without him she felt vulnerable. It took a very long time before Philomena managed to bury the memory of what happened in the wood that evening deep enough so that she no longer stifled the urge to cry out or throw up. She never told a single soul what she'd seen.

3

The wind was fast. The palm trees swayed, each narrow trunk bending in a southerly direction. Philomena pulled her shawl tighter around her shoulders as she staggered uphill towards home. Close to her house, even above the ferocious rushing wind, she heard her friend, Mrs Williams, coughing. She glanced at the battened-down shutters on her own house. It was safe in there, warm, protected from the lashing strips of rain that ran down her face and soaked her clothes. But she'd heard Mrs Williams cough like that before, and she knew that she was alone in the house.

The gate had already blown open, so she walked cautiously through the fallen twigs and branches up to the front door. She knocked, but there was no reply. Just more coughing.

'It's me, Mrs Williams, you all right?'

As Philomena entered the house, there was the smell of camphor. On the old dresser, cumbersome and left in the house by the previous occupants, were burnt-out candles. Gregory's camp bed in the living room had not been slept in for several days. Mrs Williams was in the bedroom. She was lying in bed wearing a blue checked headscarf, tied with a knot on top of her head. In her hand was a pure white cotton handkerchief—the same colour as her nightdress. The knitted shawl she'd been wearing had slipped off and lay strewn across her pillow. The quilted bedspreads were dishevelled and barely covered her.

'Oh, Mrs Williams. You must be cold?'

Mrs Williams nodded, her coughing eventually subsiding. 'Phil. You come? Oh, dear—God will bless you.'

Philomena proceeded to rearrange Mrs Williams' shawl and straighten out the quilts so that they rested neatly on top of her. 'What can I get you?' Philomena asked.

'Nothing, I don't need nothing.' She held Philomena's hand as the young woman knelt by the side of the bed. 'Sit, sit.' Mrs Williams patted the covers.

'No. My clothes are wet.' Philomena had been drenched by the rain. The wind had blown off her hat, and she hadn't bothered to chase after it. Her skirt and blouse clung to her body, her shawl she'd left by the bedroom door.

'Philomena?'

'Yes, ma'am.'

'Pray with me.'

The two women closed their eyes. As they began to recite the Hail Mary, Philomena wondered if her mother might be worrying about her. The storm had been a lot stronger than anyone had anticipated, but she knew she could not leave this woman now. Before they'd said more than two lines of the prayer, the wind picked up again, howled around the house and the sound of something toppling in the front yard stopped them both.

'Your mother know you here?' Mrs Williams said this as though she'd read Philomena's mind.

'No, ma'am.'

'You go. Go home. When the storm pass, come and say your "good nights" to me.'

'No, I should stay with you. You're weak, Mrs Williams.'

'I tired of telling you, Philomena, you are a big woman now, a teacher, call me Evangeline. I know. You too respect-ful to call me by my first name. I only wish that son of mine was like you.' Mrs Williams closed her eyes again and looked as though she were in pain. But this was the expression she always held whenever she thought of or talked about Gregory.

'I'll come back,' Philomena whispered. 'As soon as I tell Mum I'm here.'

'You get dry before you catch cold. Get something to eat and come later. But not before the storm pass. You hear me?'

'Yes, Mrs Williams.'

Philomena gathered up her soaked shawl, turned back to look at her sick friend and waved a feeble hand. Mrs Williams smiled. A full, wide smile. Philomena always wondered how she managed them.

Back in her own yard, the kitchen and toilet outhouses were bolted shut, yet their foundations looked barely lodged into the ground as though they could fly away in the wind and rain. She opened the front door to see her mother sitting huddled at the dining table, drinking a cup of bush tea. She leapt up when she saw Philomena and hugged her.

'I couldn't eat until I knew you were safe. You're so late back from work. Go and take out the wet clothes you have on you. Quick before you catch cold in your chest.'

During dinner, Philomena chewed slowly as if she were being forced, wondering if Mrs Williams had eaten. She supposed not and kept some food back, praying for the storm to pass quickly so that she could go back to her.

It was completely dark outside when the storm passed. Philomena left the house and turned on her torch. The ground was sodden and squelched underfoot. She did not bother to knock on Mrs Williams' door but went straight in. Thankfully, it would seem that her friend's coughing fit had stopped for the time being.

Philomena tapped the bedroom door and went in with the plate of food she'd brought from home and placed it on the side table. Mrs Williams appeared to be sleeping. Her head was turned to one side, and her lips were parted slightly. Philomena saw that the hanky she'd been holding lay on the floor beside the bed and was spotted with blood. She bent down over Mrs Williams, who lay very still. Philomena placed a trembling hand near her nostrils. No breath. She put her head on her chest. The chest that normally rattled so loudly when she breathed was silent.

On her knees now, Philomena put her head next to her neighbour's and closed her eyes, too. With one arm loosely draped over Mrs Williams' body, she continued to recite the Hail Mary left unfinished from earlier on. Philomena whispered the name, 'Evangeline', the tears falling from her eyes. She stayed like this a long time. She would have to call the doctor, find Gregory, tell him what happened. She had no idea where he might be.

4

It was the stormy season when Mrs Williams died. The night of her death had been the worst of all of them. Dark sky, rain like sheets of water falling directly down onto the rich soil, drenching it, running down roads, into gullies, making the rivers rise and flow onto the rocks of the river banks. And then, as if someone had waved a magic wand, a bright blue sky appeared, the wind died down and the island steamed with heat. Then another torrent would come and then the next.

The doctor had little to say about Mrs Williams' death and had been just as vague about how to treat her illness in life. Mrs Scott had offered her different types of bush tea, but none had any real effect. What she had needed was sound medical help. Help she could only have received if she'd had money and could travel abroad. America or somewhere in Europe.

The sad truth was that she had expected her son might help her. He made half promises but had taken what little money she had saved to go to Martinique and stayed there for six months. Each month, his mother grew weaker so that she was unable to look after herself and relied on the kindness of her neighbours. When Gregory returned, it was with a new suit and nothing else to show for his time away, and still he watched as his mother's health declined.

Philomena waited a long time by her neighbours' gate the day after Mrs Williams' death, craning her neck towards the bend in the road, waiting for Gregory, wondering what he'd been doing and where he'd been for almost two days.

'I have news,' she said when he finally arrived, smelling of stale booze, his eyes red from too much drink and not enough sleep. He brushed past Philomena as if she were one of the pecking hens in the yard and went to close the door on her. She pulled at his shirt sleeve.

'Before you go in, you have to know … your mother. She's in there—'

'I know!' Gregory pulled her troublesome hand from his arm.

'They told you she died?'

'What?' Gregory's eyes widened. He turned his gaze back to the open door, faltered for a second but swung away from the darkened interior. He looked wild as though he could run out of the gate, but Philomena blocked him, their bodies colliding.

'You have things to take care of. They can't take the body before you sign a paper. Gregory, you have responsibilities.'

'All I have is the shirt on my back.' His voice was low and gruff. He turned back to the house, slamming the front door behind him.

After his mother's funeral, Gregory went home, locked the windows and drove nails into the door. Philomena looked out when she heard the commotion.

'That man has gone completely mad now. I don't know what he thinks he's doing.'

Gregory shot an angry look in her direction, and she withdrew from the window as quickly as possible. He picked up a heavy looking holdall, grandly slammed the gate and waltzed off down the road. The gate sprang open and swung to and fro for a while, creaking on its hinges.

Philomena crossed her arms, not surprised that he would take off. She wondered if she'd seen the last of him.

Two years had gone by since Gregory locked up the house and walked away without a word. During that time, Philomena's older brother, Pearson, who had left home long ago, married and left the island. Philomena continued working as a teacher and living with her mother in the house.

Next door, the weeds began to grow up high around the house once more. Philomena set off for work at the school in town each weekday morning. She would admire the oleander bush, which had grown taller and more beautiful each year, and would kiss her teeth as she passed the withered mess that Gregory had left behind all that time ago.

One Saturday morning, the sun had not long risen and Philomena sat in her living room, reading a book next to the window. The sprinkling of rain she had not noticed was falling began to dot her shoulders as the breeze picked up. She closed the window and continued to read. Very soon the rain was tapping on the glass, but it was another sound that caught her attention.

There was laughter, shrill, happy laughter, rising above the sound of a horse and cart trundling up the road. She put her book down and looked out of the window. The sun was shining through the rain, and Philomena could see a young girl sitting next to the driver of the cart. The girl looked like a teenager but certainly not older than twenty. She had two thick plaits that lay neatly down on each of her shoulders. On her head she wore a straw bonnet. Her bright smile and cheerful laugh drew Philomena closer to the window until her forehead was touching the glass. This girl was the most beautiful Philomena had ever seen. She was graceful. Her frame was light and delicate, and she sprang down from the cart as it stopped at the Williams house, like a blossom falling from a tree.

Philomena found herself in her own yard. It was still raining as she walked closer to the oleander to get a closer look. The girl turned and smiled at her. Her skin was the colour of honey and her eyes burnt raven black as she waved to Philomena. Philomena lifted her hand but held it there in mid-air. The girl was standing next to Gregory. He was not waving, neither was he smiling. In fact, he pulled this girl by the shoulder and angled her to face his front door. He went to the cart to find some tools. A hammer to pull out the nails and a hoe to hack away some weeds.

Philomena crossed her arms and walked the width of the oleander's branches so that Gregory couldn't see her. The young girl fidgeted like a child who had been told to face the wall, away from the rest of the class. Her head kept twitching towards Philomena, and she giggled with her hand over her mouth. Then, without warning, the girl placed her hand on the top of her bonnet and ran towards the oleander.

'Hello,' she called to Philomena. 'Are we neighbours?'

'Um, yes, sorry. Yes, we are.' Philomena looked over at Gregory. His face told Philomena very little, but the way he bundled and pulled suitcases and odd bric-a-brac from the cart, she could tell he didn't approve of the young girl being so familiar with the next-door neighbour. He worked noisily to dislodge the nails which had rusted. The girl looked over her shoulder at Gregory and then back at Philomena.

'And what should I call you?'

'Me—oh, my name is Philomena.'

'My name is Junie. Junie Williams. I am Gregory's wife.'

'You, you and Gregory? Married?'

'Don't look so surprised. I'm not that ugly.'

'What?' Philomena became flustered, trying to imagine how Gregory could have met and married someone so full of charm and grace as Junie. Her smile covered the whole of her face as she stood being framed by the orange petals. Her dress was shabby, but her petite shape was well poised, dainty, Philomena thought. 'No, of course not. You're far from ugly. How could you say that? It's just … I never imagined Gregory as the marrying kind. I suppose I am surprised that he ever came back here. It's been years since he left.'

'Two.' Gregory appeared at Junie's side and drowned her shoulders within his arm.

'Not so rough,' Junie told him.

'The door is open, we should go in,' he said, pulling Junie to look at him. She nodded, glancing back once around the arm that guided her away.

Philomena nodded at Junie who entered the house first followed by Gregory, who had not bothered to look back. He hadn't said hello or asked after Philomena and her mother, she realised. She crossed her arms, warming the cool breeze that picked up from nowhere as she stared aimlessly after the couple. She tried to imagine how Junie would settle in there with Gregory. Had he bothered to clean the house before he'd left so abruptly, or were the white linens and colourful quilts his mother used to lie in still on her bed since she died? Were there still burnt-out candles on the big dresser in the main room, plates on the dining table? There may have been empty whisky bottles lying around. After Mrs Williams' funeral, she couldn't imagine that Gregory did anything else other than consume alcohol and formulate a plan to leave the house and his life in it behind. She expected he'd sell it, take the proceeds and what money his mother had left and gone for good. That was what she'd hoped, Philomena realised. The last thing she expected of Gregory was to find a wife and come back. Perhaps he needed someone to cook and clean for him. She was sure Gregory had never learnt how. Junie had an island accent, possibly she was from the north. How they could have met, Philomena couldn't imagine. No doubt she'd discover the mystery surrounding this union.

She walked slowly back to her house. Her mother was out on the veranda.

'He got a girl?' Mrs Scott's voice was grave. She was as disbelieving as Philomena about Gregory's ability to find someone willing to marry him. As Philomena climbed the veranda steps, still clinging onto her arms, the night she had tried hard to forget came barrelling back to her mind. The menacing rage she'd witnessed in Gregory in the woods, the hate and anger that must have driven him to behave in that way, crowded her thoughts, and she thought of that innocent girl alone with a man like him.

'Do you think he loves her, Mum? I mean, is it possible when he showed so little love for his mother? I know he hates me, and I didn't do anything to him.'

'Love is a strange thing, Phil. You'll find that out one day.'

'I hope he found it. He married her after all. So maybe he has changed.'

'We'll have to wait and see, but right now, that's his life.' She held a palm up to the Williams property. 'Over there. You leave them to it.'

Philomena nodded and went inside with her mother. She couldn't help feeling a kind of warmth for the girl. Philomena knew she wouldn't just leave them to it. At least, not Junie. She wanted to get to know her.

5

The once-abandoned house next door was transformed. Gregory fixed the windows, and between him and Junie, they added a coat of white paint to the outside walls. It was a fair job, but it was the transformation of the gardens that was the most remarkable. Junie had a way with plants and flowers, and in her hands, the front and back yards made the house look like a home.

The stumpy lime tree that Mrs Williams had planted seemed to grow larger limes in greater quantity than before. Junie cut back the rose bushes that stood on either side of the front gate. They grew out into the road, prickly and wild, their petals littering the ground. Now the bushes grew fuller, sending branches of red roses over the front fence like warm arms to welcome visitors. From her mother's garden, Junie had brought several cuttings of bougainvillea which she planted in the front yard. They flowered in an array of colours. Cerise, hot pink, lilacs and purples, adorning the yard like a patchwork quilt, comforting and inviting.

Along the pathways leading from the gate to the house, and up to both outhouses, the kitchen and the toilet, Junie planted crotons. Their red and gold leaves hung low and bushy. Along the front of the house she'd planted rose pink frangipanis with blushes of bronze in the centre of the propeller-shaped petals. Their essence was strong and fragrant under the windows of the house. By night, if the breeze permitted, their scent floated over to the neighbours' yard and into any open windows.

Each time Philomena saw a new flower or shrub appear, she would smile to herself. She smiled, too, at Junie whenever she saw her. Junie would wave back but never ran over to Philomena as she had on their first meeting over a year ago. Philomena had wanted her to. She remembered Junie's thick plaits, how her hair had been neatly parted and combed and how her dress, as drab as it was, was clean and well pressed. Junie now wore her mass of hair in a messy bundle on top of her head as if she had no time to care for herself because she was devoting it all to the beauty of her garden. That same dress, the floral pattern of the fabric more faded and the collar beginning to fray, was the one she wore most days. It was as if it were a part of her skin, a part of her identity, the girl who was there only to grow flowers, feed the few chickens she'd acquired, sweep and keep the front door closed shut at all times.

One Saturday morning, Philomena saw Gregory leave early with a large bag over his shoulder, leaving Junie on her own. An hour later, Philomena set off to go to the market by the port in the village below. As the place for obtaining news and spreading gossip, the market was as busy as usual. Philomena preferred to rush her way around the stalls and into the grocer's, trying to escape inane chatter about the local scandals. She would often be accosted by people who called, 'Teacher Scott, Teacher Scott, how my child is doing at school?' She would stop long enough to ask that they come to talk to her after class. Ever since Gregory brought home his young bride, more than a few people wanted information about them and in as much detail as she could spare.

They concerned themselves with how little they saw of Junie and how rare it was for Gregory to come down to the village. Someone once asked if they were both still alive up on the plain.

'They are both fine. The house looks lovely, and I believe he is working away from home at the moment.' Philomena picked up her pace and almost ran from the market to avoid any more questions about Junie or to listen to made up stories about the couple. She had heard everything from Gregory got her pregnant and was forced to marry her by her father, to Gregory had been paid to marry her because she was half mad and her mother couldn't control her. Philomena would love to have put the gossipers in their place, but she knew so little about Junie herself, they had barely exchanged two words in all this time.

Philomena returned home to catch Junie in the garden, the front door slightly ajar. Junie was bent over, observing the croton bushes. Through the crack in the door, Philomena saw the old dining table Mrs Williams had brought on the cart the very first day she arrived with Gregory, the boy. She knew it was old and wobbled if it was leant against, and she wondered if Gregory would make it his business to fix up the inside of the house in the way that Junie had made so much of the outside.

Junie stood and waved to Philomena. This time she greeted her with a Hello Neighbour and then asked after her.

'Me?' said Philomena. 'I'm fine thank you. I noticed Gregory leaving with a big bag earlier.'

'Yes,' said Junie. 'He have a job to go to.'

'I see, so, have you been shopping yet? You see I, er, I bought a lot of fish at market, maybe too much for me and Mum. It won't stay fresh. I could spare a few.'

'Really?' Junie hopped up to the gate and stood on her side of it.

Philomena hadn't realised how much weight Junie had lost since moving in. Her dress was looser, and her eyes looked hollow. She hadn't offered the fish for that reason. It was just a friendly gesture that came to her to take advantage of Junie's obvious attempt to make friends. Something her mother would do when Mrs Williams was alive. But this was the new Mrs Williams, and she certainly looked as though she could do with extra food.

'Or I could make broth with it and bring a pot for you and your husband?'

'He won't be back for a few days.' Was that relief Philomena detected in Junie's eyes? 'He's gone to Martinique. He used to work there a lot. He said there is nothing here for him.'

'Well, maybe if he tried to make friends, he might...' Philomena stopped herself, afraid she'd say too much against Gregory. She had a lot to say, to him and about him, especially since seeing the once-vibrant Junie having become so gaunt. Yet, despite her appearance, Junie beamed a full smile and opened the gate.

'Come in. If you really have enough, I'd be happy to accept your kindness.'

Philomena followed Junie to the outside kitchen at the side of the house. It was dark inside the small holding, the shutters were closed, and when Junie opened them, Philomena noticed that there were no fresh food supplies. Plates and cups were turned over and clean. The ceramic pitcher had water in it, and there was a half loaf of bread on the counter, probably days old, with a clear plastic bowl covering it to keep ants from crawling into it.

'You know, I bought so much food,' Philomena said, placing her basket on one of the surfaces. She began to take out some apples and a hand of bananas from which she pulled off three to leave in the fruit bowl. She put a small loaf beside the stale-looking one and separated half the amount of fish she'd bought.

'That's too much, Philomena,' Junie declared, placing her hands on her cheeks. 'I couldn't eat that much if I tried. I think my appetite cut off.'

'Well, that wouldn't wash with my mother. She would force-feed you if you even mentioned such a thing, and then she would go out and fetch some leaves to make you a bush tea.' Philomena exaggerated the island accent and said, 'You must eat, girl. Before food waste, better belly burst.'

The two began to laugh and didn't stop until tears rolled from Junie's eyes and she began to cough from the exertion. A memory of the older Mrs Williams flashed through Philomena's mind. She gathered herself.

'But are you all right, Junie?' She regarded Junie from beneath her brow, the way her own mother would.

'I'm more than all right. I have food. I mean, more than usual. It's been a bit of a struggle, I have to say. So thank you, Philomena. I can eat like a queen tonight.'

Without warning, she threw her arms around Philomena's neck and squeezed. At first, Philomena left her arms at her sides, shocked by the outburst of affection. She hadn't been on the end of an embrace like this in a long time. She'd had cuddles from her mother as a child, but her mother's was the only physical contact she had. At school, as a teacher she might pat a child on the shoulder for work well done and she had received the odd spiky hug from some of the younger children after she'd read them a story. This, coming from Junie, felt like a welcome home from a long lost friend. She put her arms around Junie's waist, feeling the willowy outline of her form and had an overwhelming desire to throw off her cardigan and start cooking for Junie straight away.

'Here,' said Philomena. 'I have some vegetable soup in a tin. It's a whole meal that you don't have to chop, season or make yourself. I'd never seen it in the shop before, it's from America. It tells you how to cook it.' She held the can up towards Junie who glanced at the label briefly and smiled up at Philomena without taking the can.

'I'm not sure.'

'It's very easy. Look, it says, empty contents into the saucepan.' Philomena looked around for one. 'And warm over a medium heat. See?' She offered the can to Junie.

'No, I can't.'

'I insist. Be my guest. I don't think Mum would have liked it, anyway.'

'Philomena, no I can't.'

'The instructions are simple. Here.' She put the can under Junie's nose. Junie pushed it aside and leant back against the counter, crossing her arms.

'Philomena, I can't read those words no matter how easy they are. I can't read.'

Philomena swallowed quickly and placed the can down.

'I see. I'm sorry, Junie, I didn't mean to make you uncomfortable. It's all right. You didn't get the opportunity to learn. You know I'm a teacher, don't you? I could help you.'

Junie's eyes widened. 'But, no,' she said. 'I'm not sure Gregory…'

'Well, Gregory went to school. I'm sure he'd be happy for you to learn.'

'I don't know. I'm not sure he would. He can be a bit…'

'A bit what?'

Junie straightened her posture. 'Well, I would love to learn my letters. If you really don't mind.'

'Of course I don't. It would be a pleasure.'

Junie looked as if she might burst. 'But let's keep it to ourselves. Find a way to do it so he doesn't have to know who teach me.'

'He doesn't like me, does he?'

'Well, he doesn't like anyone.'

Philomena packed up her bag.

'You need to clean this fish, cook it so you can have it at its best. You could eat today and tomorrow on this. Only, make sure you do.' She left the kitchen with Junie following behind. 'And I will teach you to read. Gregory doesn't need to know. It will be useful. For your future.'

'Thank you so much. Teacher. Maybe we can take our washing to the river at the same time. Find a little moment to read.' Junie skipped along the front path behind Philomena. 'Our little secret. Right?'

'Yes. Our little secret.'

'He's gone for the week. Could I learn in a week?'

'We'll do as much as we can. I'll find a good book to start.'

Junie reached to touch Philomena's arm as she closed the gate. 'Thank you, Phil.'

Junie skipped back to the kitchen, humming. Philomena climbed her veranda steps, smiling.

6

Although she hadn't made a habit of it, Philomena sometimes accompanied her mother to church on Sunday morning. This morning, she wondered if Junie might like to come.
Gregory was away for now, and she knew he didn't attend
the sermon. She wondered if he'd told Junie she couldn't, either. But Philomena tapped on her neighbour's door early the
next morning, anyway.

Junie's hair was loose, a mad bush of velvet black framing
her face and brushing her shoulders. Junie yawned as she
tentatively unlocked the front door and opened it enough to
show her face. She smiled at Philomena, rubbing her eyes as
she allowed the door to open a fraction more.

'Is it time to read already?' Junie wore only a thin white
full slip, one that was likely to have looked smooth and
pretty once but the white was closer to cream and the lace at
the bodice was coming away from the rest of the fabric. She
didn't try to cover up or hide her dishevelled state.

'I thought we could go and bathe before church,' Philomena said. Over her arm was a towel, some soap in a pouch
and a smart dress.

Junie looked at the dress and stepped backwards. 'You
know, I stopped praying a while back. I don't know if I still
have faith.'

Philomena didn't know what to say. She felt certain Junie's
decision might have a lot to do with Gregory. She thought

31

she remembered Junie wearing a small cross and chain on the day she met her. Perhaps she'd invented the memory.

'Well then,' said Philomena. 'That's fine. We could bathe, dry off, read for a little while and then eat some breakfast?'

'That would be wonderful.' Junie closed the door while Philomena ran back to her house to find a book. She grabbed the first one she laid her hand on and ran back to Junie's house to find her leaving in her usual dress, an old towel around her shoulders. She was busily trying to catch her wild hair and tie it up in a headscarf.

'My mother says a woman's hair is her beauty,' said Junie. 'If she could see mine now, she would tell me to cut it and start again.'

'It's not so bad,' said Philomena as the two walked in the direction of the river. 'It just needs to be greased and combed.'

'It's so much to manage.'

'I can help you.'

Junie turned to take Philomena's hand, and they ran through the clearing up the hill and down the grassy slope leading to the wood.

It was warm, even for eight in the morning. The trees along the river cloaked the sun, but tiny flecks of yellow light broke through the branches causing a kaleidoscope effect on the river bed. Light glinted off the dark river, the water barely moving. The odd bird cawed overhead, but otherwise it was quiet, peaceful. Close to the large and leafy white-wood tree, the women sat on the grass and leaned against a row of rocks. A little way along was a deep pool in the river and was the place Philomena and her mother washed their clothes by hand. The soft water became soapy easily, and a large boulder was where they laid wet clothes to take in the sun and start the drying process. Philomena realised she'd never seen Junie taking her washing there. She and Gregory probably had little to their name in terms of housewares. Philomena wondered if it would be too forward of her to offer to help in some small way, buy them a few things they might need. She dismissed the thought knowing Gregory was bound to refuse.

'So calm, so heavenly,' Junie said with a smile. She sat up. 'Should we go in?' Before Philomena had a chance to respond, Junie was pulling off her dress. Naked, she ran to the water and tentatively touched her toes into it. She waded deeper, her ankles disappearing, her knees, thighs. When she was in the middle of the river, Junie sank below the tame ripples and remained submerged for several seconds. When she jumped upwards, swallowing a gasp of air, her headscarf had gone, her hair hanging like willow branches. She pushed the water upwards from her face and ran her hands back over her hair. Bobbing in the water, she laughed and called for Philomena to join her.

'It was your idea to bathe.'

'I know,' Philomena called back. She got to her feet, turned her back to Junie and pulled her dress up over her shoulders. She placed it onto the rocks, picked up her soap bag and walked into the river as far as her knees, stopping to hold a twisted branch overhanging the water's edge.

'You're not scared of water, are you?' Junie sank beneath the surface, shooting water from her mouth like a fountain when she emerged. She laughed like an amused little girl, not like a married woman and not like the thin woman bending over in the garden, working tirelessly under the sun all day.

Philomena washed discreetly and plunged her body into the water. Junie took the soap to wash her hands, neck and face and left the water to dry off.

'I don't know what you can do with my hair now,' she said to Philomena who hurriedly dried herself and got dressed. Philomena sat on the rock to put her sandals back on and saw the bush of Junie's pubic hair disappear beneath her old dress as she eventually slipped it back on.

'I'll try and comb it when we get back,' said Philomena. 'You mustn't let it get too dry otherwise it'll become very tangled and impossible to manage.'

'But we can't go back until I've done some reading.'

'Of course,' said Philomena. She picked up the book. She'd brought a copy of *Little Women*. 'Ah, this one is going to be difficult to start with.'

Junie sat beside Philomena against the rock, their legs stretched out in front of them as Junie fanned through the pages of the book.

'I have books I read as a child in a box somewhere,' said Philomena. 'I should have checked properly.'

'You can read this one to me for now.' She handed the book back to Philomena. 'I might be able to pick out some words.'

She nestled close to Philomena, the way her young pupils did at story time. All of them wanting to sit close to teacher so that they could see the pictures.

Philomena ran a finger under the title and read it aloud.

'Are they children?' Junie asked when she heard the title.

'At the start of the story, but they do grow up.'

'Okay. Please start.'

Philomena opened the book and began to read slowly, conscious of her speaking voice and hoping she could make the story come alive even though she felt nervous reading aloud to a grown woman. But Junie was not like a grown woman in that moment. She was a curious child, her nose close to the pages, asking where on the page the word Philomena had just read was. She looked from the page to Philomena's lips as she spoke. She smiled when Philomena gave the characters different voices. When their stomachs began to rumble, Philomena closed the book.

'I love this book,' Junie said with her eyes closed.

'Me too. And just think, you'll be able to read it for yourself one day.'

Junie jumped up and picked up her damp towel. Philomena gathered her belongings and they walked back through the woods, holding hands.

'We'll go to my house,' said Philomena. 'Mum will be at church until late, so we can make breakfast and leave some for her.'

Junie did not reply. She was taking slower steps, pulling Philomena back, forcing her to stop.

'What is it?' Philomena saw a trickle of tears on Junie's cheek.

'I never had a friend before. I never had someone be so kind to me like you.'

'Not ever?'

'Never in my life. You are my first real friend. My only one.'

Philomena liked the idea of being the only one and vowed from that day that she would always be that special person for Junie.

7

On Monday morning, Philomena arrived at school in the best mood she'd been in for a long time. She had always loved teaching and was usually the first member of staff at the school and, apart from the head teacher or the caretaker, she was the last to leave. But since having spent the morning and most of the day with Junie, she had been buoyed by the thought of helping her to read and wanted to get home as early as she could. She didn't think anyone would mind if she borrowed a few books from the school. She had worked out a practical and accelerated way of teaching her friend, thinking that Junie would be less dependent on Gregory if she could read and write and that had to be a good thing. She imagined how much happier Junie could be if she was free of Gregory. They could become real friends. She could help Junie find a job, a new place to live. With her, perhaps. These thoughts excited her. The Junie she'd met that first day had come back, but she knew that on Gregory's return, Junie's exuberance would be extinguished. Gregory would cast his dark, oppressive shadow, and they would go back to communicating with stolen smiles, discreet waves and short clips of conversation.

For the rest of the school day, Philomena's mind flitted from her morning at the river with Junie to her actual job of teaching.

She took pride in her work, her heart was in helping the children get a good education. Growing up she always dreamed of becoming a teacher so that she could pass on the same opportunity to learn that she had had. Philomena had loved to discover the world through books. She had come to realise how small her island was and to know there was always more for her if she ever chose to leave it. She had no idea where she would go. Maybe Norway where there was snow or perhaps to Africa to explore its history. She hoped she could open the world up to Junie one day.

The school had changed since she was a student there. Instead of one classroom for all ages there were now three. She had taught in all classes, but this year, she had been spending her time teaching the younger children, the ones who hadn't yet learned to read, write or express their creativity in the arts or their physical skills in the school yard. She pondered over how much of this Junie missed out on as a child and had to bring her mind back to the maths lesson or to the child reading aloud in class several times during the day. The children were astute, they'd catch her out if she didn't pay enough attention. Each time she thought of Junie being able to learn as much as she knew, she smiled.

Her good mood hadn't gone unnoticed by Saul Mattherson, the head teacher. He taught science and mathematics to the older children. When he wasn't teaching, he would enter or walk by the classrooms to keep abreast of how things were going. Saul ran the school with precision and care. It was because of him that the school obtained the funds to expand and to have awarded to them the official signage at the school gate: a large wooden board with a royal blue background and the name of the school painted gold. The news made the local paper, and everyone was in high praise of Head Teacher Mattherson. They patted him on the back at church, they talked about him in the market, wondering if he would ever marry and if so, who would the lucky woman be? They commented on how young he was to have such a prestigious job. At thirty-five years old, ten years older than Philomena, surely he'd want to take a wife soon. Philomena had often found herself in the midst of a conversation about Saul Mattherson in the market where tongues wag and very little is accomplished, in her opinion. But by the close of business, they had obtained most of what they needed to know about other people's affairs. Philomena entertained herself with the notion that it was quite possible to set up a stall selling gossip and rumours and becoming a rich woman with the proceeds.

'What would you do if he ask you to marry him?' one woman asked directly one day, catching Philomena off guard as she held a watermelon to her nose to check for freshness. She had only grinned and moved on to the next stall and bought six large oranges before hurrying off home.

Philomena did find Saul handsome. He was kind, too, and one of the few people she could talk to on subjects other than what their neighbours had for breakfast. Sometimes after school, they chatted over tea with the newspaper in front of them. They'd talked with interest about the war, the number of Caribbean casualties there had been and the effects it had on their fellow West Indians returning home. Saul had never wanted to be a part of the war effort. He'd lost a brother and a cousin. His plan was to carry on teaching and perhaps take a job abroad once the war had ended. But five years had passed since then, and he was still in Dominica. He loved the island and the school, but with limited funds and a lack of enthusiasm from the government, he found it hard to keep the school well equipped and it broke his heart to see his students struggling to achieve when they had to share exercise books between three.

'Don't you think it's the easy way out?' Philomena had asked him. 'Going to a rich school where attainment is easier because it can afford books for all and special lessons for the struggling and the brighter students?'

'Perhaps,' he'd replied. 'But sometimes I become disenchanted. I feel as if I'm banging my head against a wall to do right by these children and end up feeling unappreciated by them and their families. Let's face it. We're a poor country. We need to develop, and no one seems to care. If you can't care about your own country then what's the point?'

This topic had ignited many heated debates between them, but they would always end the conversation laughing, their tea growing cold before, as Saul put it, 'They had set the world to rights.'

'Someone is happy today.' Saul entered Philomena's classroom as she was hanging some of the children's drawings on the wall and taking down some sketches and paintings that had hung there since last term. She was humming and wasn't aware of him coming in until he spoke. It occurred to Philomena that in order for him to know she was happy, he'd have to have been observing her. She knew that Saul did that a lot.

'I'm in a good mood,' she replied but continued to hang the drawings up.

'Need any help?'

'Isn't that a lowly job for a head teacher?' She sighed a light laugh.

'I don't mind lowering my standards, Phil.' He had a nice laugh, Philomena noticed. Everything about him was either nice or pleasant. Everything about him made her enjoy being in his company, and she looked forward to their little meetings after school.

They put up the artwork in an amicable silence until Saul commented on the talent of some of Philomena's students.

'I wish I could take credit, but my art leaves a lot to be desired. I think I'll stick to being an admirer.'

'I'd like to see some of your work one day,' he said, stopping to look at her.

'No, you wouldn't. I've never been very good at painting or even colouring in a picture. My brother, Pearson, he was the artist. He's good with his hands. Good at mending things, good at making things. He returned to his studies, even though he has a wife and a small child. He's at university in America, studying architecture. Mum is so proud. Me too.'

'I wouldn't mind a job in America. How about you? Would you ever go?'

'And leave Dominica?' She stopped to consider it. With Pearson living abroad, there would be no one to look after her mother when she was older. Philomena brought the money in. How was her mother going to cope? She thought about taking her to America, too. She could work there as a teacher and still look after Mum. She'd get away from all those small-minded people, their petty arguments and their familiar conversations. Their need to pry into her life and wonder about her finding a husband, or worse, putting their sons or grandsons up for consideration. One woman had suggested her well-educated, or so she claimed, nephew as a suitor for Philomena. It turned out he was only nineteen. The truth was that Philomena knew of all the eligible men down in the village and in the surrounding areas and she knew she would never give any of them the time of day. Saul was the exception, though. At least she could talk to him and laugh with him. But she had never considered marriage with him.

'I suppose,' she said after contemplating this. 'If the circumstances were right, I would consider leaving Dominica.' Then in a split second, something else occurred to her. Something she hadn't even considered. If she were to leave, what would become of Junie? Would it be enough to teach her to read and hope that she could then move on from Gregory, or would she have to stay next door in case Junie ever needed her help to leave her husband? Though Junie hadn't asked for an escape, Philomena was already convinced that given time, Junie would see she needed one. Since the night in the woods, after she'd witnessed the horrific ritual that Gregory had performed on that poor animal, she couldn't believe that anyone was safe in his company. Not a fragile creature like Junie.

'So,' said Saul who sat on the edge of one of the low desks. 'If you got a good proposition to leave here, you'd take it?'

She hesitated before answering. 'It would have to be a very good proposition.'

Philomena continued to clear away and tidy up in the classroom, preparing for the next day. She wasn't aware of Saul following her every movement with half-closed eyes, a wide smile on his face.

'I think that's all,' she said looking around, satisfied with her preparations. 'Head Teacher Mattherson, I will see you tomorrow.' She slipped on her thin jacket and collected her bag.

'Head Teacher?' Saul grinned. 'Are we being formal now? It's after school hours.'

Philomena laughed at the innocence of his handsome face.

'Okay, Teacher Scott.' He chuckled when Philomena shook her head and giggled to show she'd been joking. 'I will see you tomorrow.'

He watched her leave, and mirrored the short wave she gave him before leaving him alone in the classroom.

8

Gregory returned home unexpectedly, and Philomena ached for the day she could knock for Junie again. She waited for a sign from her friend to know when it was a good day to read together. They kept up the pretence of ignoring each other, not exchanging words but furtive glances and tiny nods of the head that said *Hello* or *How are you*? Philomena never looked in Gregory's direction if she happened to see him in the village, in town or if they passed each other on the road. The days of wishing that the school children would be kinder to the young Gregory and not tease him so much about his wild hair and the freckles on his skin seemed a lifetime ago. How she had longed for Gregory to find at least one friend at school, even though he'd made it clear he hadn't wanted it to be her. Just one person he could talk to, play with, smile with. Years ago, before his mother died, all Gregory did was scowl at Philomena; when he spoke, it was with disdain or he did nothing more than grunt. She had no idea why he detested her so much. All she'd ever done was try to be kind, helpful. Though they ignored each other now, Philomena felt afraid of Gregory. She tried to disguise it, but it had been there since that dreadful evening in the woods.

Gregory had returned on the Monday afternoon while Philomena was at school. She hadn't been aware as Junie wasn't in the front garden and the front door was closed shut when she came home. She rushed indoors, placed a reading book from school on a side table and, just as she was about to tell her mother she was popping over to Junie's, she spotted Gregory out in the garden. Her heart sank. Days later, when Philomena returned from school, Junie was in her garden. She thought it might be a good opportunity to at least mention the book, but the front door opened with a muted creak by the smallest amount. Philomena thought she saw a shadow behind it, so she said nothing, her eyes staring hard at Junie. Junie, though facing Philomena as she walked by, had her eyes trained on the gap in the door, her expression wordlessly telling Philomena not to stop, not to even look at the house. It wasn't safe. This confirmed everything for Philomena. Junie was also scared of Gregory, but it went so much deeper than her own fears. She detected the shiver of Junie's thin body, the rise in her temperature as her cheeks burnt red. She was sure, too, that she saw Junie's heart pulsing against the threads of her dress, that she could hear the thud of it as if it might explode at any second. She breathed a sigh of relief as she entered her own house and then rushed to the side window to see if Gregory had raced outside to grab Junie and force her back inside. Junie was kneeling, tending to her flower bed, Gregory's shadow blocking the afternoon sun from her back.

On the Saturday, Philomena, inspecting the flowers of the oleander that separated her garden from her neighbours', made a grand statement about wanting to go to the river every Sunday morning at 7.30 for a bath before church. She'd said it to her mother who was on the veranda, smoking a small pipe.

'But you don't come to church these days.' Her mother relit the pipe and puffed on it.

'I thought I might start again. There's a lot to pray for these days.'

Mrs Scott looked puzzled and shook her head. Philomena smiled to herself. She knew Junie was just on the other side of the tree and had heard every word. She had made sure the Williams' front door was closed and that Gregory wasn't likely to have overheard. But her plan to meet Junie was set.

For the next few Sundays, Philomena tucked a book within her towel and hurried past the Williams' house to take the path to the river. Sometimes Junie would be there already, either in the water or sitting nervously on the smooth rock they leant on, shoulder to shoulder, arms pressed together so tightly they had to make a big adjustment of their bodies every time one of them turned a page.

'I told Gregory that I wanted to start going to church and would he buy me a new dress,' Junie announced one Sunday morning.

'What did he say?'

'He only looked at me and asked what was wrong with this one.'

'But we're not going to church, we're reading.'

'I know that, but we spend more and more time here every Sunday, so if I pretend to go to church after, he won't keep asking why it takes so long to bathe. I tell him I love to swim, but all he does is ask question after question. Like he's a policeman.'

'Or your jailer,' Philomena said under her breath. Junie pretended not to notice. 'I'm sorry your marriage turned out to be this way.'

'No one is more sorry than me, Phil. Let's read.'

The Sunday morning reading sessions began to expand to three hours. Gregory was usually sleeping off a hangover, so he didn't always notice the time, and now that Junie was pretending to go to church afterwards, he stopped asking why she was away from the house for so long. Having bought more time, Junie was less nervous and fidgety. They talked for longer, Philomena telling Junie all about her work at school, her friendship with Saul and how he had asked Philomena if she would ever consider leaving the island.

'Don't you go and leave me.' Junie had looked pleadingly at Philomena and then burst out laughing as though she hadn't meant a word of it. Philomena had looked deep into the mahogany depths of Junie's eyes and whispered the word, *never,* while Junie laughed off her concern.

The river reflected the green of the willowy trees along its side. Their branches hung low, leaves brushing the water like slim fingers swishing and rippling the surface. In places, the taller trees kept the fierce rays of the sun off the women so that they didn't burn, they didn't swelter, they didn't melt beneath it. Birds flapped through the branches, landing sometimes, the occasional caw or the flutter of leaves. For Philomena and Junie, they felt as though the river was theirs alone for the three stolen hours of Sunday morning.

Philomena brought breakfast. Sometimes pieces of roast breadfruit with fish from last night's supper. Or there was bread and salad, fruit, sometimes chicken or porridge which had turned cold by the time they got to eat it, just like the coffee she brought. Always tepid by the time they got to drink that. Bathing, reading and chatter filled their stomachs, and only when the forest sounds grew with the waking and movement of fish or curious animals did they realise it was getting to the time a person returning from church should leave. Then they'd hurriedly eat breakfast and clear up after themselves, leaving at separate times. Occasionally, Philomena would take a longer trail back where the wood was more dense, where boars might be passing or snakes might be trailing along the ground. If they should ever arrive together and Gregory spot them from the window, he would know instantly he was being deceived and she couldn't take the risk.

Junie could read now, although slowly. For months, they had fooled Gregory and the women had grown closer. Even more than sisters Junie had once said, although neither of them had sisters to compare the experience to. Whatever it was they felt for each other, it ran deep.

'What happened to you, Junie? You not eating properly?' Philomena said one Sunday.

'What you mean?' Junie looked away and hurriedly put on her shoes before helping Philomena clear away their breakfast, towels and books.

'You look thin. I mean, more than usual. Like you changed overnight.' She regarded her friend closely.

'To be honest, I don't have much appetite. Keeping the house and the garden is a lot of work for me, and I suppose I don't put on weight.'

'There's a difference between not putting on and losing. Don't think I can't see what is happening.' Philomena sat still on the rock while Junie flapped around their things like a bee seeking pollen.

'Oh Phil,' she said. 'Sometimes you sound like an old lady. Fuss, fuss, fuss. I'm fine.'

'Is Gregory providing for you? For you both? When did he last work or give you money to go to market?'

'He finds it hard to get work.'

'You know, maybe you could find work for yourself. One of those rich people's gardens. They could pay you. It would help with groceries and things like that. A new dress.'

Junie stopped buzzing, weighing up the idea in her mind.

'Gregory wouldn't like that. You know what men like him are. Have to be the one out making the money, won't see their wife go out to work.'

'Just try him.'

'He won't listen. Gregory is a law unto himself.' Junie smiled at Philomena as they picked up their belongings. 'You not pleased?'

'Pleased?' Philomena asked.

'Yes—"law unto himself"—I learn that from the book you read for me, and I know what it mean now. Yes, my dear, that Gregory is a law unto himself.' The two laughed and held hands as they left the riverside.

It had been exceptionally hot that morning. They'd stayed longer in the water. Junie's fingers crinkled, and Philomena playfully scolded her for being lazy about her studies. The wood was quiet, no breeze to move the branches, animals and birds dozing, lazy in the heat. Slowly, the women walked home unaware of a tiny snap of a twig, a faint rustle in the low branches, a person coming upon them. This person moved swiftly like the tiny snakes slithering through the dark soil and the fallen leaves. Snap. A louder one this time, clumsy enough to make them turn to see where the sound came from.

Gregory was behind them, staring at Junie as though he couldn't believe it was her. Beyond the look of shock, anger grew. His cheeks burned as though the sweltering wood had suddenly caused him to overheat. His trousers were baggy, dirty, a large buckled belt holding them up. His short sleeved shirt was open. The vest underneath it had a brown stain down the front like old vomit. His hands clenched and loosened, clenched and loosened. His tight jaw caused a large vein to protrude from his neck.

'Gregory, you make us frighten.' Junie let go of Philomena's hand, a nervous smile coming to her lips. 'What happen? Why you not asleep?'

'Why my wife is here in the river and not at church or in her bed?' He completely ignored Philomena and came to stand only inches from his diminutive wife.

'E-every Sunday I bathe in the river before church. I did tell you.'

'What happened? Did they close the church today?' His eyes turned towards Philomena. 'All I see here are sinners.'

'Gregory, I... ' Junie stepped back as Gregory moved in an inch closer. Philomena could see his clenched fist. Junie gave a quick glance to Philomena who in turn bowed her head and continued home on her own. Philomena could hear the two walking slowly back behind her but was too afraid to open her mouth and say the wrong thing. Her arms felt weak, she could barely move her feet forward. The look in Gregory's eyes had silenced her. She had heard the tremor in Junie's voice, seen the look of sheer panic. Guilt gripped her, she knew something bad was going to happen, she could feel it, but she didn't know what else to do but walk away. Not make things worse for Junie. She tripped on loose stones, felt her dress catch on a twig. Dropped the book. The book. Had Gregory noticed? He looked as if he'd been in a deep drunken sleep, perhaps that detail might escape him. She hoped.

Inside her house, Philomena went directly to sit at the window seat facing the Williams' house. Not a thing moved nor a sound came from next door. What could they be doing? The sound of her front door opening startled her, and she

swivelled her head to find her mother standing in the doorway in her best clothes for church. She took the scarf off her
head and stared questioningly at Philomena.

'What?' her mother said in a whisper, but Philomena put a
finger to her lips. Her mother came to the window and
stooped to see. 'What?' she repeated.

'It's them.'

That's when the commotion began. At first, it was reminis-
cent of the days when they would hear old Mrs Williams and
Gregory quarrelling. Usually this would result in Mrs
Williams having a coughing fit, followed by more shouting
from Gregory, punctuated by the slamming of the door and
the hinges of the gate almost rattling off when Gregory
stormed off down the road. This time they heard sobs, not
coughing. The sobs were loud, coming from the kitchen.
Philomena heard the crashing of plates and Gregory's voice.

'Did you hear me?' he shouted. So loud, so stark. Philomena stood but kept her eyes on the window. She couldn't
move though her impulse was to rush over there and … do
what? She was too afraid. Too stunned and shocked. Her
worst fears gathering. Gregory wasn't only going to shout at
Junie, he would punish her. Physically. Philomena could tell
this was happening. He was beating her friend.

'Answer me!' Philomena heard. This time the creaky door
to the kitchen swung open and Philomena ducked back from
the window, her mother stumbling in the same hurried motion. Footsteps, two sets, moved with speed from the kitchen
to the house. The front door slammed.

'No, Gregory, no!' And then more crying. Philomena
started towards the door, but her mother stopped her. She
gripped Philomena's upper arms and shushed her.

'It's not your business,' Mrs Scott said.

'How can we stand here and do nothing?'

'Nothing we can do. This is their business. Best to leave them to sort it out. I don't want you walking in on that man. I can't let you take that risk. He sounds mad.'

'Exactly. I have to help her.' She shrugged her mother off and bent towards the window. 'What if he kills her?' At those words there was silence. All the noise, screams and crying from next door suddenly ceased.

'Do you think he killed her?' Philomena spun around to her mother, desperate. The front door of the house next door banged open and then the gate slammed. Philomena saw Gregory disappear down the road and promptly rushed out of her house.

'Philomena, you be careful, you hear?' her mother called.

As Philomena pushed open the front door, she saw Junie on her knees in the corner by the large dresser, her head against it. Her lip was cut, her nose bled. Dark red contrasted against honey coloured skin and mingled with tears that streamed down without a sound from Junie. Philomena knelt in front of her. She had started to cry before she'd even entered the house, but only then could she feel the warm tears on her own face. She touched Junie's cheek, tried to wipe away a tear, blood, but Junie flinched. Her eyes were like hollow wells. Expressionless. Her feelings hidden in a bottomless pool.

'Junie, I'm sorry. It's my fault. Come.'

Philomena helped Junie to her feet. She had to lift Junie who fell like a heavy stone against her. She sat her, though awkwardly, onto a chair beside the dining table. Philomena went out to the kitchen and came back with a bowl, half-filled with cool water from the barrel beside the house, and placed it on the table. Next, she looked around for a cloth which she dipped in the water and began wiping blood and tears from Junie's motionless face.

'I will get something to rub on these cuts. Get the swelling down. Mum will have something.' Philomena rose and walked to the door, stopping as she heard Junie take a deep breath.

'She warn me,' Junie said.

'Warned you?' Philomena returned to Junie's side.

'My mother,' Junie whispered through the swelling of her jaw. 'She tell me that Gregory is a bad man. She already see it in his eyes. She beg me not to marry him.'

'I'm sorry, Junie.'

'She tell me if I marry him and leave her house then never come back. She don't want me anymore.'

Philomena realised that Junie rarely spoke about her family and knew next to nothing about them. No one from home had ever come to visit Junie, either. No relative or friend. Philomena knew there would be no use trying to hide Junie next door because when Gregory came looking for her, probably intoxicated, she and her mother would be no match for a drunk and raging Gregory. Nothing as delicate as Junie was safe in his hands, and the local police would refuse to intervene in a fight between a man and his wife. That was the way of things.

Philomena tried to hush Junie who had begun to sob, softly, as though she hadn't the energy to cry hard.

'She doesn't mean it.' Philomena comforted her. 'I could go to your mother and explain everything. Plead on your be-half, tell her she was right but that she didn't know just how bad a man Gregory is. I can tell her he's a monster. I can tell her about this and what I—' Philomena caught herself and stopped short. She drew a deep breath. 'If I go now, I can bring your mother back while it's still light. Then I'll help you pack. Wait until she sees you.'

Junie bowed her head and turned her body from Philomena.

'You don't know her,' Junie whispered. 'She's nothing like Ma Scott. I can never go back home. She'll never set a foot here.'

'Then let me find somewhere for you. I can ask Saul, he's a good man. He has his own house. He is educated, kind. He'll help if I ask him.'

Junie looked back over her shoulder.

'Look, I made Gregory angry. But it's the first time he hit me. The only time. He's usually happy to just bang his fist on the wall or the table then go and have a drink. Then he's fine. But you'll see, he'll have a drink, he'll sober up and see what he's done and learn to control his temper better. Please don't stir up trouble for me, Phil. Please.' She reached for and squeezed Philomena's wrist. Philomena stared down at her bloody hand.

'Then let me clean you up. Fix this room up. And you go and lie down.'

'Yes, yes. Thank you, Phil. Knowing Gregory, he'll probably forget about today. But maybe it's best if we don't … if you and I go back to the way it was. No more reading. For now.'

Philomena nodded and went about tending to Junie's wounds. Junie chatted as if all Philomena was doing was sewing a button on her dress. Philomena wept inwardly, and her heart raged with hate for Gregory. Anger at herself for being too weak and so afraid of him. She had to find a way to stop this, a plan to get him to stop. This may have been the first time Gregory had used physical violence, but she knew, as sure as Junie probably did, that it wouldn't be the last.

9

It wasn't Junie's injuries that woke her from a troubled sleep but the tight muscles of her shoulders and the nerves they must have pinched because of the awkward posture she'd fallen asleep in. She had waited, interminably, for Gregory to come home, hoping he'd be less angry than when he'd stormed out. Philomena had left, placing a glass of water on the table for her after having done all she could to reduce the swellings on her face, the bruises on her arms and stopping the blood seeping from the cracks in her skin. She'd told Junie to rest and to make sure she ate something and should she bring over a plate of supper. Junie had insisted she'd be fine and that it was best no one else was home on his return. What she meant was it was better not to have Philomena there, aggravating Gregory. She knew that for some reason Gregory did not like his neighbour. In fact he hated her. He'd said so himself. He said Philomena interfered in his life too much. She was judgemental and thought she was superior to everyone because she was a teacher. Reading books is not the same as knowing about life, real life, he'd said. Philomena should just find herself a husband and get the hell away from him. Junie had asked if he wouldn't prefer a wife who could read, it must be nice to know half of what Philomena must know. A rage had erupted from her husband when she'd asked him that day. It had been over dinner. Gregory hadn't finished eating but had sent his plate of food flying across the room and into the sofa against the wall. He brought both of his meaty fists down onto the table. She knows too much, Gregory had shouted. Remnants of masticated food showered out from his mouth.

'I don't want to hear that name in my house, and I don't want you to have anything to do with her. You understand?'

Junie had been so shocked by this outburst that all she could do was nod her head. She wondered if she should carry on eating or pick up Gregory's plate. There was nothing else to cook, no food in the kitchen pantry. But he had risen to pick up the plate himself, letting it clatter onto the table. Junie got up then. She went to fetch a damp cloth and began rubbing gravy from the sofa and floor. She picked up the scraps of food and offered Gregory her plate. He ignored her, fuming as he grabbed for the day-old newspaper he had brought back from the store in town. Now, all she could do was think about what her mother had said.

It was just after light, Junie heard a car pull up close to the house. She wondered if Gregory had slept off his rage and someone had driven him back. Getting up, trying to stretch the stiffness from her shoulders, she went to the living room window and hovered far enough back so as not to be seen. Outside, a tall handsome man with skin as dark as Philomena's stepped out of the car and smiled as he watched Philomena leave her house. He bowed and swooped to open the car door. Mrs Scott stood on the veranda and waved as the car backed up, turned around in the small patch of flat land and went back in the direction of town. This must be the teacher from school Philomena had talked about. The one who could help her, hide her from Gregory. He had never come to collect Philomena before. Her friend looked so dressed up in her teacher clothes, carrying her big bag, her hair immaculate and being escorted by a good-looking teacher. Junie felt pride seeing Philomena like that, but something else pulled at her heart. She thought Philomena only cared about her. She had liked the idea of having Philomena all to herself. She wanted to rush out and accuse Philomena of letting her down. There would be no more visits to the river, and now she would lose Philomena completely to that teacher. Closing her eyes tightly she tried to shake the thoughts away, but that only made her aware of her aching face and head.

Junie's eyes were still on the road, long after the car had disappeared and the sound of its engine had grumbled away down the hill. There was still no sign of Gregory.

She ventured out to the kitchen and brought in the metal bath. She boiled a large pot of water and then another and then a third, filling the bath and adding some cooler water from the rain-water barrel outside. Rose petals danced on the surface of her bath water, their scent only just present, but she focused on it because it was much better than the smell of congealed blood. She splashed her face, careful not to open a wound, then rubbed some of the scented bar of soap Philomena had given to her onto her face. It lathered up, and she splashed the soap away. She rubbed the soap gently along her bruised arms, cleaned her armpits, her feet and hands. The water was shallow. It only came up to her waist, so she couldn't plunge into it as she did in the river. This would have to do. She put on clean underwear and then picked up her old dress. It was ripped, bloody and smelt of sweat. She cast it aside and opened the cupboard in the bedroom. Inside it she found a blouse and a skirt she'd had since she was twelve. It still fit, and she wore it from time to time though it brought with it memories of her overcrowded house, the fight for food with her older brothers and the lumpy bed she'd had to share with her two younger brothers. The blouse was newer, it was the one her father bought for her wedding. She'd given back the nice skirt she'd worn on her wedding day because it had belonged to her aunt. Her something borrowed.

Next, Junie emptied the bath, one large pail at a time. She cleaned the house. Cleaned the kitchen and frowned at the lack of food. Not enough to make a nice meal for Gregory for when he returned. If he returned. It was already late afternoon, and her stomach rumbled. She made some coffee, ate some dry crackers and went out to her garden to sit on an old wooden stool, painted light blue, to watch the road, waiting for Gregory to come home.

10

Philomena had never thought about the night sky. Black and endless. Not even a deep shade of blue as if all someone had done was dim the brilliant blue of daylight, its many shades from topaz to aqua to violet. At night, a black veil blocked out all the blue, the moon and the stars sometimes, too. When she was younger, she had a lamp lighting her room so that she could see to read. When she put it out, her eyes were half closed and she'd be asleep before she even noticed the inky well above the house. But this night, the night she saw the injuries on her friend's face and body, she couldn't sleep.

She had paced the house all afternoon. She had tried to take her mind off the smell of blood, the sight of snot running down such a beautiful face and the look of shame and sadness in Junie's eyes. It wasn't her fault. It wasn't anything to do with her this bitter and aggressive streak Gregory had within him. What was it exactly that made him so angry, so ready to express violence before love? Before kindness and appreciation? Nothing that she could see. Yes, there were the taunts and teasing at school. But that was school, and that kind of thing happens. It doesn't make you want to hurt a person, torture a defenceless creature, to brutalise someone who is nothing but goodness itself. He had been raised without a father, but in any case so had Philomena. That hadn't made her objectionable, violent. Mad. She decided that he must be mad. She knew that Junie was at risk, but she didn't know what to do about it.

Earlier that day, Mrs Scott had bumped into Head Teacher Mattherson after church. He had asked after Philomena. Mrs Scott had said that Philomena didn't always come to the service and neither did he, come to that. She had asked what brought him there. Had it been, perhaps, to see Phil. He had grinned and tugged at the collar of his white shirt. He had wanted to show Phil his new car and what did Mrs Scott think of the idea of him picking her up to drive her to school the next day. Mrs Scott asked if it was not a bother to come so far out, pass the school and drive all the way up to their house. He said it would be his pleasure. But when Mrs Scott relayed this to Philomena, she took no pleasure in it. Her mind was only on Junie, and she imagined her sitting in the house, afraid, alone, waiting for that mad man. She had been keeping an eye out for him.

'You have to come away from the window,' Mrs Scott said. 'You can't keep staring at their house.'

'He hasn't come home. What if Junie is suffering concussion after what he did? We don't even know what he did.'

'You saw her. Cuts and bruises never killed anyone. Maybe she's at home packing.'

'She has nowhere to go.'

'Everyone has somewhere. Someone.'

Mrs Scott put a plate of food on the table. She had cooked dinner, a large one, and kept talking about Saul Mattherson, but Philomena wouldn't be distracted.

'One of these days, you'll have your own husband to worry about,' Mrs Scott said. 'Come and eat. Junie will be fine. When you're out at school, I'll look out for her.'

'But you told me not to interfere.'

'Only because I don't want you near him. You let me sort that Gregory out. He wouldn't dare trouble with me. I cooked most of his meals. I washed his dirty bedclothes. If he gives me any trouble, I'll have a few men up from the village to tell him what's what.'

'Violence is not the answer. I have to find a way to get her out.'

'And I'm saying that Junie is not your problem. Now eat.'

Philomena nibbled at her food. She chewed until the sweet potatoes had liquidised and then forced herself to swallow. The meat she merely picked at. Cut off two small slices but found it impossible to swallow another mouthful. She sipped guava juice and kept her eyes on the window and her ear trained for the movement of the front gate.

By the time night fell, Gregory hadn't come back as far as she was aware. She listened out for him until her body closed down and she slept four hours before the cockerel down at Miller's yard crowed loudly into the morning air. She remembered what her mother said about Saul coming to pick her up in his new car, but her excitement was feigned. When he arrived in his new car, Saul puffed out his chest and grinned and held open the door for Philomena to jump in. It was a second-hand Ford Deluxe Roadster. It was shiny and red and in good condition. Saul said it had a sound engine, made before the war. Philomena knew she should ask questions about the car, but all she could do was nod and smile and thanked him for picking her up.

'This is such an honour.'

'It's my absolute pleasure.' Saul closed the passenger side door with a flourish.

Out of the side of her eye, Philomena thought she saw Junie at her window. The desire to jump out, run to her, drag her into the car and tell Saul to drive as fast as he could was immense. She kept her eyes on the window the whole time as Saul manoeuvred the car, turned it around and headed back towards the village. The vision of a fragile woman with a swollen face haunted her for the whole day.

At the end of the school day, Philomena rushed around the classroom picking up the torn, discarded and crumpled pieces of paper that she'd already told her class to deposit into the bin. She fixed the chairs and tables, but she didn't have time to set up for the next day.

'Are you in a hurry to leave?' Saul asked.

'Yes, I need to get home early today.' She closed her bag and put on her light cotton jacket.

'Anything special?'

'A friend in need,' Philomena said quickly.

'Oh?'

'Just my neighbour.' Philomena stopped short at the door where Saul stood with his arm out wide, holding the door open but not moving for Philomena to leave. 'She had some problems yesterday, and I need to know that she's all right.'

'Oh, yes, of course.' Saul quickly stepped aside. 'I won't keep you.' He followed her to the main doors of the school, a set of double doors with windows in the top half of each side. On the inside of the door there were handmade posters by the children outlining the rules of the school: no shouting inside; no running inside; no ball games inside; no swearing; no rudeness. On another poster, this one with lots of pictures, We Must: Love God, Be Kind To Our Neighbours, Be Generous, Study Hard, Be Polite, Try Our Best. The same message had been there since she was a child here herself. She wondered if Gregory had ever bothered to read them as he slithered out between the doors, determined to spend as little time at school as possible.

Saul was still following, chatting to her.

'Um, I was hoping we could go out.'

'Out?' Philomena said absently as she walked across the school yard. Someone had left a shoe there. Saul picked it up.

'Yes, that's my way of asking if you would like to go out somewhere with me. We could go into town. A meal perhaps?'

She swung around, realising she was being rude. *We Must Be Polite.*

'A meal? Um, yes, Saul. That would be lovely. But I do have to run. I'm sorry.'

'No, no. Yes, yes, of course. You run. We'll arrange something another time. Tomorrow. When you can.'

'Thank you. See you tomorrow.' She smiled as fully as her distracted mind would allow and walked away quickly in the stifling late afternoon heat. At the bus stop, she stopped a truck not carrying too many passengers. She jumped on the back and gripped a panel in the inside carriage. The people on board were coming back from town: workers, shoppers, all too tired to converse, and Philomena was glad of that. The truck rocked and rumbled towards the village and stopped close to the port. She dropped some money into the driver's damp hand and headed up the hill towards home. She was hot, and sweat stained her blouse as she slowed in front of Junie's house to try to gauge the situation within. As usual, the door was closed. Junie wasn't in her garden.

Mrs Scott signalled for Philomena from the veranda.

'He's home,' she whispered as Philomena climbed the steps. 'He hasn't been shouting. He came back with some provisions. Food but I think a few bottles of booze, too. He nodded at me. I nodded back and asked if everything was all right.'

'What did he say?'

'He only grinned. That smile with no life behind it. He makes me shiver that man.'

Mrs Scott had no idea.

11

It became harder and harder to catch even a glimpse of Junie. Everything had changed. Junie was very rarely in her garden, Gregory seemed always to be outside the house. He prowled the front yard like an animal stalking its prey whenever Philomena returned from work, back and forth the width of the house as if he was marking out the line she must not trespass. The front door remained shut so Philomena couldn't catch a glimpse of Junie if she dared to look towards it. When she did happen to see her friend, Philomena could tell Junie had changed. It had been a gradual transformation over the subsequent days following the attack, and she kept on changing as the weeks went by. Apart from Junie's looks, she appeared more guarded, nervous. She looked wiry, tougher but not hard and certainly thinner. Her youthfulness wore away, and she smiled less. Gregory bought a cart and an old mule. Philomena had heard the gossips talking about a small patch of land in the fields further up the hill from her house that Gregory had bought, or won, so that he could grow crops. Junie began to wear work trousers and an old shirt, sometimes denim dungarees because now she had land to harvest, taking her away from her beloved garden.

At the start of this food-growing venture, Gregory used to drive the mule himself, but very soon he was up to his old tricks, disappearing for weeks at a time or staying out so late drinking that he was fit for nothing in the early hours when people usually worked their allotments. Now Junie drove the mule up the hill and tended to the land herself. Philomena imagined he'd bought the land, the cart and the old mule that brayed loudly from the back garden and trampled the beautiful landscape of Junie's garden, to keep her away from the house. Away from Philomena so she couldn't see what he was doing, what Junie had become. He lashed out at Junie from time to time both verbally and, from the sound of her agonising shrieks and cries in the night, physically, too. Philomena wouldn't expect to see Junie for days after one of Gregory's assaults.

Once in a while, the paths of the women would cross. That mostly happened when Philomena orchestrated the departure from her house to school at the same time as Junie was on her way to the allotment and only ever on a day she knew Gregory wasn't home. Sometimes she might run into Junie at market on a Saturday morning. Gregory had begun allowing his wife to go down to the village on her own. She wore her denim overalls, her mass of hair beneath a headscarf. Her hair bunched out at the back and was never combed. Philomena caught people whispering about her behind their palms, discussing a fresh bruise or the dried blood on Junie's spilt lip.

Junie's garden was still lovely, though she spent less time in it and more time behind the closed front door, whether Gregory was home or not. Philomena thought back to the time she'd found the makeshift shed, deep in the woods where Gregory kept the wounded goat and carried out the horrific torture on the defenceless animal. She often wondered how many people had their animals go missing, how many times Gregory carried out that ritual. What was it all for? How was a person satisfied by this sick way of being?

Now, she feared Junie was his captured animal. Small, frightened and alone and afraid to reach out to her only friend. A friend who was failing her.

'You can't help someone who doesn't want to be helped, doesn't ask for your help,' her mother would say. But Philomena didn't believe that. She knew Junie was afraid to ask. Like the frightened goat, Junie couldn't speak up for herself, either. Philomena's only chance at saving Junie was to extract her tormentor or find a safe place for Junie that her tormentor could not penetrate. She could only rely on the kindness of Saul to help. Though they had been to dinner together, talked a lot about a future as teachers in America, marriage, setting up a home together, Philomena had never mentioned Junie. She was waiting for a sign or the permission of her friend to bring Saul into her confidence. That had yet to happen.

Philomena always looked out for Junie at market. Once in a while, she would spot her, but Junie had a way of slipping in and out of the crowds and vanishing before Philomena could catch up with her. Gone as though it had been a dream or some hopeful imagining.

One Saturday morning, Philomena did see Junie, and she waited for an opportunity to walk up to her head on, stop her before she vanished.

'Good morning, Junie.' Philomena was breathless having weaved around the market, ducking out of sight and trying to avoid being caught up in conversation. 'I haven't seen you in a while.'

Junie stopped, immediately turning sideways on to Philomena as if she was about to hurry away or had something to hide. Philomena gently tilted Junie's face towards her own.

Around Junie's eye were dark blue marks left over from a previous contusion. Philomena stroked Junie's forearm. Her shirt, an old one of Gregory's, was rolled up to the elbow. Philomena took Junie's hand and softly lifted her chin.

'You don't have to hide from me. I am your friend.' Philomena spoke close to Junie's ear so she wouldn't be overheard, speaking hurriedly in case Gregory happened to be around. 'But honestly, I feel less and less like a friend. I hear you cry, and I don't do a thing. I feel terrible, and I'm sorry, Junie.'

All eyes were on them, now. Both women saw the attentive expressions on the villagers' faces.

'Come,' said Philomena. She reached for Junie's bag and led her towards the port.

They sat on a low bench overlooking the wild sea. It was noisy, waves beating in rapidly. Philomena deeply inhaled the freshness and felt the cool air enter her expanded lungs. She wondered how the boats had arrived on such choppy waves. There were clouds in the sky; it was a greyish blue. Birds silhouetting the clouds dived and dipped in the air, sweeping gracefully in circles above their heads. There were two large boats from a nearby island moored along the pier. A few people walked idly by carrying baskets of food; a woman carried a full pail of fish on her head, walking in the direction of the shops and the main supermarket. They ignored Philomena and Junie who sat close together, their eyes straight ahead, looking out to sea. Philomena let out a deep sigh and turned to Junie.

'I miss our Sunday mornings.'

'So do I.' Junie's voice was soft, almost lost when sailors started to return to the boats and getting ready to set sail.

Philomena's eyes travelled the coastline to her right. Rocks overhung the sea, the beaches, not suitable for leisure activities, forming a curve several miles long, the sea seeming to vanish behind the hazy veil of the sky in the distance. Philomena's view focused back on Junie.

'I miss you.'

Junie finally met her gaze.

'Oh, Phil. I miss you, I miss everything. It was so much better before. When I first met him, he was nice enough. He didn't treat me like this. He's never been this cruel.'

'*This* cruel. That would imply he was a little bit cruel.'

'Not cruel. Not really. Bad tempered. Troubled, Mum said. Too many thoughts running deep. But I felt sorry for him. He told me no one had ever given him a chance. He said I was his chance, to be happy, to have a normal life. And I believed him, Phil. I believed what he said even when I knew he drank too much, swore too loudly. Got upset.'

'You thought you could heal him? Tame him?'

'Something like that.' Junie looked pleadingly at Philomena. 'He isn't impossible to love, you know.'

Philomena shuddered.

'But how, Junie? How did you even meet him?'

'He stayed at my uncle's house. He worked for him for a month, and he used to take me out when he was driving my uncle's van. That's how I come to know him.'

'But your mother warned you.' *I could have warned you*, Philomena thought.

'You know what love can do to a young girl.'

'I suppose I can imagine.'

Junie was still only twenty, still a young girl, but she spoke about the past and meeting Gregory as though she was an old woman now. One who'd made a silly mistake. Fell in love with the wrong man. And what of love? It had had an adverse effect on Junie. Not that it had made her unlovable or unable to love but unable to protect herself from the type of love Gregory was inflicting on her. Surely she wasn't too young to know the difference between love and hate. Hate had to have been in Gregory's heart, no one who loved could do the things he did. Philomena refused to believe it. Some Sundays, Philomena would sit in the church service, her mother on one side, Saul on the other, and while the priest talked about God's forgiveness and how we should forgive the sins of others, Philomena couldn't find a way to do this. She could never forgive Gregory. Not in her heart or her mind. Gregory couldn't be forgiven. Gregory would kill her friend one day, and she would never be able to forgive herself for not trying harder to help. But what could she do? All she could do was pray.

'How is the garden going up there?' Philomena asked. 'The food you're growing in the allotment?'

'Oh, it's just a few potatoes, lettuce, onions, tomatoes. He had the big idea of making money selling things at market. I planted limes from a cutting. I'm hoping they will come through. I thought about turning the limes into preserves or cordials. Maybe both.'

'You mean a business?'

'It's a dream I have. It won't be anything big.'

'You never know, you could become a big business woman one day. Have a factory.'

Junie laughed, her cheeks flushing, her white teeth gleaming. She rested a hand on Philomena's lap. Philomena felt the warmth of it and covered Junie's hand with her own. She missed the curls of Junie's hair in the crook of her neck when Junie rested it there while listening to her read.

Philomena read from *One Thousand and One Nights*, A *Tale Of Two Cities*, *Jane Eyre*. She missed Junie lying with her head in her lap, holding up a book Philomena was helping her with. The book in the air as she read about the boy and his sister playing with their dog who barked, who ran and rolled over. Philomena would stroke Junie's damp hair, running her fingers between the curls while they were still loose with water and the sun had not dried them out yet. Philomena would gather Junie's wet tresses and bind them in a thick ribbon, plait the ends and wrap them into a neat bun. Junie was like a child and hadn't learned how to care for her hair properly. Philomena had taught her how, but it was obvious Junie was no longer looking after herself. Her beautiful skin, her beautiful hair, both looking dry and uncared for.

'I would like to see you have a business one day,' said Philomena. 'That would be the day you left him. Especially if you don't tell him what you have planned.'

'You mean like the reading lessons? He found out about that.'

'Gregory is cunning, but he isn't intelligent. You are. And you have me. Use me, Junie. Use my friendship to get you out of there. You only have to say the word, and I can have my friend, Saul, come and pick you up.'

'He'd find me. Wherever I go, it has to be far. Not a place he can find and not a person he can beat or punch to find out where that place is.'

'Like me you mean? He'd think I was complicit. Of course he would.'

'Complicit? You mean he thinks you will know where I went? That you helped me?'

'Exactly. But no matter what he did, I would never tell.'

'I have to think. My mind gets so cloudy. Like I'm the one drinking all the whisky, not him. My head is so blocked and painful some mornings. It's a pleasure to get the old mule and get up into the mountain where the air clears me. Unblocks me. I can talk to old Mr Reynauld up there. He helps me with the gardening. I don't have to go every day, but I do. Especially if Gregory is gone. Pa Reynauld invites me to his house. We drink tea or coffee, and we talk. About everything. About nothing. He has a bible. He can't see too well, and I read to him.'

'I haven't seen old Pa Reynauld in ages. He has children, doesn't he?'

'Yes, and grandchildren. Grown up. But Pa says they're all too busy to come by.'

An unpleasant feeling cloaked Philomena at the thought of Junie finding friendship with Mr Reynauld. But surely he deserved a friend like Junie. And Philomena should be happy that Junie wasn't completely alone.

'I have to go,' Junie said eventually. 'He's not here, but he could be back any day. I'll cook supper.'

'We can walk back together.' Philomena reached for Junie's hand again. 'We could find a way to read again. I noticed that if he goes away, he almost never returns sooner than three days. That could be our day. Day one of his travels, we read together. What do you think?'

Junie's smile returned.

'I think, yes, please, Phil. You see how clever you are. I didn't even count the days. I should have.' They both laughed and shook their heads at such an opportunity wasted. 'Let's go. We can decide on a new book.'

They linked arms like school girls, giggling helplessly about nothing. They impersonated some of the women in the market, giggled some more. Pulled each other closer, practically skipping. The walk up to their houses was far too short. Philomena wished the moment could last for her lifetime.

12

It wasn't easy to see Junie after that day in the market. Their plan to meet when Gregory was away hadn't been enacted so far. He seemed to stay put in the house like moss growing on a mountain, sticking to Junie's side if she was working outside the house or accompanying her to the allotment. It was as if he knew. Philomena couldn't imagine for a moment that Junie would give anything away, yet there he was like a hulking shadow trailing her every move. Philomena tried to communicate something, anything to Junie if a chance meeting, albeit at a great distance, should arise. She wanted to tell Junie she was on her side, she was there for her, waiting for their opportunity to fool Gregory, recapture those moments under the hazy sun, resting against their rock, discovering new words and new worlds. Mostly, Philomena could only watch from her window or glimpse Junie from the side of her eye if she was gardening. And there was Gregory, ever hovering by the door smoking a cigarette, screwing his face as smoke billowed around him.

In a moment of hope and, by now, nostalgia, Philomena left the house one Sunday morning to go to the river. She brought a towel and some clean clothes so that she could swim and pass a few hours reading the way she used to in the years before Junie arrived. She was aware that she needed some exercise. Saul was collecting her for school every day, escorting her everywhere, to town, to meet his parents, to go shopping. If she wasn't with Saul, she was teaching or sitting and reading, hardly moving and having too much time to think about Junie.

As usual, the riverbank was quiet and calm. Fewer people needed to use the water for washing clothes and themselves any more. The village at the bottom of her hill had moved on. They had indoor plumbing, baths and sinks and they could wash clothes by hand in the comfort of their homes. It was only the people located up towards the mountains and along the roads winding up to the centre of the island that lived as in olden times. Country 'Bookies' the villagers and townsfolk called people like Philomena and Junie. The large pipes needed to bring Philomena and Junie's house up to date hadn't been commissioned by the government as yet, and all they had was a tap on the side of the road and large barrels to collect rain water. Philomena could easily afford to move her mother and herself into somewhere modern, but her mother refused to leave the picturesque plain up the hill from the village, so Philomena stayed with her.

Philomena arrived at the river, perspiring after walking briskly from home. She took off her shoes and pulled off her skirt. She stood and unbuttoned her blouse, and as she did so, she thought she heard movement. She smiled and looked up, thinking it was Junie, that she'd escaped for a few minutes because Gregory was sleeping off yet another hangover. There was no one there. She scanned the bushes, squinting to see if Junie might be hiding, too afraid to come any closer. After standing still, listening for what she thought had been tentative footsteps, she gave up on the idea that Junie would dare to come to the river with Gregory still in the house.

She waded into the water in her slip and underwear and swam right out to the centre. She sank beneath the surface of the river for several seconds. The water was clear, cool at first but feeling like her body temperature the more she got used to it. When she emerged, she rolled onto her back, floating with her eyes closed so that the water lapped at her arms, her legs and her face. She gently moved her limbs, letting the water carry her along. She would roll back and swim at some stage, back to her belongings, read her book as she dried off. She would test herself to see how fit she actually was. As fit as when she used to walk to pick up transport to take her to school? Or when she and Junie spent their Sundays racing each other in the river? Sometimes they swam far, all the way to the place where there are large rocks on the river bed and water gushes so quickly you struggle to swim against it. But they would try. Their arms and legs kicking and splashing, but their bodies barely travelling. They would laugh and measure how much further they got each time. Philomena was strong then, physically. Happier, mentally. The Sundays with Junie seemed to have occurred a lifetime ago though it could not have been more than eight months since they were last together. It wasn't that she was unhappy with her life. Saul made her smile a lot. He was gentle with her, kind, and they did have a lot to laugh about. They still talked about moving to America. She loved Saul. Saul had asked her to marry him. She had told him she had her mother to think about, so it was a big decision. She hadn't made one yet.

When her body grew cool, Philomena swam back to the rock where she'd left all her things, gliding smoothly for the fifty metres or so she had drifted. She had left a bright towel over the rock, but the closer she got to that spot she realised the towel had gone. Vanished. And so had her clothes. For a moment, she thought she must be mistaken, that she'd floated further away than she imagined. But no, she knew this place. Right by the large whitewood tree. But someone had moved or taken her things: her bag with dry clothes in it and her book.

Philomena waded out of the water. She was out of breath, confused and afraid. For the first time, she saw the intimate setting as a lonely place, somewhere anything could happen to a person, and there'd be no one there to call to for help. She wanted to call out, ask the air, the trees and bushes if anyone was there. She was sure she could feel someone around. Goosebumps crept up her arms, and her teeth chattered. Her slip clung to her wet skin. She guarded her body with her arms and tried to look in and among the trees because whoever moved her clothes could be watching her right now. She ought to change her body language. She looked vulnerable, half undressed, arms around her torso and the chattering of her teeth becoming more pronounced. She corrected her posture and looked around her feet along the river bank for evidence of someone having been there. Inside, she prayed that she'd made a mistake, that she'd put her things somewhere else, not on the rock at all. And then she spotted them. It was the blue towel she noticed first, behind the large rock. It had merely slipped down. She'd waded out of the water thinking the worst and stayed frozen in one spot, hadn't bothered to check properly. Behind the rock, the rest of her things lay scrunched in a tight ball. But this still was not right. She knew for sure a large towel couldn't have blown off the rock, and she would never ball up her clothes like that. Someone *had* been here and deliberately moved her bag, her blouse, her shoes, her skirt and the blue towel. She bent to pick them up and hurriedly rubbed her face, arms and legs, her hands shaking. She could dress quickly, gather everything in her arms and just run. But whoever had played this nasty trick on her was still there. Looking at her right now. Gregory knew these woods, he could navigate them in the dark. He must still be there, enjoying this, watching her, wanting her to feel afraid. Fear crept over her like an ice cold shroud, her flesh unable to warm up, the towel ineffective to dry her skin.

She took a deep breath in and sat on the rock. She stopped searching the gaps between leaves and branches but kept her eyes down. She wrapped the towel around her body and then took her time, rubbing her skin with care and attention so that the water did respond, it dried, the goosebumps disappeared. She knew that there was no point in running half dressed through the wood because Gregory would see her as one of his frightened animals. He wanted to torture her, scare her, take his time, and she refused to let him win.

Calmly, she took off her wet clothes, discreetly so that she didn't expose herself. Then she sat on the ground, leaning up against the rock, facing out to the river. She took out her book and a small piece of cake. Nibbling her cake, her eyes scanned each line and she turned each page, trying not to let the tremble in her hand show.

Philomena sat for a while hoping Gregory would get bored and leave. He had succeeded in frightening her, and now it was time to go home. She hoped she had fooled him into believing that she was not afraid. She would walk as quickly as she could back home. Whatever it was Gregory had in mind, he could do it to her any time. She was powerless to stop a man that size, especially one who obviously hated her and might still be drunk from the night before.

She gathered everything and placed her wet clothes into the bottom of the bag, then the damp towel, next her blouse

and skirt followed by the book. All the time she steadied her
hands. She walked swiftly, not looking back, not even to her
sides; her eyes remained just a few feet ahead, but she kept
listening out for the crunch or snap of someone following
close behind. Then, she heard it, a shuffle in the bushes, a
sound of someone rushing. She stopped dead, her heart racing so fast she found it impossible to breathe. She couldn't
scream even if she wanted to. In an instant, she realised that
the footfall was retreating, running away from her, not towards her. She looked around, gaze darting to each angle.
All she could see was a green haze, various shades, punctuated by earthy brown and flashes of vibrantly coloured flowers. They blinded her, made her dizzy until she couldn't hear
the footsteps, just her own heartbeat pounding in her ears.
She thought she would pass out. Slowly, she regained control of her breath by extending her exhale until she finally
felt that he was gone. She continued on towards home. When
she passed the Williams' house, the door was tight shut, her
heartbeat back to normal. Gregory could have done anything
he wanted to her, and no one would have been any the wiser.
Perhaps Junie would know, but she would be too afraid to
say a word. This was his warning to Philomena. She understood it clearly.

13

Junie woke early, she thought, but Gregory had already left the bed. She sat up and let out a dry, raspy cough. When she rubbed her throat, it was sore, the skin still red and tender from the night before when Gregory came home drunk and demanded his dinner was brought to him immediately before he died of hunger. Junie had looked at him on her way out to the kitchen noticing the girth of his waistline. He was developing a round, paunching stomach. He must be eating somewhere else to grow a stomach that large, she thought. Their larder was usually empty, or the food over ripe or spoilt in the heat. Maybe it was the effects of the booze. Maybe another woman. She didn't care. She hoped he'd get sick of her and toss her out, then she could go to Philomena for help. But for now, she was trapped there. He'd trapped her, told her not to utter a word about what happened in their house to a single soul, especially Philomena. He hated that woman, hated her, and Junie had no idea why. Something from their past, she imagined, though Philomena hadn't said anything about their falling out.

She'd lit the stove and tried to heat some water in a pan so that she could warm Gregory's dinner plate. Being in the kitchen gave her some breathing space, time away from him so that she could think. She thought about the last time she'd spoken to Philomena. They'd stared out at the ocean, held hands and talked. She'd felt human again, like a real woman and not a caged animal, a wild creature only there for Gregory's pleasure. The thought of the things he'd done to her—in the bedroom, in the living room late at night when he'd thought the Scotts were fast asleep—made her shudder. Yet, she couldn't leave. She had nowhere to go, and if Gregory had to force her back from anywhere, he'd make sure she never left the house again. That's what he'd said, and she knew exactly what he meant by that.

Trapped, she was thinking when the kitchen door was kicked open, trapped. The sound of the door banging open against a stack of empty shelves made her jump, but she didn't turn around. She kept her back to Gregory and looked at the steam rising from beneath the plate of food. It wasn't warm enough yet, the ground provisions took ages to reheat, and the fish broth would still be tepid.

Gregory approached and towered above her. He stood close to her so that his stomach pushed at her back. She tried to lean away. One thing she had learned was not to speak first; if she did, she was bound to say the wrong thing. It was a trick of his because no matter what she said, he'd find a way to twist her words and get angry with her. Any word, any wrong look would provoke an argument, and if she didn't speak up for herself, he'd remind her what a fool she was, how stupid, what an idiot who had nothing to say. She was not fool enough to retaliate, knowing that a slap with the back of his large hand was all she'd get. *Don't say a word*, she thought. *Don't even breathe.*

'What the hell you think you doing?' Gregory's breath was rancid and clouded the air around her. She said nothing. 'You can't hear me?'

'I'm just warming the food.'

'You're staring at the plate. That's all you're doing.'

'Yes, I know, but I'm waiting for it to be warm enough for you.'

'And how would you know if it was warm enough?'

'It's just the time it takes. I just know you have to wait a bit longer or it won't be hot enough. Not even a little bit.'

'And you think I don't know that?'

'I'm sure you know, I was only saying…'

'Do you even know what you're saying? Because it sounds to me as though you're preaching to me, telling me I don't know something so simple as warming up some food. If you can call it that.'

In a small voice she said, 'It tasted fine earlier.'

Gregory pulled Junie's hair so that she stumbled back from the stove. He swung her in the small space and pushed her by her throat so that her back jammed into a cupboard. She looked down at a stain on his shirt and not into his eyes. Gregory squeezed her throat, digging his nails into the skin on her neck. She whimpered but didn't cry out for him to stop. She tried to be still and make her breath quiet. Maybe he'd continue to squeeze until she could no longer breathe, until her eyes closed and she passed out and she never woke again. She waited for that to happen, but Gregory released his grip and stepped away.

'You can't teach me a single thing,' he blasted at her. 'You're too stupid. You see?' He brought down his fist hard at his side without realising how close he was to the stove. The plate collapsed off the pot, the steaming water spilling out, a few splashes catching Gregory's hand which he shook and then cursed with a roar. He lunged at Junie, pulled the collar of her shirt and dragged her down to her knees by the upturned pot.

'Clean this up, you damn idiot. Don't just stare at it.'

He had stormed back to the house, leaving the kitchen door wide open. Crickets were singing outside, the sky had turned black. She heard Gregory stumble into something and swear before entering the house. She let out a long breath and cleaned the kitchen in silence and without shedding a tear. She washed all the utensils in a bucket outside the kitchen before drying them and packing them away. The kitchen lamp flicked and flickered but stayed alight long enough for her to cut some bread and pour some milk into a cup to bring for Gregory. She balanced the plate of bread on the cup and carefully took down the lamp to light the way to the house. She looked up at Philomena's house; the side window where Phil sat and read sometimes was empty. Seeing her frame at the window seat was always a source of comfort. But the lights were out in the Scott house. They were safely tucked up in bed and hopefully hadn't heard the commotion in the kitchen. Every cry or bash or bang that could be heard from her house was like a moment of shame for Junie. Philomena must think her weak, have given up on her. She thought of Philomena being at the river and almost cried aloud for the pain of missing their Sunday mornings together.

Quietly she entered the house, but Gregory had retired to the bedroom. She put her head around the door to see him sprawled on the bed on his stomach, one leg dangling onto the floor, the side lamp dangerously close to the edge of the small table next to the bed. If that tipped over, it would catch on fire, she'd thought. She walked over to the bed and heard her husband snore, a feral, unleashed growl coming from deep within him. How deeply he was sleeping, he'd have no idea if the lamp tipped over. She could go back to the kitchen. Clean up some more and not look out the window and never know if there were flames leaping up into the sky from inside the house where Gregory slept like the dead.

Junie blew out the lamp and returned to the living room. She blew out both the kitchen and house lamps and sat in the darkness, her eyes trained on the still of the night time and the peacefulness of the sky she couldn't see. When she was tired enough, she lay beside Gregory, falling to sleep in the stale air he produced and the ugly sound he made.

Now he was gone and it was light, and though she was glad he wasn't beside her, she couldn't understand how he could have roused himself from his drunken slumber and be out of the house so early.

She got up and gathered her hair into a large bunch on the top of her head and tied it with elastic before putting on a headscarf. She had slept in her clothes—an old shirt and a pair of boys ragged trousers that came to her shins—clothes Gregory had found for her from somewhere so that she could work the allotment. The bread and milk she'd brought for Gregory was still on the dining table in the main room. She went to open a window and saw her husband running fast up the path to the front door. She thought someone must be chasing him. He slammed open the door and closed it quickly, his back against it as he tried to steady his breath. He looked at her briefly before staggering to the bedroom. He smelt as if he'd been running all morning and looked ex-hausted. His back was wet with sweat, and his hair looked crisp from perspiration.

'Shut up and be quiet today. I need more sleep.' He closed the bedroom door. Junie heard the bed creak under the weight of a grown man who had flung himself onto its thin frame.

She stood for a while, waiting for him to fall asleep again before she went out to wash her face, check on her garden. Through the window just as she heard heavy breathing from the bedroom she saw Philomena. She must have come back from the river. Junie raised her hand to wave, but Philomena didn't look her way, her gaze fixed straight ahead. Junie followed Philomena's progress up to her house, but as she climbed the veranda steps, she disappeared from view. Junie quietly let herself out of the house and heard Philomena's door gently close and felt a warm tear release itself from the well of tears that had formed there.

14

Philomena tried hard to stay in the moment, but after seeing the girl with honey skin and the aqua dress walk past their table, she found it hard to concentrate on what Saul was saying. He'd gone to a lot of trouble with his appearance, making sure the restaurant had Phil's favourite fish—it was in season now, and so demand was high. He called to ask how it was cooked, how it was served and to ask what was on the wine list. The person who had answered the phone when he made the reservation grew weary of his questions and in the end demanded to know if Saul wanted to book the table or not.

Their table was well positioned. It was out on the decked ground-level balcony furthest from the restaurant. It overlooked the sea and was a lot quieter than being inside where a band played music with a fast rhythm and a swirling riff. There was a lot of energy being generated by groups of well-dressed islanders and red-faced foreigners. It was hot, and the smell of food was both intoxicating and inviting. The aroma of spices in the air was making everyone perspire, cocktails and rum flowed freely and at some stage Philomena expected everyone to get up and dance in a waving train of hot bodies, colourful clothes and peppery breath.

Their waitress showed them to the table outside, and Philomena sighed with relief, fanning her face.

'Are you all right?' Saul asked her as he held her chair for her to sit down. The waitress left the menus on the table and said she'd be back to take their order. One of the guests grabbed the waitress before she could go back inside and made her dance with him. The mayhem was already beginning.

'Yes, I'm fine,' Philomena replied.

Saul picked up the menu. Philomena rested her elbows on the table and looked out at the sea. There was a large boat moored by the small pier. The restaurant's outside lights extended along the handrail that led along the pier. The lights glinted on the dark waves that danced and rippled and splashed at the boat's side. On the beach, someone had started a fire, and where the smoke rose into the sky, tiny yellow sparks ignited and crackled. The group of people around the fire were young, perhaps in their early twenties. Philomena, at twenty-six, felt old compared to them and admired their loose-limbed movements and the playful way they chased and teased each other. Someone had brought a grill, and they were cooking. One of them was the young woman in the aqua dress.

Philomena scanned her vision from the young crowd by the fire, back to the dark rolling waves of the sea onto the cool sand. They were not so far away that she couldn't take off her shoes and wade into the water. But there was nothing to see in the distance only the vague idea that there was a horizon out there somewhere.

'Well,' Saul was saying, 'you see they have your fish?'

Philomena shook her head and looked across to Saul. He was beaming at her, his face a little shiny, and she wished he would undo his top button and remove his tie. She smiled at him. 'I'm sorry, I was far away.'

'Where were you?'

'I don't know. Just far.'

Saul reached across and placed his hand on hers. He squeezed gently on her folded hand. She loosened and held his hand which made him beam all the more. Philomena's heart beat a little faster. She knew he was making an effort for her. She knew how much Saul loved her and how much being with him made everything that was not good in her life so much more bearable. He was a good man. She was lucky to have him, to be with him. Her mind flitted to the nights in his bed, his warm strong body pressed close to her and the sound of his breath, the smell of him. All of him made her body feel beautiful, desired. With Saul she felt safe.

'Well, come back to me,' he said. 'To here, and choose what you want to eat.'

Finally, she opened the menu, and Saul leaned forward in anticipation. *Red snapper (when in season)* it said.

'Very nice.' She looked up, and Saul could not resist kissing her.

They chatted as they ate. The portion sizes were enormous, and Philomena took her time, sipping a fruit cocktail laced with rum. A slow and lazy intoxication began to take her over, and she was happy to sit and listen to Saul who talked about his idea of moving to America. New York to be exact. He'd been there only recently to visit his brother, also a teacher, who had taken him to jazz clubs and crowded bars and to shops selling food from around the world, and there were people from all around the world living in New York.

'You'd be surprised to see the number of black people there,' he said. 'And there are opportunities, lots of them just now. It's a good time to think about leaving.'

It was at that moment the girl in the aqua dress came into Philomena's view. She had left her group of friends and was walking towards the restaurant. She had no shoes on,

Philomena noticed, and she walked slowly, with slim hips and confident shoulders, the clavicles clearly defined. Philomena had wanted to call out Junie's name, but she knew it wasn't her. The girl just looked an awful lot like her. Suddenly, Philomena felt guilty about having such a good time, to have eaten so much she had to take deep breaths to expand her waistline. She had drunk so much her cheekbones were numb and she was happily smiling at nothing. Saul's talk was of something very serious, but she grinned helplessly as if she wasn't listening. And she wasn't listening, she realised, because it was as if she could hear the soft footsteps of the girl and the small swirls of sand that she kicked up with every step.

'Phil. I've lost you again, haven't I?'

'No, not at all. I think I might have had too much to drink.'

'We'll talk about it again another time. Maybe I'll start making applications. Once I have a job and we're married, it will be easier for you to find something over there.'

'Over there?'

Saul laughed patiently.

'How far back in my dialogue did I lose you? I was talking about moving to New York. You'll love it, Phil. Why don't we just go for a few days? Next school holiday, you and me. What do you think?'

Philomena patted her cheeks and blinked quickly to release herself from her reverie.

'I think it's good, Saul. But as usual, there are all the things I have to consider. My mother … finding work … adapting to somewhere so different…'

'Marrying me.'

'What?'

'I knew you didn't hear me drop that word in earlier.'

'I'm sorry, Saul, but shouldn't we talk this through? I—'

'Phil. You know I love you. I've said it a million times. You?' He let out a short laugh. 'I suppose I can count on my hand how many times you've said it to me.'

Philomena reached over and held his willing hands.

'I do love you, Saul, but I… But I need time to think.'

'About Junie?'

Philomena's head jerked upwards, her eyes meeting his.

'Why do you mention her?'

'Because you always do. I understand she's a close friend and that you worry about her, but I hope you won't form your decision based on a person you are not even allowed to talk to.'

'It's a lot more complicated than that.'

'Explain it to me then, this friendship. Because from what I can see it's not so much a friendship but you worrying about an unfortunate girl who could remove herself from a bad situation if she would only see sense.'

'And you're not seeing what's going on.'

'Then tell me what's going on. What is it about Junie that has you so distracted and so unlike yourself whenever you mention her?'

Philomena let go of Saul's hands and sat back in her chair. The sudden movement jolted the effects of the strong alcohol, and for a moment, she forgot where she was. She turned to see that the girl in the aqua dress was at the restaurant doorway, talking to the waitress. They giggled, held hands. The waitress laughed helplessly at something the aqua girl said. Philomena could see now that she looked nothing like Junie, not really. This girl was carefree and easy in her demeanour. She kept her attention on her conversation, she never looked furtively over her shoulder, she didn't wince when a man at one of the outside tables roared uncontrollably at a joke being shared. His fierce laughter took Philomena by surprise. It was as if the girl in aqua had deepened the trance-like effect the cocktail had pulled her into. Now she jolted forward and became aware of Saul sitting patiently. Waiting. For what? she wondered for a moment. Ah yes. Her answer. What was the question? No, she was the one with the question.

'What is my normal self, Saul? Who am I? What am I? Sometimes I'm not sure.'

'You're the woman I love.'

'But that's not a character trait.'

'No, but it means you don't have to worry.'

'Because you want to take care of me.'

'Is that so wrong?' Saul leaned forward, his voice soft. 'I want to marry you. You, the woman I love. The woman who is intelligent, gentle, kind, thoughtful and strong. The woman who cares for her mother, loves the children in her charge and is dedicated to their future. The woman I want to grow old with, have children with. The wife I choose.'

'I'm all those things except for when I talk about Junie?'

'You're still those things. It's just that your mind travels elsewhere when you do talk about her. I know you want to help her, and I will help, too.'

'You would?'

'Of course I would. Anything you need me to do. But just how big is this husband of hers?' He grinned.

'No, Saul, I would never ask you to tackle him. That man is capable of anything. I just need a refuge for her. If I can persuade her to run away, leave him, then we could hide her away. Just until he gets sick of looking for her. Maybe even too drunk to remember he had such a beautiful wife. Maybe she could come to America with us.' Philomena looked at him pleadingly.

'Phil, you haven't even said you'll marry me, let alone leave your mother, leave Dominica. But for Junie you'd give everything up.'

'Oh Saul, if only you'd seen how much he has changed her. Would it be so terrible for us to offer her a way out of her situation? A new life?'

'If we could do it, that would be a good thing. A Christian thing, but there are things we need to discuss first.'

Philomena looked at him, questioningly. Just then, the girl in the aqua dress walked by her again. She tiptoed onto the sand and followed her footprints back to her friends. For a moment, she disappeared between the space where the lights from the restaurant didn't illuminate the sand and where the flames from the fire glowed.

'Phil, Phil? Did you hear me?'

'I'm sorry, Saul, I am. What did you say?'

'I said, Philomena Ann Scott, will you marry me, be my wife and make a life with me in America?'

Philomena smiled broadly at the idea of taking Junie with them and helping her find her way; perhaps she could finally convince her mother, too. The love she felt for Saul swelled in her heart, and she knew this was right. Saul was the man she must marry, and everything else that followed from there would be perfect.

'Yes,' she breathed. 'Yes to all of it. You're a wonderful, beautiful and kind man, and I've never loved you more.'

She stood, unsteadily. Giddy from the decision she'd made, giddy from the drink, giddy because she had found a way to make her dream come true. Saul stood, too, and allowed

Philomena to take him into her embrace, stooping to wrap his arms around her waist.

'Is this a celebration?' The waitress was back at their table.

Philomena nodded enthusiastically.

'We're getting married,' Saul said, holding Philomena's hands.

'Congratulations,' said the waitress. 'When is the big day?'

'Soon,' said Saul.

'Very soon,' Philomena added.

15

In the early hours of the morning, Junie woke and sat up in bed. Gregory was on his back, snoring loudly and filling the air with cheap nicotine and rancid booze. She screwed up her face and wondered when in God's name he'd take off on one of his trips again. Wherever he went she didn't care, she just wished he would go. Let her breathe for a while, have time to take a bath, do something about her hair which was growing long and wild. She was so aware of how awful she must look, it was in a way a blessing that she hadn't seen much of Philomena. She'd be ashamed of her, and Junie didn't like that. Their last proper conversation had been the highlight of the last few weeks. Since then, Gregory had hung around the house like an uninvited guest, the relative no one looked forward to a visit from. She just wished he'd leave.

The living room was still, a film of dust rested on every surface, including the wooden floor. The room was dingy despite the start of another bright day, the sun lighting all the parts its rays could reach in a room that looked deserted or housed inhabitants who cared nothing for their surroundings. Or perhaps they were phantoms who moved around the house without stirring the dust. These phantoms had abandoned an unsightly pile of washing that overflowed from a wide wicker basket in the corner of the room.

Junie ignored the washing and stepped quietly outside to fetch water to wash her face. She had nothing clean to wear, but Gregory had forbidden her to go to the river without him. Whenever she suggested it was time to do the washing, he swore, pulled up a chair and poured himself another whisky before lighting a cigarette and going outside to sip booze and puff white smoke from his chest. He was on duty outside the house; she couldn't go anywhere unless he said so. It was understood that the only trip she was permitted to take without him, aside from fetching water or going out to the latrine or to cook in the outside kitchen, was to the allotment, no stopping anywhere or talking to anyone.

She set off for the allotment in a sweat-stained shirt and her usual trousers after gathering her gardening tools from the kitchen. She hung the bag of tools over her shoulder and began to walk up the hill to the allotment. Gregory had sold the mule and cart weeks ago. Now she was the mule, the cart, the gardener, the prisoner.

She passed the Scott house—her heart sank whenever she even looked in its direction—and continued on her way.

Several of the plots where Junie grew food lay neglected. Weeds sprouted up everywhere. Wild flowers of all colours, whose petals took off in the wind and attracted small birds to feast on the berries, lined the forest that bordered the plots. Junie didn't know the names of them, but old Pa Reynauld did. He told her about them, and she sometimes picked the brightest flowers and brought them to his tumbled-down house where she'd arrange them in a glass jar while he brewed tea.

Pa Reynauld knew nothing about Junie's life on the plain below. Junie couldn't hide bumps and bruises from him, but he said nothing about them. He would occasionally comment and say, 'Looking better today,' when a bruise on her face appeared less angry. He was already there when she arrived, bent over in two, wearing loose-fitting trousers and an open shirt. He was sucking on a pipe at the same time as pulling up the weeds surrounding his patch of spring onions. Junie marvelled at his flexibility and wondered how old he actually was. She knew he had grown-up children and his grandchildren were all adults. Some of those had children, too. She'd got confused about how many and their names and where they all lived when Pa tried to explain. So had he, chuckling helplessly before saying, 'Oh, let me just start again', then he'd begin the long twisting tale about his bloodline with the name of his firstborn, the only name that came to mind easily.

'Morning, my precious girl,' he called when he saw her arrive.

'Good morning, Pa. I see you already working hard. Don't tell me you've been here since yesterday and haven't been home.' She spoke to him in their native patois because Pa Reynauld never spoke in English and claimed that he'd forgotten how.

'Oh, you know me. Up before the cockerel and still awake when the moon arrives. I think you have several of your veg ready to pick and sell.'

'Well, my husband will be pleased. He bought this land so it could make a profit. I have lemons and limes in the garden down there. They just fall and rot into the earth. I already told him I could make something of them but I need a way to get them to market. But he still went and sold the mule, so I don't know how he expects I can carry food to sell.'

'Mr Newton comes up here regularly and takes baskets of my produce to market. He could take yours, I'm sure. I'll talk to him.'

'I had the idea of making pickles and jams, you see, but I'm afraid to tell him.'

'You mustn't be afraid of a good idea. But it will be a lot of work for a little thing like you. You'd need help. Money. He could help you.'

'I don't know about that.'

'Only way is to ask. Or do what my wife used to do. Plant the idea in his head and let him think it was his.' Pa Reynauld laughed with wild abandon. His toothless smile broad, the creases in his skin deepening. He began to talk about his wife, making his way to his tool shed where there was a wooden rocking chair outside. He sat down with a sigh and told Junie, again, about the time he met his beloved Valeria.

The hours ticked away as Junie sat cross-legged on the earth beside Pa Reynauld. The sun poured heat onto her back, and the smoke from the pipe that Pa continuously re-lit made her woozy. Her stomach grumbled with hunger, and Pa stopped to look at her.

'Is it breakfast time, my precious girl?'

'It must be. I haven't done a thing all morning.'

'Who says a person has to work every day? Come on.' He eased himself up out of the chair and began to head to the lane leading to his house.

'Maybe I should get home to make him some coffee.' Junie hesitated.

'And he doesn't know how to do that? A grown man?' Pa laughed and continued on. Junie felt she had no choice but to follow him. It wouldn't be the first time she'd gone to Pa's house. Gregory would be none the wiser. As far as he knew, Junie was up in the allotment working on the future earnings of his investment. Junie knew that simply bringing lemons, limes, tomatoes, peppers and a few small potatoes to market would not be enough to make the kind of money that Gregory expected. But to make them into something that could sell would be more profitable. Pa was right, she had to find money to put into the venture, but she doubted Gregory had any. What he earned, when he earned it, would mostly support his drinking. She didn't want to let go of the idea of a business. It was the only hopeful thing in her life, and there was always the possibility that if they made good money, Gregory wouldn't get so angry all the time. He'd have a reason to get up in the morning. She would, too.

It always amazed her that given the size of Pa Reynauld's house, he and his wife raised six children there. It was well kept and comfortable inside. Just a living room with a dining table in it, a couch and an easy chair and two bedrooms. One he slept in, the other was filled with broken furniture and boxes of his wife's clothes.

'Sit, sit, sit,' he said. On the table were two large plastic bowls that covered some food that Pa must have prepared before heading to his allotment. There was cold fried fish, salad, bread and a covered jug of juice.

'You expecting someone, Pa?' Junie didn't sit, she helped Pa as he reached for plates and glasses from a side cupboard.

'I have one of the grandchildren coming to help me repair that.' He nodded towards the ceiling. Junie looked up but couldn't see anything specific wrong with it. 'Rain is getting in so the roof has to be fixed.'

'I see. So your grandchild is a builder?'

'Has his own business in Roseau. Or is it Portsmouth? Maybe both. Anyway, they been promising for months one of them would come. The last one who came said if a hurricane pass, this whole thing will come down. They want me to move into town, to go live with one of them. I said no.'

'It's not a bad idea to be close to family. You'll need someone to look after you one day.'

'And when that day come, the Lord will take me to look
after me and I will be with my darling again.' He chuckled
and sat down.

'Should I go out and make us a pot of coffee?' Junie asked.

'That would be very good.'

By now, Junie had lost all concept of time, like the mornings by the river with Philomena when the seconds, minutes
and hours didn't matter because the two women would be
busy laughing, talking, escaping into their books. She
thought about her friend again, her love of books and her
closeness to her mother. So close she was still at home
whereas Junie bickered with her siblings and fell out with
her mother. She wondered, as she waited for the water to
boil, if perhaps she forced herself to love Gregory. Did her
need to get out of her house make her blind to some of Gregory's distasteful ways, the ways her mother saw quite
clearly and that she had since discovered for herself. Junie
had never got on with her mother. As soon as she'd reached
puberty, her mother had talked about 'dirty' girls. Girls who
spread their legs before marriage and were a disgrace to their
family. She had kept Junie out of school for many years and
had never noticed that Junie could barely write her name.
Her mother would call on her to help clean the house, go on
errands, help her with the day-to-day running of her cleaning
business. Her mother cleaned for the rich folk who occupied
the grand plantation houses from the past. Some of her rich
clients were white, others were influential black business
owners or speculators from overseas. Junie's mother had
overstretched herself, cleaning several business properties
locally and in town. She came home tired and miserable and

took her frustration out on her daughter who was showing all the signs of developing her mother's beauty which her mother had long since abandoned, working tirelessly for a modicum of status in her village. Her mother had taken Junie on cleaning jobs since the age of ten. By the time she'd met Gregory, she'd had enough of the back-breaking work.

Gregory hadn't asked anything of Junie other than she come away with him and be his wife. She was about to turn eighteen. She was tired of her mother, tired of cleaning until her hands were red and raw, worried that she would become a carbon copy of her mother one day. Little did she know that she had swapped one tyrant for another. Her mother knew. She knew who Gregory was deep inside, but Junie was too eager to escape to take her time and find out.

The water boiled suddenly, and Junie prepared a pot of strong coffee. She thought about the food on the table and her stomach rumbled again. She couldn't remember when she last ate a full plate of food. What had she done with her life? How could she have been so blind?

Junie carried the coffee inside and set it on the table. Old Pa Reynauld looked as if he had fallen asleep. His head sagged forward as he sat in the dining chair, a grey cloud masking his usual sunny disposition. He must be having a serious dream, Junie thought and went to pour herself some coffee. If Pa's grandchild didn't come soon, Junie might be tempted to make a start on the breakfast that had been laid out for him. She imagined that one piece of fried fish wouldn't be so bad to help herself to. She was invited after all. Just as she reached to uncover one of the bowls, Junie heard a truck arrive, the wheels bumping over the rough terrain of the road and onto the smooth patch of grass at the side of Pa's house before the driver stopped and pulled up the handbrake. She shook Pa's arm to stir him.

He woke with a start and stared through Junie as if he was only imagining she was there.

'Sorry,' she said. 'I had to wake you.'

'My precious girl. You still here? What time is it?'

'It's still morning, and I'm still here, Pa. You invited me to have breakfast with you and your grandchild. He's here.'

The truck door slammed, and a man whistled as he walked up to the door. There was a brief knock before it was opened, and a tall man in jeans and a checked shirt came in, saying, 'Hello, hello. I'm here.' He greeted them in English before deferring to patois.

'Papa! Look at you, so handsome. You already been to garden?' The man was tall and sturdy looking. Broad shoulders with a good posture. His hair was trimmed short, his skin the colour of cinnamon, a slight sheen to it from the hot drive up from Roseau to the mountains. His eyes were bright, and he smiled broadly at Junie. 'Don't tell me you already take a new wife, Pa?'

Pa Reynauld chuckled like a child behind his hand, his toothless smile obscured. His shoulders shook until he gained control and put his hand on Junie's.

'This is my precious girl. I told you about her last time you came.'

'I didn't come last time, that was Dad.'

'You all are the same person to me these days.' Pa laughed again. 'Come and sit. We been waiting for you before we could start eating.'

Pa's grandson walked to the table where he stood with his hands on his hips.

'Oh you shouldn't have waited for me. You know I would always eat before I come here, Pa. Go on, go on. You two go ahead.'

'Can I pour you a coffee?' Junie asked timidly.

'Yes, please,' said Pa's grandson. 'And what do they call you?'

'I'm Junie.' She smiled and shakily poured some coffee into the China teacup whose blue printed paintwork was almost worn away. He put out a hand.

'Vincent,' he said and gave Junie's hand a vigorous shake. He took the cup to the easy chair by the window and sat down with a grand sigh. 'Please,' he said, smiling at Junie. 'Eat.' He slurped some coffee and let out a satisfied, 'Ah.'

'Can you do the whole job in a day?' Pa asked.

'No, no. Today I'll survey the whole house and surrounding land. See what else needs to be done around here apart from the roof. Maybe come up with one of the labourers to help. I think it might be a long job.'

The room was quiet except for the sound of Pa trying to eat with very few teeth and Junie nibbling at the fish and drinking guava. She tried not to stare at Vincent who sat looking around at the room and taking sips of coffee. He was sizing up his work and appeared to be ignoring Junie until their eyes met. He grinned at her, and she blushed under his gaze.

Pa tried to persuade Vincent to eat something, but he continued to refuse.

'It's not so bad, is it Junie?' Pa asked her.

'You are an excellent cook, Pa.' She had eaten a lot more than Pa had, she couldn't stop helping herself to portion after portion.

'Well, you're certainly enjoying it,' Vincent commented. Immediately, she felt shame. Had it shown to the men just how hungry she was? Was she being too greedy? 'You have a good appetite,' Vincent said. 'How can you be so small when you eat like that?'

'She is a hard worker,' said Pa. 'A very hard worker.'

'Maybe I can find some jobs for you around here, then,' said Vincent. 'What do you say?' Pa began to laugh again, Junie following suit, imagining herself climbing up a ladder and Gregory actually agreeing to it. Vincent returned his empty coffee cup to the table and stood with his hands on his hips again, his back to the door. With all the laughter, neither heard it creak open.

'So this is where you get to.'

They all turned to see Gregory's large dark figure standing at the door. Junie caught the smell of stale cigarette smoke and a night of alcohol oozing out of Gregory's pores, out of his mouth, curled as it was in a grimace. Junie sprang up.

'You stay and finish your breakfast,' Pa said holding up a shaky hand. He eased himself to standing. 'I don't remember anyone knocking on my door before it open. I don't say to come in.'

Junie went to make introductions, but Pa shushed her.

'Young man, this is my home. It is open to friends and family. Are you either?'

'I came looking for my wife. I haven't seen her all morning.' Gregory shifted his weight, looking awkward at the open door. Behind him a cloudless and glorious sky contrasted with his drab and dirty attire, his clumsy stance and the odour he emitted.

'And isn't it you who send your wife to come and work on your garden?'

'She stay so long,' said Gregory. 'I thought something happen.'

'Can I interest you in a coffee or some water before you take yourself back home?' asked Pa. 'Junie still have things to do up here. Now you know she safe, with friends, you're not compelled to stay.' Junie had never seen Pa stand so straight or keep a serious face for so long. He always had a smile dancing close to the surface, but he found no humour in the situation. This stranger in his house.

'How much work you have left to do?' Gregory asked moving his gaze to Junie. He had never sounded so gentle, so well spoken.

She looked at Pa. 'I have a little weeding to do. Not much, and I think we are coming close to having some peppers and tomatoes.'

'Then I'll see you at home?' Gregory gave Junie a lasting look. There was no malice in it. Nothing for her to fear. Gregory nodded in turn to Pa and his grandson before leaving and pulling the door shut.

'Your husband? Really?' said Vincent. Junie nodded, heat in her cheeks and the back of her neck. 'I would have said you'd be married to someone less...'

'Maybe I should go.' Junie turned to Pa.

'You sit down and finish eat.' Pa was still looking serious. 'When you are satisfied, then you go. Not before.' He sat again. 'And I think you need to give him time to cool off.'

After a few moments of silence and an exchange of glances, Vincent dismissed himself so he could start work. Junie picked up a piece of bread and began to chew, but the dough no longer tasted sweet on her tongue.

<h1>16</h1>

Not long after Gregory left the house, Junie became anxious. She hoped Pa was right, that Gregory needed time to cool off, then he might not lash out after finding she'd disobeyed him and spoken to someone other than him. One thing for certain was that the exertion of walking up to Pa Reynauld's would have been too much for him and he was likely to have got back home, slumped on the bed and fallen asleep. He spent his days in a drunken fog, slipping out of it to buy more drink, to make Junie's life a misery or to disappear off, claiming he was working away and she'd see him when she saw him. If she was lucky, he'd sleep for an hour or two, wake up and forget what happened and she could avoid an argument with him, or worse.

Junie stood outside the house with Pa watching as Vincent climbed his ladder up to the roof and looked at the damage that time and the elements had raged on the old house. They were out of hurricane season, but there would be another, and Junie feared for the old man's safety. Vincent climbed back down the ladder.

'Pa, you'd be better off knocking the whole thing down and building a new house.'

Pa chuckled and waved his grandson away.

'I'm serious, Pa. This place is a death trap, and the glass in those windows isn't fixed in securely. They could blow in, and you'd have no protection from the wind, the rain.'

'I'll take my chances—as usual,' Pa said.

105

Vincent rubbed his chin. 'Daddy said you were stubborn and that you wouldn't listen to my advice. All I can do is fix it up the best I can. Pray for kind weather.' He looked at Junie and raised his eyes at her as if she could do anything to convince Pa to move in with one of his children. She shrugged and patted Pa's arm.

'I best be going. I haven't done any work on the crops today, but I have things around the house to do.' She thought of the dusty living room, the washing, the empty larder in the kitchen. She had done so much cleaning in her life, she knew how to keep the house spotless, but Gregory would insist on her doing nothing until she was told. She mustn't make a noise when he was trying to sleep; the house could look after itself. This was all well and good until he turned on her, called her a disgrace and pushed and shoved her as she tried to get the place back in order.

'Are you sure you don't want to stay a while?' Pa looked worried.

She kissed his cheek. 'No, I must go.' She began to skip back to the path. 'Work to do. Nice to meet you, Vincent.' She waved. Vincent waved back and looked as though he wanted to say something to her but changed his mind.

Junie hesitated when she got down to the allotment, deciding whether or not to collect her bag of tools but thought it easier to leave them until tomorrow when she'd come back again and start picking the ripened fruit. She didn't want to delay getting back any longer, and besides, no one but Pa would come up there; her tools would be safe.

Her tummy was full for once, and she smiled up at the late morning sun, thirsty and thinking how nice it would have been to have stayed longer at Pa's. He was great company, and his grandson seemed nice, too.

Closer to her home, she spotted Mrs Scott sweeping the steps of the veranda. She called out to Junie as she neared the Scott house.

'Junie, I have some seed cake I bake earlier. Would you like some?' Junie stopped, briefly pondering the idea of cake but moved her eyes to her own front door. It was closed. 'One little piece of cake won't hurt.'

Mrs Scott had stepped down from the veranda and was approaching her. 'You too skinny, Junie. Come inside, I'll cut a piece for you.' Then she motioned over her shoulder towards Junie's house. 'And him if he's home.'

'I've just come from having a big breakfast, so maybe I'll say no this time. But thank you for your kindness, Ma Scott. You and Phil enjoy it.' Junie glanced at her front door. She couldn't sense any movement inside. Had he gone out? Was he asleep as she'd hoped? 'And how is Phil? I haven't seen her in weeks.' She was a little shaky now, nervously looking at the front window, thinking she saw a shadow. Gregory did not want her talking to Mrs Scott any more than he wanted her to talk to Phil, Pa or anyone else. But she couldn't be disrespectful. Mrs Scott was trying to be neighbourly.

'Oh, my goodness.' Mrs Scott put one hand on her chest and took the hand Junie had on the front gate. 'Phil is getting married. She and Saul. Can you imagine? I thought I would never be rid of that girl.' Mrs Scott laughed playfully. 'I'm just joking. She has been a real blessing to me, but it's about time she had a family of her own. Time to take her head out of her books.'

Junie contemplated this. Phil was getting married. That meant she'd be leaving home. She'd be leaving her behind. Junie glanced at her own house again. It was generating a message, a warning, *Come inside before he catches you talk-ing to her.*

'Wish her congratulations from me. I should go.' Junie pulled her hand away from Mrs Scott and waved her fingers lightly at her. She bowed her head as she pushed open her own gate, aware that Mrs Scott hadn't moved from her spot.

She touched the door handle and took a deep breath before opening it. Inside it was quiet, still, dust motes settled and the dirty washing looking forlornly at her. But he was gone. She exhaled in relief. Before Junie could take another breath, the door flew open behind her and Gregory was there. He grabbed her up by her elbows and kicked the door closed with his heel. She closed her eyes tight, waiting. For what? The back of his hand? A fist? An almighty shove that sent her flying across the cluttered room and into the big old dresser again? She would always crash into something. The dining table, a chair, straight onto the floor or, if she was lucky, the matted easy chair. She dared to open her eyes after several seconds of Gregory saying and doing nothing. His face was as she'd expected, eyes bulging, mouth drawn into a scowl. He was almost comical now. As if he'd learned to look menacing from a picture in a book. He shook her and then released her. She stepped back, into the dining table which shuddered on its wobbly legs but supported her weight.

Gregory pointed a finger straight between her eyes. 'Who do you think you are now?'

'I...'

'Well? Who told you to go and make acquaintance with that old bastard up there?'

'You know I see him up at the plot sometimes. I did tell you. You want me to stop going?'

'I never said that. What I want is for you to do your work and not go troubling anyone.'

'He invited me, I couldn't exactly say no.'

'You couldn't exactly—' He slapped her face. The force of it rattled her ears and stung her cheek, her hand immediately flying up to cover the mark it made. '*I* tell you exactly what you can and cannot do. You hear me?'

She nodded quickly and tried to duck away from him. He pushed her back against the table and moved in so that she was pinned against it.

'I said…' He drew out each word. 'Do you hear me?'

'Yes, Gregory, I hear you. I'm sorry.' She closed her eyes.

'And what have I told you about *them*?'

Junie opened her eyes to see he was pointing in the direction of the Scott house.

'It's just so hard. Mrs Scott is an older woman. I was taught to show respect. It's hard to ignore someone.'

'The only person you respect around here is me. Do we have an understanding?' His arms circled her body, trapping her escape as he gripped the table with each hand. Junie cowered backwards, trying to move her face away from his.

'Yes, Gregory. I understand. I have to go. I need to use the toilet.'

He breathed heavily into her face for a few moments.

'Go.' He unlocked the prison his arms had made. Junie rushed to the door and ran out to the toilet. She held her hand against the door and swallowed air until there seemed to be none left in the small shed. She stood for several minutes and heard the front door open. Shortly the gate banged closed. He was gone. For how long she didn't know. She opened the toilet door and peeped out before venturing outside. It was such an ordinary day. The sun warm, the birds singing, wind through the branches across the other side of the plain, Junie's eyes smarting from the slap she'd received. She dragged her feet back to the house, and through the oleander that separated their houses, she could make out Mrs Scott sitting on the veranda. If only Mrs Scott had chosen this moment to speak to her, now that *he* was gone.

17

Philomena was excited. There was a plan, loose as it was, to get Junie out of Gregory's clutches and off to America with her and Saul. Saul had told her that as professionals it would be easy to find jobs and gain citizenship. He had already started sending letters of application and was very positive about his prospects because of the contacts his brother had made for him. As a married man, his wife would be permitted to enter even if she hadn't found a job yet. It was all set. Philomena only had to find a way to bring her mother over with her, as well as Junie, and the circle would be complete. Convincing her mother would take time, but Junie would be happy to come. That much she was certain of. All Philomena had to do was find a way to speak to Junie about this plan. She just needed to bide her time and wait for Gregory to be away from the house.

Saul had convinced Philomena that it would be a good idea to plan the wedding for that year: the summer, when school was finished. He was so sure he'd find a job in the coming months and they could be in New York by September. It was February; not much time to plan a wedding, but she would try. Her mother was more than pleased to help but constantly shied away from the idea of going to New York herself.

'I can come on a holiday, next year, when you've had time to settle in,' her mother said, lighting up her small pipe after dinner. They hadn't cleared away the dishes yet. She'd cooked a large meal of boiled fig and yams in a fish broth.

As usual, Mrs Scott had cooked too much and, as usual, had planned ways to sneak a plate across to Junie. But Gregory had been sitting in the old wooden chair outside the house all evening, smoking a strange-smelling cigarette and calling out nonsense to an invisible intruder. It was dark when they'd finished eating, and though Gregory seemed to have fallen asleep, slumped over in the small chair, she and Philomena knew there was no way they could get past him without him stirring and waking up.

Mrs Scott lit a lamp and went onto the veranda to continue her pipe.

'Oh, Mum.' Philomena followed her outside, grabbing a cardigan because it was a cool night. 'Why would you want to stay up here in this backward part of the country when you could be away and discovering something new?'

'There isn't anything I don't already know. I have nothing new to learn at my age.' Her bones creaked and cracked as she sat in a high-backed chair and let out a satisfied sigh. 'Besides, what man wants his mother-in-law staying with him and his new wife?'

'Saul is very keen for you to come.' Philomena leaned back against the veranda gate and crossed her arms around her body.

'He's keen to marry you, that's all I can see. He's left a big burden on my shoulders to organise a wedding in just a few months.'

'Mum, you are the one who took over the arrangements.' Philomena pulled an exasperated face at her mother which Mrs Scott chose to ignore. 'You know I don't want a whole big thing. Just you and Pearson and maybe his family would come over. Saul only has his parents. His brother might come from New York, bring his family, but that would be it.'

'No, it won't be it!' Mrs Scott exclaimed. 'You have aunts, cousins. And aren't you going to invite the other teachers from school? They'll want their families to come. And I've got the women from the church group. Let's see ... how many of them are there?'

'No, Mum. It's not going to be a big thing. Before I know it, the whole village will be invited. Saul and I are paying for it, and we'll need all our money for when we go.'

'Have it your way.' Mrs Scott threw up her hand.

Insects were flitting and buzzing around the lamp. Mrs Scott tried to shoo them by flapping her hands at them, but they circled away only to return seconds later. She slapped her forearm after being bitten.

'Stupid flies.'

'Maybe we should go inside,' said Philomena. She looked across to her neighbours' house. There were no lights on. She wondered about Junie and what was going on in the darkness over there. Nothing good, nothing you'd expect between a husband and his wife who had turned out all the lights so early in the evening. There wasn't a sound from within. There was every chance that Gregory was still out on the chair, but she couldn't see a light from his cigarette, neither could she smell the thick tobacco he'd been polluting the air with earlier. Maybe he'd polluted his body enough and was in there asleep.

Was Junie sleeping, too, she wondered or was she standing alone in the front room, looking out into the shadows of her garden? Outside maybe, shivering in the coolness of the air, planning her escape? Something moved in the Williams' garden, and Philomena squinted to see if she'd been right, that Junie was there and could hear her making plans for the wedding. It was Mrs Scott who'd told Junie about the wedding, and she hoped that Junie wouldn't think she was abandoning her. It would be easy to think that. They hadn't seen each other properly in weeks, so it was more important now that Philomena tell Junie about her plan to take her to New York.

'You coming in?' Her mother got up from the chair and held the lamp.

'I just want to take in some more air.'

Crickets chirped noisily in the background of her thoughts. Her mother left the lamp out on the veranda table and went in to clear up the plates. Philomena heard the china and cutlery being piled up and offered to take them from her mother when she came outside.

'Let me,' said Philomena. 'In New York, the kitchens and toilets are inside. Hot water in your bathroom. Toilets that flush.'

'All that is for kings and queens. I'm just a simple woman.' Mrs Scott turned her back on Philomena and went inside.

'Oh, Mum.'

Trying to find her footing in the dark, Philomena carried the crockery to the kitchen. She placed the plates down, but with no lamp, it was pointless trying to wash them up. Again, she wondered about Junie. It was clear they hadn't had an evening meal. Gregory, as usual, had had servings of alcohol to satisfy him and now drugs, it would seem. No wonder he never thought about what Junie needed, the nutrition, the love, the affection. She could give her all of that.

Instead of going back to the house, she stepped carefully towards the oleander, just to see if she could make anything out at all over there. It was far too still and dark for her liking. She crept closer to the oleander and leaned into a gap in

the leaves. She pulled a branch to one side and squinted, trying to let her eyes adjust to the shapes and shadows. She
couldn't quite make anything out until something moved,
stirred on the other side of the tree. A large object, an old
shirt, a tall figure. Gregory. She stood up, heart pounding.
He did nothing but stand there. She saw him as clearly as if
it was day, or at least a silhouette of his body, his square
shoulders. Her mouth was dry, not that she could have found
anything to say. She was spying on *him*, not the other way
around. She stepped back, once, twice and turned to run. She
hurried up the veranda steps, grabbed the lamp awkwardly
and entered the house, locking it behind her.

'You look like you seen a ghost, Phil.'

'It's him,' she whispered. 'He's been out there all this time,
listening to everything we were saying.'

Mrs Scott looked towards the window. 'That man should
learn to mind his own business. Anyway, we didn't say anything on him. Just talked about the wedding, but that's not
something we can hide.'

'I know, but it makes me feel horrible.' She rubbed her
arms. 'And you want to stay here with him as your neighbour?'

'I want to live in my house, that's what I want.'

Philomena drew the curtains, picked up a book and sat
down. 'I'd hate myself if anything happened between you.
Please, Mum, just think about it a bit more. You didn't have
to come straight away. Maybe in a few months, even a year.
We'll be settled by then.'

'Enough, Phil. That's enough.' Mrs Scott took up her knitting and smiled as she picked up where she'd left off.

Philomena held her book open, but all the time she was thinking of ways to change her mother's mind. She didn't want to leave her behind, she didn't want to leave Junie.

18

Gregory was gone, for how long Junie didn't know, so she decided to make the best of her time without him standing over her like a dark cloud for the whole day. He had grumbled something about a job in Belle Maniere. Junie didn't ask about it or who offered it to him. Gregory did make trips to the village from time to time, so maybe he found out about the job then. He had stopped allowing her to go to the market and had decided he'd go out and buy the things they needed. Most of the time he'd stagger home with a basket of booze and what looked like leftover food from the market stalls that couldn't be sold because it had been left out in the sun all day. That included fish. When she had to cook fish that wasn't fresh, the kitchen smelt for days, as did her hair and her skin.

Once Gregory had left for his job, the house stood dim and deathly, the way it usually did but without his stench and his oppressive mood darkening her day further. The bed she sat on smelt of stale, sweaty bodies, sex and very likely the tears she cried herself to sleep with most nights. She pulled her hair to her nose, sniffed it, lifted her arms and gasped at her own odour.

Junie got out of bed and looked at Gregory's clothes in a heap on the bedroom floor. She took out the only two items hanging in the wardrobe—her dirty work dungarees and a stained shirt—and put them on. She loaded a small basket with some of the dirty laundry and a large block of carbolic soap from the kitchen, hoisted it onto the side of her hip and headed to the river.

It was still early, the air was fresh after a light rain, the heat building slowly but not at its hottest yet. Junie lay the basket of clothes very close to the river's edge, stripped off her old clothes and tossed them onto the basket before gliding out into the water. It was cold on her skin. Closing her eyes tightly she sank beneath the surface for as long as she could hold her breath. She swam back to the clothes bundle and pulled the soap out. She rubbed it onto her arms, her face, her hair and tried to generate as much lather as possible. Foam built on her face, into her hair as she massaged her scalp. She knew Philomena would disapprove of using this soap in her hair: it would be too drying and cause tangles. She would hand her some simple shampoo, a bar of scented soap from town for her skin. She would have a moisturiser, a wide-toothed comb to de-tangle her hair for her. Philomena had soft towels, and Junie hadn't even brought one this morning. All she cared about was washing Gregory off her, out of her pores.

She watched the foam on the water drift away, begin to dissolve and become nothing. Junie wished she was like the soap bubbles, flowing in the river, running out to sea and vanishing into the vastness of it. It would be a satisfying way for her nightmare to end. Far better than what her mind told her would happen, that Gregory would end her life one day with his hands, and it wouldn't be as simple as floating away. It would be enduring, painful and more blood and anger than she had already suffered. Yes, Gregory would kill her one day, that much she knew.

The water soon felt warm. Junie continued to float, glide, swim. She didn't want to leave the water. Time ticked serenely as Junie called on the good memories she had of being in the water with Philomena. She felt the pride of learning how to read. She and Philomena had made a plan to continue her lessons as soon as Gregory went away, to seize the opportunity her freedom afforded her, even if it was only for a day. But she was too ashamed to go and knock on Philomena's door looking the way she did. Besides, Philomena would be at school now, and she hadn't seen her pass by in ages. She must be spending time with this man she planned to marry. Junie had seen him driving the big car that whisked Phil away at a time she needed her. And now she was going to marry him and never be there for her again. It seemed pointless to start up their lessons, try to re-kindle a friendship that played out sporadically and would be gone altogether when Phil moved away.

Junie shook her head, driving away images of what life would be like if she no longer had the possibility of seeing Philomena, if only briefly. Never at all was too painful to think about.

She dressed in her old dungarees and carried her dirty clothes to a large rock jutting out from the river where the water formed a deep pool, perfect for standing in and soaking clothes. She spent hours rubbing soap into stains and grime, rinsing and laying them onto the rock to dry. Her stomach growled, hunger pains slowed her progress, but she worked steadily to finish washing all the items she'd brought. She allowed them to dry as much as they could on the rock and lay down at the place she and Philomena used to read together and fell asleep.

It was hunger that woke her two hours later. Her old, fraying dress that she'd washed earlier was almost dry, so she put that on. She left her old dungarees hidden by the drying rock and gathered her washing into the basket. Most of it being still damp made the basket heavy, and she heaved and panted as she walked back home, the basket in front of her, her arms straining to carry them.

She hung the washing on the line in the back garden and sized up her tasks for the rest of the day. In the kitchen she made some coffee, ate the last of a stale loaf of bread and went about cleaning the interior of the house. Layers of dust motes floated in the hazy light coming in at the window. Little by little the house was looking more presentable, but sadly she was not. In her old dress with her hair now dried into a frizzy mass around her face, she went to find something to bind it all away in. She found a hair tie that she'd hidden away, a gift from Philomena, and then she put on a headscarf. As she knotted it at the back, she heard a truck pull up outside. Her heart sank when she thought it must be Gregory and that somehow this job of his had fallen through. She sat at the table waiting for his footsteps and for him to come bursting into the house demanding to know what she'd been doing all day.

Seconds past but Gregory didn't appear. The truck had idled for a while and then the engine was switched off. She got up to look out of the window and saw Vincent, Pa Reynauld's grandson, entering the gate, carrying a lumpy Hessian sack. He called, 'Hello' and continued up to the door. Junie slapped her hand to her mouth. She didn't want Vincent to see her in her old dress, a thin headscarf trying to mask the fact that her hair was wild looking. He knocked on the door and then she thought of Gregory. What if he had been home? Junie would have suffered for Vincent's visit, no matter how much she tried to convince Gregory that she hadn't encouraged it.

Vincent knocked and called out again. She opened the door and found Vincent stooping to put the sack down and stepped outside.

'Vincent, hello,' she stuttered.

'Oh, you are here.' Vincent wiped his shiny forehead with the back of his hand. 'Pa sent me. He picked some of your produce before it got overripe. You didn't do it that day, and you haven't been back.'

Junie swallowed, looking over her shoulder. She hadn't quite finished cleaning the house. The floor could be washed, she hadn't moved the rest of the dirty laundry out of sight. She pulled the door closer to and continued to smile sweetly at Vincent.

'Everything all right?' he asked.

'Oh, yes. Fine. I was just … I … well, doing some cleaning, so you didn't catch me at a very good moment.'

'It's fine. Pa was hoping to see you soon. He sent a few extra things that he hoped you'd like. Some cabbage. I think even some eggs in a box, there. Goat milk.'

'Oh my goodness. Please thank Pa for me.'

'You can do that yourself. Next time you're up. I'm there.' He fidgeted as he talked. Hands on his hips then briefly into the pockets of his overall and then he'd scratch the side of his head. 'Yes, working on Pa's roof. As well as other things, so I'll be there a while.'

'Oh I can't, I mean, I don't usually call in at the house.'

'No?' Vincent looked disappointed. 'All the same, maybe you'll change your mind.'

'No, Vincent. I…' She looked over her shoulder at the small gap in the door. 'It's my husband you see? You met him. He can be a bit, how can I say, short with people. And he doesn't want, or doesn't like it if I'm away from the house too long, and he isn't very fond of visitors.'

Vincent laughed nervously and shook his head.

'What I mean is, Vincent, he wouldn't be happy for you to call on me here. Not a man, coming here to see me.'

'I was only passing on a message.'

'I know, and I am so happy Pa thought of me. But, can you see? Jealous husband. It can be a problem for some women.' She hadn't meant to but she had touched her hand to her face, the last place Gregory had hit her, then rested her hand on the bruising on her wrist that was fading but clear to any- one that they had been made by a large hand, squeezing tightly, coming close to snapping her delicate bones.

Vincent's eyes moved down to her wrist.

'Pa told me. He's worried about you,' he said. 'He wants you to know that he will do anything he can for you. You only have to say the word.'

'I know.'

'You know? So why haven't you called out for help? Don't you have people? Friends, family nearby?' He looked at the Scott house.

Junie's eyes swept over to Phil's house, too. She thought about the lack of feeling her mother showed her and how alone she felt. She was alone and trapped in a prison where the bars were invisible but the opportunity to escape was not there. Where would she run to? Who or what did she have apart from this life? This life she'd chosen and had been warned against. It was too late to go back. What good would going to Philomena's house or Pa's do? He'd find her there. He could do anything to her if she made him angry enough.

'Vincent, I know Pa means well, but I have to work this out for myself.'

'I don't want to intrude, I have only met you once, but I can see how afraid you are. I know you don't know me, but you know Pa so you know it's true when I say to you, I can help you.'

Junie contemplated this. A salty tear escaped from the corner of her eye. She couldn't stop the few more that followed and tried to dry her cheeks with her knuckle. She sniffed as Vincent nervously put his hands in his pockets. She didn't want Vincent, as gentle as he was, to come to blows with Gregory. Vincent was tall, looked strong, but Gregory was a much bigger man. If Vincent tried to reason with him, Gregory would use the only thing he knew how to use: his fists. No, she couldn't allow this to go any further.

'I know what you're thinking,' Vincent said after Junie had gathered herself and stopped sniffing. 'You think it is hopeless. But have faith, Junie, and learn to trust people.'

She looked down at the bag.

'I will go,' Vincent said, 'and I won't come back because I don't want to cause a problem for you. But I do want to help you. And I will.' He nodded and backed away from the door. He waved and said nothing more before he turned, jumped into his truck and drove off.

19

No matter how hard she tried, Philomena couldn't disguise the knot of guilt that lay in the depths of her stomach every time she thought of Junie and did nothing to help her. The wedding was happening soon, in time for Saul to take up the new position he'd been awarded at a school in New York as a teacher of mathematics. It was a step down in position but paid a lot better than his head teacher salary at the current school on the island. Philomena was glad of the new job, she had been excited for it as much as she'd been excited for the wedding because it was the only way she could see of extricating her friend from Gregory's clutches. It was the ideal way for Junie not to have to live in fear, and they'd no longer have to look over their shoulders if they wanted to meet. In New York, Philomena could be with Junie all the time.

This much was true, yet a conflict of emotions stirred inside Philomena. She knew she loved Junie in a way that went beyond friendship, a way that she didn't quite understand. And here she was in Saul's bed and it felt right, comfortable, good. She loved Saul. That she was sure of but couldn't understand why it felt as though Saul would be in the way when the three of them went to New York. This was a trip for two people, a chance for something new, a life of possibilities and advancement, but she didn't know which of the two she wanted to start this new phase of her life with. Was it with Saul? Was it with Junie?

She lay in Saul's bed, aware that she spent a larger proportion of her week at his house than she did at home. At home, all she did was wring her hands and pine for Junie. With Saul, the feelings of anxiety lifted because of how he made her feel. But then those moments passed and the guilt took over.

She curled into a ball, hugging her knees to her chest as she lay on one side. She hoped to ease the knot, but her mind whirred with confusion. She and Saul had spent the day talking about the wedding. Everything was in place now. It had been a reasonably quick courtship, a short engagement period and now a wedding just months away. For someone who had never planned on getting married or going much further than the market in town, she wondered how she got to this point.

'Good morning,' Saul said in a sleepy voice. So caught up in her turmoil, she hadn't heard him stir. He wrapped his arms around her and pulled her body into his. It was warm and comforting. They'd taken a shower together the night before, had lazy sex in his bed and fallen asleep exhausted, their fatigue added to because of the amount of rum they'd drunk while cooking a meal together. They'd eaten late and gone out walking to let the enormous meal settle.

Saul's house was on a mountain slope. It was a beautiful mountain, green and rocky, and his car bumped and juddered as it climbed it. The car wasn't suitable for the terrain, but he drove it just the same. Outside his bedroom window, a never-ending forest grew upwards to the sky and off into a distant place that only the soaring birds with their blue, red and gold feathers knew. She would miss this view, she would miss this island.

She allowed herself to be rolled onto her back; Saul smiled down at her.

'I think Mum was expecting us at church this morning?' she said to him.

'Are we too late?'

'Perhaps. But she won't be happy that we arrived together. Everyone will know I was here.'

'Is there anything that goes on around here that no one knows about? Everyone knows everyone's business. Plus, we're getting married so that should keep the gossips at bay. Most of them are coming to the wedding, anyway.'

'This wedding.' Philomena sat up in bed and pulled the covers over her naked torso. 'It's out of hand. I told Mum, I don't know how many times, that I only wanted a little thing.'

'I don't think that word exists in the vocabulary of a Dominican mother who is seeing her only daughter marry.' He rolled onto his back. 'Let her have this. We can afford it.'

'That isn't the point. I just wanted to keep a low profile. Not make people feel uncomfortable.'

'You mean jealous because of how grand it's going to be?'

'I just don't want people to think we're putting on a show. Airs and graces. You know they'll all talk about us behind our backs.'

'Yes, while they're drinking all our drink and eating more fried fish than is good for them. Oh, let them have this. Let your mum be happy for the day. We have the rest of our lives.' He turned to pat her thighs before springing out of bed.

Philomena took a deep breath and sank back into the warmth of the covers. She thought about Saul's words: Happy for the day. She would be happier if Junie could come to the wedding, be a part of the wedding, somehow. She already had a Maid of Honour. A cousin she rarely saw but that her mother insisted had to take the role. Even if she could invite Junie, Gregory would never allow it. She closed her eyes tight and imagined how beautiful a bride Junie would have been. An excited seventeen-year-old, in love for the first time, blind to the fact she was marrying a monster. How Philomena wanted to weep for her right now, but she had made her best effort not to constantly talk about her to Saul who couldn't fathom Philomena's attachment to her at all. Apart from the fact Philomena pitied the girl and wished she could help her, he could never imagine that Philomena's feelings for Junie ran any deeper than that.

She heard Saul rattling around in his small kitchen. He would be making coffee, nice and strong. They would sit outside and drink it on the two wicker chairs that faced the tall forest. Rays of warmth would surround them, caressing their skin, the brightness of the sun making their spirits soar, or so Philomena hoped. She would try to find ease and relaxation as best she could, but somewhere in her mind, in her heart, she would pledge to try harder, to do more for Junie.

20

It was stomach ache she complained of, said that she was on the verge of throwing up and that if Saul could only drop her home, she'd go straight to bed and see if Mum had a tea that would help her.

'Are you sure you won't just stay here?' Saul said, not long after breakfast and before they were due at school. 'I can have Mrs Peters come by and look in while I'm at work.'

Philomena had never missed a day of school, not as a student, neither had she as a teacher. But if her plan was going to work, she needed the element of surprise.

'No, Saul. I promise I'll be better off at home. Mum will be so upset if she thought I was ill and on my own and she couldn't do anything to help me.'

'She'll have to get used to that now she's decided not to come to New York. If you get sick, she can't exactly comfort you all the way from here. There isn't even a phone up where you live. What if it gets worse? You won't be able to call anyone.'

'Oh Saul, you worry too much. I'm sure it will pass. I just want to be home. Mum will love to take care of me, make me one of her teas. And they usually do work, you know?'

'Well, if you insist,' Saul said. 'We better get a move on because I have to come back most of the way, and I can't be late. I'll have to organise cover for you.' He tutted and Philomena laughed inwardly at how like her mother he was

128

acting himself. She hated to lie to him, to be away from her students, but she couldn't see that she had much choice.

Saul sped away after dropping Philomena home. Her mother was surprised to see her.

'What's wrong?' She felt Philomena's head with the back of her hand and tested the temperature to the back of her neck. 'Well, it's not a fever.'

Her mother had made Philomena sit on an easy chair once Saul had delivered her safely into her care.

'It's just my stomach. But you know, I think it's easing off now.'

Her mother eyed her suspiciously. 'Are you sure that's all it is. You not pregnant?'

'No, Mum, I know for a fact I'm not.'

'Well, you shouldn't be staying at Saul's house. You are a young girl. You should marry first. Do the right thing.'

'Oh Mum.' Philomena got up. She'd had enough of the pretence, it was time to enact her plan. 'I just need to go for a walk.'

'A walk!' her mother declared. 'Two seconds ago you come here holding your stomach like you are a patient in a hospital, and now you want to walk!' She shook her head.

Philomena picked up an umbrella to her protect from the hot sun.

'It will be a long walk, Mum, but don't worry about me, I'm perfectly fine now. Just a walk, and I'll see you soon.'

'All right.' Her mother hung on the words, a question behind them that asked what her daughter was up to, but she let it pass. 'Is there any point in brewing you a tea?'

'When I come back. It'll grow cold if you do it now.'

Mrs Scott raised her eyebrows as a goodbye gesture, and Philomena left the house. She took a quick look at the

Williams' house but had no intention of going there. She suspected Junie would be up at the allotment, so that's where she headed. She knew Gregory didn't go up to the allotment these days, so it was a safe bet that she'd find Junie alone. As Junie was only there on weekdays, this was the only opportunity she had of seeing her. Her plan was to finally talk to Junie, tell her everything. Tell her that she hadn't forgotten her, even if it seemed that way. She was marrying Saul, but she had a plan, and when Junie heard that there was an opportunity to get away from Gregory, she felt sure Junie would jump at it. She would finally be able to make Junie happy, not for a few stolen moments by the river or the briefest exchange that they hoped Gregory wouldn't see. Every day they could be together. The best part was that Saul fully supported the idea.

Philomena had been right to bring the umbrella. The walk up the mountain road towards the allotments was steep, and the sun was at its highest. She fanned herself with her fingers and tried to slow her pace so she could catch her breath. She hadn't realised how fast she was walking in her excitement and desperation to see Junie.

As she got closer to the plots of land, she was disappointed not to see Junie out there working. She saw Pa Reynauld sitting in the shade of his tool shack, rocking away and smoking a pipe, enjoying his solitude.

'Mr Reynauld, good day,' she said as she approached him. She realised then that Pa had been asleep. His pipe in hand and the momentum of the chair had probably been imagined by her. 'I'm sorry. I didn't mean to wake you.'

'And who do I have the pleasure of greeting?'

'It's me, Pa. Philomena Scott?'

'Philomena Scott,' he exclaimed. 'The last time I saw you, you were this high.' He raised his pipe hand to signify a height. The pipe hadn't been lit. 'You were running around with your brother while your father was in his garden. I remember you. I remember everyone who used to come up here. But no one comes any more. I don't know what will become of this place if I die.'

'Well, Junie will come.'

He turned suddenly, a look of worry on his face.

'What is it?' Philomena asked.

Pa shook his head. Had she left it too late to come to her friend? Had Gregory done something? Just then, the engine of a truck came down the mountain from the direction of Pa's house.

'Well, I send her some food the end of last week,' said Pa. 'She hasn't been up here in well over a week now. Maybe longer.'

Philomena turned to the truck which had stopped close by. A tall man walked towards her and Pa.

'Hello,' he called. 'I saw Pa had a visitor. I thought for a moment it was Junie.'

'You know Junie?' Philomena closed the umbrella.

'Oh yes, well, she has her garden here, and I met her at Pa's house, what, a couple weeks now?'

'And how was she?'

Now this young man looked worried. He looked at Pa who was shaking his head.

'My apologies.' The young man outstretched a hand for Philomena to shake. 'I'm Vincent, Pa's grandson. I'm working on his house, and I met Junie there. I did go down to bring a bag of food from Pa and picked some of her limes for her. Some were getting overripe.'

'So you saw her last week? At her house?'

'He wasn't there,' said Vincent quickly. 'I offered to help her.'

Philomena was lost for words. *He* offered to help Junie. Why would he do that? Inwardly she chastised herself. Junie needed help, and she hadn't been there to help her. Of course someone else was bound to step in. It made her more determined to find Junie and speak to her today. This young man and Pa were doing the things she was supposed to do. Helping, bringing her food. That guilty feeling wound a tighter knot in her stomach.

'I thought she'd be here,' Philomena said with a dry throat. 'I'm already helping Junie.'

'We're here,' Vincent said. 'For anything she or you need. Remember that.'

'I will,' said Philomena who turned to leave.

'I can drop you back down,' Vincent offered. 'Are you her neighbour?'

'Yes, and thank you.' She didn't like the idea of riding with this young man who seemed to be stepping in where she had failed, but she was hot and tired and still had to find her friend. She must be trapped in the house with Gregory, so she had to come up with a way to draw her out. Maybe her mother could help. 'Goodbye, Pa. Have a nice day.'

'You as well, Miss Scott. Mind how you go and look out for my precious girl.' *His* precious girl?

Philomena followed Vincent to the truck and jumped aboard. She wanted to ask him who he was exactly, where he lived and how he thought he could help Junie, but she calmed herself and tried to stay cool in this heat. She must be level headed if she wanted to help Junie and do battle against Gregory. She mustn't let feelings of envy cloud her judgement. Of course Vincent went to call on Junie, he was free to do so. She on the other hand was not permitted onto the property, so she had to find a way to overcome this obstacle.

'Can I drop you here?' Vincent asked.

'Yes, thank you. And don't worry. I'll look out for Junie.'

'Are you going to knock for her?'

'No, I'll have to see how the land lies first. You understand.'

'I do. Well, good luck, and let me know if you need me. I told Junie I'll be at Pa's for a good while working, so…'

'That's good of you.' She jumped out of the truck and slammed the door. 'Thank you, Vincent. Drive safely.'

He took off towards the village, and Philomena hovered by the front gate. Her mother came out onto the veranda with her arms crossed.

'Did your walk help?' Mrs Scott was looking in the direction of the moving truck.

'Yes, I'm feeling much better.' Philomena climbed the veranda steps and lowered her voice. 'I walked as far as the allotments. I wanted to talk to Junie without him around.' She rolled her eyes in the direction of the Williams' house. 'But she wasn't there.'

'No, she wasn't because just after you left, Junie walked off with a large basket of dirty washing on her head.'

'The river?' This was perfect. 'But what about him?'

'Well, if you'd have been here, you would have known that he isn't home. Gone for over a week now. God only knows what become of him. He's never usually gone so long.'

'I have to go.' Philomena leapt down the steps despite being hot and perspiring.

'Where you going at this time? It's a hot day and you already looking flushed. You sure you well?'

'I need to speak to Junie. It's urgent.'

Philomena rushed away, leaving her bewildered mother alone on the veranda, shaking her head.

Philomena had already wasted over an hour traipsing up a mountain in pursuit of her friend. If she'd only known Gregory was away, she would have knocked on Junie's door earlier. But it was all right now. She'd see Junie, tell her about New York and start arranging how best to get Junie over there. She could read now so finding work would be a lot easier. Though Philomena hadn't taught her how to write yet, there was time for them to work on that together.

There was a welcome coolness on the path to the river. The soil was still soft and not baked by the sun, her feet made no noise as she made her way to the pool in the river where Junie was likely to be washing clothes. Wild bushes growing low to the ground, their flowers in shades of violet and magenta carpeted the way. She ran through them rather than staying on the well-trodden path because it was quicker.

'Junie!' Philomena couldn't help but exclaim from the joy of seeing her friend.

Junie swung around in surprise. She dropped the sheet she had been swishing in the water and touched her chest, sagging forward as if she'd been winded.

'Philomena, you nearly frighten me.'

'I'm so sorry. Mum said you were here, and I ran most of the way. I've been looking for you.' Philomena walked to the water's edge, unable to contain a broad smile.

'Well, here I am.' It was only a half smile Junie gave Philomena who dropped to the ground to take off her sandals. She waded in a little way but not as far as Junie who was immersed up to her knees and who kept her back to Philomena.

'Is something wrong?' Philomena stopped.

'No more, no less than before.' Junie spoke over her shoulder.

'How long has he been gone?'

'A few days. I've been washing and cleaning the whole time. Where were you?' She turned slowly.

Philomena couldn't answer at first, sensing a quality in Junie she hadn't seen before. So, she had been right to worry that Junie would feel abandoned by her. She had needed her around, they'd vowed to find a moment to read together, and the first chance they got, Philomena was absent. Away with her fiancé, a man she had not told Junie she intended to marry. She wondered if Junie would be too angry to be happy for her.

The women stood in silence a long time, Philomena looking into Junie's thin face. Her skin looked patchy and pale. Her hair was tied very tightly with a headscarf. Her eyes looked sunken, the outline of her cheekbones more prominent. Junie turned her eyes downward and Philomena waded in deeper, drawing closer to Junie so that she could hug her. At first, Junie held herself like a wooden board. Gradually her body softened as she laid her head to rest on Philomena's shoulder. Eventually she wrapped her arms around Philomena's waist, warm tears trickling down her cheeks and wetting Philomena's dress. She sniffed several times, blinked, then closed her eyes as though she could fall asleep in the comfort of Philomena's soft, warm body.

The women stood like this for a while, neither daring to speak and break the silence and beauty of the moment. The river made no sound around them, nothing along the river's banks stirred, not even a leaf on a branch. Suddenly, they both heard the loud crack of a twig a short way off. They pulled away from each other. Junie's heart pounding was audible in the stillness that followed. Their eyes darted towards the trees on either side of the riverbank. They looked frantically for shapes behind the bushes. Philomena looked harder, deeper into the wood, but there was no one there. Gregory hadn't crept up on them. Junie's breath faltered as though she might pass out. Philomena pulled her closer, but Junie shrugged her off.

'Why you here? Why you don't go and teach today?'

'I wanted to see you.' Philomena smiled. She wanted to tell her everything, but Junie walked back to the large rock at the river's edge dragging the wet sheet through the water and throwing it over the rock. She proceeded to unravel the other sheets and clothes from her basket, pulling some out, immediately replacing them and tossing some aside to grab for another buried item. She decided on another sheet and grabbed up her large bar of soap before wading back out. Philomena watched the exaggerated, spiky movements.

'I busy,' Junie huffed and threw the sheet into the river. Standing sideways on to Philomena, she began to rub soap into the sheet, then scrubbed it hard between her hands. Philomena went to sit on a small empty space on the rock.

'I know you're angry with me, Junie. I know I haven't been here very much, but when I was, I tried so hard to see you. You have to believe me. I'm your friend.'

Junie continued to work on the sheet. She swished it around in the water and pulled it up to wring it out. She was hurrying and being careless. Her blouse was soaked now and clung to her body, revealing the outline of her tiny breasts, nipples reacting to the cool air sweeping the river.

'You know I'm getting married. To Saul. Mum told you, I know,' said Philomena. 'It's just that I … I love Saul. He loves me a lot. But Junie, I also love you. So much. It's been killing me to know you have to suffer that man and you feel you can't get away from him.'

Junie waded back to the rock and threw the sheet onto the wet one, so close to Philomena she felt water splash her arm.

'But there is a way, Junie.' Philomena jumped off the rock and held Junie's hand before she could wade out again.

'What way?' Junie asked without looking up.

'Well, I'll be moving to New York after the wedding. So I spoke to Saul, and he is happy for you to come over there with us.'

'Oh Phil.' Junie pulled her arm away. 'Look at me. I have no money, I can hardly read. Don't I need papers? I don't even have clothes a person could wear in a place like that. I have nothing.'

'Don't worry, I can arrange everything.'

'I'm not a little doll you can pick up and put down and make it go here and make it go there.'

'I know … I just thought … I thought I was helping.'

'I only asked you to teach me to read. I didn't tell you to put me on a ship. I can't leave here. I'm not the kind of person to move to a big country. I'm a simple person. I can work out my life on my own, and I don't need you or anybody treating me as if I'm a poor nobody.'

'That's not the way I see you. Not at all. Junie, please.'

'I busy, Phil. I tell you before.'

'But.' Philomena fell silent. 'Well then, I'm here if you change your mind. And you know that. In the meantime, if you wanted to, if you need to get away, even for a day, I can take you over to Saul's and I'd make sure Gregory doesn't know how to find you.'

'You make a lot of promises, Phil.'

'Junie, I'm sorry. Please can you ever forgive me for not being a good enough friend?'

Junie crossed her arms. Her voice was full of tears. 'You are my best friend. But I can't go anywhere. Not now. I'm expecting a baby.'

Philomena involuntarily held Junie's shoulders and pulled her against her.

'How far gone?'

'About three months. So you see. I have to stay.'

'This doesn't have to be the end, Junie. There must be a way.'

'I want to have this baby.' Junie turned to face her, not wiping the tears that rolled down her cheeks. 'Maybe he will be kinder if there's a child. You never know. But at least I will have something. Someone I could love and who could really love me.'

Now Philomena began to cry, and the women held each other tight.

'I love you, Junie, and I always will. No matter where I am or what happens. Only know it's true.'

Philomena backed away, stumbling against some shingle at the edge of the water. She picked up her sandals and held them by the strap.

'And, I should have said, congratulations.'

'And so should I. Congratulations, Phil.'

21

In many ways, this was like a holiday for Junie. A time to re-lax, take deep breaths. From time to time, she touched her stomach; it was as flat as before, and not having had the pregnancy confirmed, she wasn't entirely sure there was a baby there. She longed for it to be true and knew she should really go to a doctor. She had not seen one since marrying Gregory, not even when she was badly beaten, bruised or had a sprain. Philomena had been the one to patch her up. Lately, she'd kept her injuries to herself, and with the absence of her husband, her body was healing again. Small bruises that had shown purple and blue had faded. She no longer had a limp, nothing hurt and she didn't struggle to get up from a chair. This was the best kind of holiday.

Each day since Gregory left, she'd stood in the garden, leaning on the front gate expecting to see him walk up from the village or to have been dropped off by someone in a truck or van as he had done in the past. She'd had no idea who the drivers were and neither did she ask, especially if he'd been drinking. All she needed to know was whether he had brought home any food.

Eight days had gone by, and he had not returned. He could be dead. She hoped he was. It would be so much easier to negotiate her life if he wasn't around. The times she'd feared he'd kill her, she couldn't count. But he would have to be different now. There was a baby. Or the chance of one. She made a silent prayer and went back inside.

She'd done everything she could in the house. All the laundry was clean and folded away in the cupboard at the back of the living room and the small wardrobe in the bedroom. She'd swept and mopped the floor. The furniture was straightened out and dusted. The cushions on each of the easy chairs were neat and upright. She'd cleaned the kitchen. She had used up all of the food package Pa had sent down from the allotments. She'd made lime cordial out of her crops and added her peppers and tomatoes to the soup she'd made with the root vegetables. The goat's milk Pa had sent, she'd enjoyed with relish. It would be a while before she had anything so nice to drink.

With her garden needing no work doing to it, she decided to take herself up the mountain to see Pa, thank him and return the Hessian sack. If Gregory saw it, there would be too much explaining to do.

Junie felt a little better about going to see Pa in clean clothes. She had combed her hair, detangled the knots and plaited a cornrow down either side of a crooked middle parting. She left the headscarf behind because she had nothing to hide: no bruises, cuts or dirty hair. She felt good in herself as she walked up the mountain road. The heat was bearable though it was mid morning. She took her time, taking the deep breaths as if she hadn't a care in the world.

At Pa's house, Vincent was on the roof hard at work. He smiled warmly when he saw her and climbed swiftly down the ladder.

'You're back!'

'Not really. I brought the sack you gave me and wanted to thank Pa for his kindness.'

'I think he's sleeping.'

She followed Vincent into the house. There was Pa, sitting in a cosy armchair, his feet on a stool, fast asleep. He snored lightly, his mouth open. Junie turned to Vincent.

'I don't know how he can sleep with the hammering you doing.' She smiled.

'He can sleep through anything it seems.'

'Here.' Junie handed Vincent the old sack. She'd folded it neatly after having shaken out any bits of soil or leaves from the produce. 'Please thank him for me. I better go.'

'Already? Can I offer you anything? Even a glass of water after that walk?'

'You have work to do.'

'I can have a break. I am the boss after all.' Vincent led her back outside. In front of the house and beyond the small gravelled drive was a wooden bench cut from a fallen tree. It had been planed smooth and varnished, though the job seemed to have been done a long time ago because the varnish was worn away in places and some of the wood was chipped. They sat side by side. Junie put her palms under her thighs and crossed her legs at the ankles. Vincent sat with his legs wide, one arm across the back of the bench. He looked at Junie, attempted to say something and then changed his mind.

'What is it?' she asked with a smile.

'It's you.'

'Me?'

'Yes. You look so different today.'

'I combed my hair.' She laughed coyly and stroked her braids before returning her hand beneath her lap.

'It's more than that. You look, I don't know. Calm or something.'

Junie touched her stomach with both hands, briefly, and placed them on her lap.

'But as pretty as ever,' Vincent continued. 'I know I shouldn't say it and I know your husband would probably want to kill me but you are. Pretty, I mean.' He sniffed a laugh and bowed his head.

'That's nice of you to say. But I didn't feel very pretty the last time you came, and I have to explain—'

'There's no need to explain. I can see what things are like for you.'

'I don't know if you do.'

'Junie, it's obvious what goes on with your husband. You can't hide it, you know?'

'I try.'

'You shouldn't have to.'

'What I mean is I try to stop it happening. I do all I can not to make him angry.' Vincent shook his head. 'No, you have to understand, Gregory is a troubled man. He is sad. I'm not sure why or what happened to him, but something makes a person like that.'

'Some people are just born bad, and you have to face that, Junie.'

'So, you don't think anything will make him stop?'

'Not one thing. I've known men like him. All of them rotten to the core. Some go too far. You know what I mean?'

Junie nodded. 'Not if they have reason to stop. If they did have a reason...' From the expression on his face, Junie could see there was no use in completing her sentence. Philomena had looked at her the exact same way when she insisted Gregory would change if she had a baby. She had no intention of telling Vincent that she might be pregnant. He wouldn't understand why she'd want to have a baby with

Gregory. Still, within her was the hope that she was right, that Vincent and Phil were wrong, that Gregory could change. He wasn't raised like this; he must have had love once, and he could find it in his son.

'Can I say something?' asked Vincent.

'Is it about my husband?'

'No, this is about you. I know you have your friend helping you, but I meant what I said about offering to help. He doesn't know me. If you ever wanted to get away, perhaps one day if it gets too much… All I'm saying is. It's a form of refuge. My house. Or someone in my family, and maybe find somewhere for you to move on from there.'

'Like America?'

'Like anywhere you choose. You just have to choose.'

'I don't know the last time I had the choice of anything. But thank you, Vincent. I won't forget what you said.'

After several comfortable minutes of silence, Vincent turned to Junie. 'So, is America a place you want to go?'

'Not really. I don't think so. I know a lot of people go there. And they go to England.'

'I have family in England.'

'True?'

'My uncle was on Empire Windrush in nineteen forty-eight. He met a Bajan woman in England and they marry. They have six children now.'

'That's a big family. And you?'

'And me, what?'

'You don't marry? Don't have babies?'

'No. My sister says I'm too fussy.'

'Maybe you are.'

'Maybe the nice ones already have husbands.'

He had moved in closer to Junie as he spoke. She saw how he studied her face, her hair and her hands resting on her lap. She felt heat rising on her face and neck and shuffled away from him.

'I'm sorry if I make you feel uncomfortable,' Vincent said. 'But I have a feeling you don't get told often enough how pretty you are.'

Junie stood up. 'Maybe, but no matter. I should go.'

'Just like that?' He stood, too. 'I'm getting good at scaring you off.'

'No, it's late. I have no idea when he'll be back so I should go.' She began to walk back towards the narrow lane leading to the mountain road home. 'Tell Pa I might see him again.' She was a distance away now. She waved quickly and headed home before Vincent could say a single word more.

22

In the weeks leading up to the school summer break, Philomena was extremely busy. She threw herself into her work, planning a graduation for her pupils that had to be the best in the school's history. She would miss the school, her pupils. Philomena loved to teach, and when she went to America, it would be as Saul's wife, not a teacher. Saul had signed his contracts of employment, resigned as head teacher and taken a short trip to New York to start looking for accommodation near the school for him and Philomena. The plan was that she would look for a teaching post when she arrived; he would help her, make recommendations at the school where he'd be teaching. He'd also hinted that if she didn't want to teach straight away, they could start a family.

Philomena hadn't, so far, entertained the idea of having and raising children. She had always been happy to be a teacher and share her knowledge and experience with her students. Soon she wouldn't be teaching, but she was eager to continue passing on her learning to Junie whom she imagined living in one of the rooms in the apartment Saul would find for them.

It seemed as if everything had come into her life at once. A husband, a new country, Junie, and it overwhelmed her. So when her mother told her that, on top of all the other wedding day arrangements, she had found an excellent seamstress to make her wedding dress and they must arrange a fitting and talk about dress designs, she felt stifled. She began doubting that she could manage to do all the things she had promised—become a wife, help Junie escape—so she put off fittings until it was becoming so late in the day, her mother lost patience with her completely.

She sat at her desk in the classroom, well after school had finished, and finalised the copy for the graduation certificates for her infant class before they went to print. She imagined how proud they would feel collecting them on the low stage in the school yard, classmates and family members watching them as they shook hands with the head teacher. She would miss all of this.

'Not going home?' Saul had been busy trying to find replacements for both their jobs. The school board had not been inundated with applicants for the roles, but there were some strong possibilities.

'I'm just finishing,' she said. 'How about you? Finished for the day?'

'Yes and hungry. How about we go out and eat?' He sat at the edge of her desk and loosened his tie.

'Oh, Mum is expecting me. She wants to talk about weddings. I have a terrible feeling that she has invited a few more guests. Last minute people she can't imagine how she forgot.' She raised her eyes to the ceiling and began to clear up the paperwork. 'Come to dinner with us. Mum usually cooks too much.'

'I'd love to.'

As they drove away from the school, Philomena had her window rolled all the way down, the early evening breeze on her bare arm. They left the town, its mismatched buildings of shops, offices, banks and houses, the streets so narrow there were traffic jams sometimes. People had to reverse their cars all the way back down a road to avoid head-on collisions.

The town was advancing; there were never this many cars and trucks when she was a child. People drove carts back then; a person was considered a millionaire if they had a car. But with all the improvements to the infrastructure and modernisation of buildings, it was still a very undeveloped country. People were leaving for England, America and Canada. Very soon, Philomena would be one of them.

The altitude changed as the car rattled up the mountain road. A backdrop of steep-sloped forests rose up to their left. Occasionally, a brightly coloured house could be seen on one of the slopes. If the house had electricity, the lights were switched on; if they had lamps, these were lit: dusk had fallen over the island. In the valleys below, Philomena could make out one or two houses among the various shades of green. Houses built in the valleys and woodlands. She saw the lights of a truck weaving its way along a narrow road just before it turned a corner and was out of sight.

They arrived at Philomena's neighbouring village. All the shops, stalls and offices were closed and the village deserted as people made their way home to cook dinner, listen to the radio, sit on verandas and talk about their day. The liquor bar was just opening, and Philomena could smell a waft of alcohol and cigarette smoke as the bar owner opened the door wearing a white apron.

Up on the plain where the two houses sat, Philomena noticed the lamp light in Junie's house and thought about asking her to dinner. She knew Junie would refuse, too afraid to flaunt her freedom because Gregory could return home at any time.

Saul parked the car, and Mrs Scott came running out onto the veranda.

'You know I worry when you're so late,' she exclaimed but clapped her hands together with glee when she saw Saul come through the gate. 'My son,' she said, linking Saul's arm. She led him into the house, ignoring Philomena altogether. Saul looked over his shoulder at Philomena, an expression of apology on his face. Philomena smiled, shook her head and looked at Junie's house through the branches of the oleander. She couldn't make anything out, couldn't tell if Junie was on her own or not.

When dinner was served, they sat at the table while Mrs Scott chattered away with uncontainable enthusiasm about the big day. Philomena kept one eye on the window. She couldn't see much beyond the oleander or through the fall of night, but she felt troubled by something unknown brewing in Junie's house. Something she could sense above her mother's one-sided conversation and the vibrations of the crickets' evening song. It was unnerving, and for this reason she barely ate and forgot to nod in agreement whenever her mother shot a glance in her direction when she needed her daughter's approval of her decision making.

'Have you finished?' Mrs Scott's question felt as if it had been fed to her from down a long tunnel, and she had to shake herself back from the far-away place she had been observing the activity in the room. She looked vaguely at her mother.

'Because you have hardly eaten. I was talking about your dress. It will fall off you if you don't eat.' Both Mrs Scott and Saul stared at her.

'I'm sorry,' she said. 'Maybe I don't have much of an appetite tonight.' She put her fork down and handed her plate to her mother who was poised to take everything back to the kitchen. 'Wait,' Philomena said and stood up. 'I'll clear this away. You sit down, Mum, and I'll make us all some tea.'

'And there is a fruit bun,' Mrs Scott said, smiling at Saul and patting his hand.

'I'll help Phil,' he said and gathered the remaining serving bowls.

'What a helpful man you've got there,' said Mrs Scott, lighting her pipe and smiling to herself.

Outside, Philomena found her way to the kitchen by the light of the lamp hanging inside it. She filled the kettle and set it on the stove. She lit the wood and waited for the water to boil. Saul wrapped around her from behind, stroking her arms as they crossed around her torso.

'You all right?' he asked her. 'Can you tell me where your mind has wandered off to this time?'

'I don't even know myself. I suppose I've listened to Mum's plans so many times, I don't need to listen any more.' He pulled her to face him, and Philomena hugged his waist, resting her head on his chest with a sigh. She thought of Junie and the amount of food left over.

The water began to boil, the steam hissed and rose from the spout. Just as Philomena pulled away to turn off the heat, she heard a loud crash from outside as if something had fallen over or been thrown. She looked up at Saul, the water still boiling.

'What was that?'

'What?' asked Saul.

'I thought I heard a noise. From Junie's.'

'Well, that's all right, isn't it? People can make noise in their own home.'

Philomena was out of the kitchen, moving towards the oleander, straining to see through the branches.

'What's wrong?' Saul asked, crouching beside her.

Philomena squinted in the dark through the tree, but she couldn't see anything clearly. The oleander had grown so much over the years, the barrier between the houses organically becoming more of a prison for Junie and a message for Philomena to keep out.

'It's nothing,' she said. 'I just thought…' She took Saul's hand, leading him back to the kitchen. The kettle's whistle was shrill. Maybe she hadn't heard anything above it after all. She set about making a pot of tea which Saul carried to the house while she took the lamp and led the way.

'Mind how you go,' she warned.

Mrs Scott, sitting out on the veranda now, smoking her pipe, followed them both inside. 'And you have a dress fitting at the weekend,' Mrs Scott said to Philomena. She didn't answer, only smiled, enough for her mother to understand that this wasn't the first reminder that week.

Just as Philomena lifted the teapot, a noise from outside alarmed her. She let go of the handle, the pot landing on its base without any tea spilling from it. The three of them all froze at a thunderous voice coming from next door. Gregory bellowed a relentless rant of foul language and slurred speech. The three of them looked from one to the other. Mrs Scott raised her shoulders. Philomena ran to the window. Then they heard a shriek, high pitched and jagged, Junie calling, 'No, Gregory, no!'

Philomena heard crying as though it was coming from outside. Too dark to see anything, she ran to the door and pulled it open, Saul close behind her.

'Wait, the two of you.' Mrs Scott stopped them in their tracks. 'If the police have to come up here, it won't look good if two teachers are involved in a fight.'

Philomena looked at Saul. He looked angry, his chest rising and falling as he looked into the night through the open door. The noise next door stopped as suddenly as it had started.

'I should just go and take a look,' said Philomena and reached for the lamp.

'Give it a moment,' said Saul. 'It might have blown over.'

Annoyed at having been stopped, but more angry at herself for not going over to the Williams house when she first heard the noise, Philomena reluctantly returned to the side window. She peered through the glass using her hands to shield the backlight from the living room so that she could see more clearly.

'It's hopeless,' she said. 'I can't see a thing past that damned tree. Turn the lamps off.'

'Philomena, after all…' her mother began.

'Please.' She turned, angry at them both. 'I can see more if the lights are off.'

Saul hurried to dim the lamps. Mrs Scott closed the front door.

Staring out of the window of the darkened room, she saw the silhouettes of her neighbours moving frenetically around the house. There were screams again, the silhouette of Gregory's arm flying up then swooping down—over and over. She stood up. Was he holding a weapon?

The screaming stopped and the neighbours' front door opened. Philomena began to pray hoping that Gregory would do what he usually did, flee the scene of the crime and storm away somewhere. Maybe into the woods or perhaps the village to cool down. They all remained in the dark room, still as statues for several minutes. They were listening for what Gregory would do next. *Please go, please go*, Philomena kept chanting under her breath. Every prayer she'd ever learnt left her lips in a whisper. Then she made up prayers of her own. Prayers for Junie. Closing her eyes with her hands still in prayer position, she dared to look out again to see what was happening out there in the dark. Before she could turn to look, she thought she heard movement in her front yard. Philomena's first thought was that Gregory had come sniffing around, probably to tell her to stay away and mind her own business. Rooted to the spot she heard a knock at the door. She didn't dare to move. What did he want? The person behind the door began to push it open. Saul ran to the door, Philomena close behind him. Just outside the door someone crouched and hovered. Philomena let out a long sigh of relief when she saw it was Junie.

'Please help me,' Junie whispered. 'I can't take no more.'

23

Junie was just leaving the bedroom when Gregory walked into the house. Her legs felt leaden; she stayed in the doorway, her mouth slightly ajar.

'Is that any way to treat a man who has been away working all this time?'

He was wearing a shirt she didn't recognise. He had cut his thick brown hair so that it neatly framed his light brown face as it had done on their wedding day. He was clean shaven, the brown freckles on his nose and brow visible in the lamp light. At his feet was a large box in which his old clothes were bundled along with a large bottle of whisky, some cans of meat and a pair of dirty boots on the top.

'Sort this out,' he said, waving an arm. 'There's more food; I left it in the kitchen. Make me something. Don't just stand up there like a person with no brain. Move.'

His voice was sharp like a punch to her gut, and she jumped to action. He smelt clean as she passed him at the open front door. He pushed her aside and took a seat on one of the easy chairs.

'I should take a lamp. It's getting dark,' she said, reaching for the one on the table.

He didn't answer, just settled himself down and unscrewed the top of the whisky bottle that he'd retrieved from the box.

Junie closed the door behind her and went to the kitchen where she set down the lamp and lit the stove before unpacking the bag of food Gregory had thrown in at the door. She hadn't heard him arrive. She had been lying on the bed, nursing a headache. She seemed to be having a lot of them lately and thought it must be something to do with the baby.

Outside, she saw a car parked by the Scott house. Saul's car. Phil must be home. Her shoulders slumped as she began to unpack the food, realising that now Gregory was back, she would not be able to go over and talk to Phil. In their last encounter at the river, she had been short with Philomena though she hadn't meant to be. It was true, she had felt let down by her friend, abandoned in some respects, but it wasn't Philomena's fault that she had met a good man and was about to be married. She had to adjust to the fact that Philomena had her own life and soon she would be far away. She would have to find a way to cope without her. It was wonderful to have been able to see her at the river again. Though the circumstances had not been like the old days, Junie knew nothing stayed the same. After all, she was pregnant now, a new phase in her life. She still believed the baby would change Gregory, and she couldn't wait to tell him that he was soon to become a father.

She smiled to herself as she went about cooking. She heated oil in a pan and scraped the scales off the small fish wrapped in paper. She seasoned it and sliced some plantain, deciding to fry it all as a quick meal. There was bread, too; she'd cut several slices. They'd eat, he'd fill his belly, feel satisfied and then she'd break the good news.

She carried two plates of food in one hand, a bowl of bread and the big bread knife in the other and hurried to the house. She heard laughter and chatter from the Scott house. Their meal had smelt divine earlier when Mrs Scott was cooking; she had salivated, felt her stomach complain of hunger and wished she could have asked for a bite to eat. Her headache had caused her to fall asleep, and she no longer had to suffer the pangs of hunger. But she needn't have worried. Here came Gregory with a bag of food, and she was going to be fed at last. Gregory would understand that she needed to eat for two, and perhaps now he'd find regular work and keep the larder stocked with fresh fish, milk and eggs. She'd need it to keep up her strength.

Gregory was dozing in the chair when she came in and laid the plates and the bowl on the table. He stirred and looked up at her, craning his neck as he looked to see what she had prepared.

'You wake me for that? Is this a meal for a man who has been working hard all week?'

'I'm sorry. I thought you might want to eat quickly. Being as you been away working all this time, I don't know when last you eat.' She started to slice the bread. 'If you don't feel full, eat mine.'

'Junie, you sound like an idiot sometimes. You think I will sit and eat my food and then eat your food while you sitting hungry?' He tore off some bread and began to chew, shaking his head at her as if he couldn't fathom her at all.

'I know, I'm silly sometimes. Anyway, I did a lot of fish. I hope you like it.'

They ate in silence. Gregory poured some whisky into a tumbler from the dresser and flooded each mouthful of food with it as if it were water. He chewed loudly, his face close to the plate, scooping plantain into his mouth with his fingers. He bit the head off each fish while holding it by the tail, never once using the fork she had put out for him.

'I hope it's all right,' she said. Again there was no response from her husband.

While she was still eating, closing her eyes in satisfaction with every much-needed morsel, Gregory finished. He let out a belch, rubbed his stomach, topped up his glass with more booze and made his way over to the easy chair. Junie carried on eating, waiting for the right moment to tell Gregory about the baby. His demeanour was prickly as though she was an irritation, and he edged his body away from her in his seat so that all she saw was his back.

She wanted to compliment his hair, his new shirt, anything to open a conversation. She couldn't tell him what she had been doing during his absence, but she would love to ask him about his time away. She looked at him, the way he shrugged and threw back his booze. He didn't seem in the mood for conversation and would probably say something like, *you have no right to question a man in his own home.* So she bided her time, finished her meal, thankful for this at least.

Junie returned the plates to the kitchen and put away the remainder of the food Gregory had bought. She brought back some water from the kitchen in a jug. She would have asked if he wanted some coffee, but somehow she thought he'd be happy enough with his whisky bottle. She couldn't help but notice the size of the bottle, and it looked like an expensive brand. She wondered how much of the money he'd made she would actually see. How much would end up as useful things for the house, food in the larder or clothes for the baby. As she brought the water jug to the house, she heard voices in the Scott kitchen. Someone was tidying up. Making tea perhaps.

'I brought us some water.' Junie smiled as she held the jug up. 'Would you like a drink?' Gregory did not answer. He knocked back some of his whisky. 'Gregory?'

He shot out of his chair, knocked over his glass, and rounded on her, shouting. 'What?' Junie was so startled by his quick and aggressive movement that she dropped the jug, its contents spilling across the floor, the jug smashing into four distinct pieces.

'Jesus Christ! Woman, you make me so angry sometimes.' He spun back to the chair, dropping his body into it with such gusto the feet shifted a few inches backwards on the wooden floor. He picked up the whisky bottle, still standing by the chair and shoved it into his mouth, chugging at the contents like a man gasping for water after a long drought.

Junie spun around, saw some cleaning cloths in a corner and rushed to use them to soak up the water. She dabbed at the floor until it was mostly dry and then picked up the broken pieces of the jug and went to take them out to the kitchen.

'You forgot something,' Gregory hissed from his chair without turning around.

'Oh?' she said softly.

'Didn't you see my glass fall?'

'No,' said Junie, timidly making her way to his chair. She had seen the upturned glass, the brown fluid pooling around it but had been too afraid to say anything in case his anger flared again. She knelt down with the jug and wet cloths still in her hand and looked at the mess.

'Jesus Christ!' he yelled again. 'How you going to clean that up if you already have your hands full?' He stood and expelled a barrage of insults and foul language at her, calling her so many disgusting names. He used words she'd never even heard of before, and all she could do was cower, scooting into the corner by the dresser, clutching the broken jug and the wet rags to her body for protection.

When she thought he'd finished, she turned to look at him.

'Don't you dare,' he shouted and went to kick her.

'No,' she said.

'What?' He hovered close to her, scowling and spitting. 'What you say to me?'

She staggered up to her feet, and something within her stirred. A voice she had never used in her life erupted from her throat, and she shouted, 'No!' She dropped what she was holding in her hand and continued to raise her voice at him.

'You cannot treat me like this any more. I am not an idiot. I am not worthless. I am not an animal.' She shook her fists at her side and felt something warm running down her arm. It was hurting, but she didn't know why. All she could do was shout in Gregory's face, and it felt good. And then—she was silenced. Gregory hit her face so hard, her head bashed against the wall. She ran towards the door, only getting as far as the window opposite the Scott house before he pulled her down and began beating her with the flat of his hand. With each blow, he cursed and she wailed in pain and begged for him to stop before he went too far.

'I waste enough energy on you,' he bellowed into her ear. He stormed to the front door and flung it open. Standing in the doorway, he puffed and panted as though he'd just run all the way up a mountain trail.

As he stood there in the darkness, Junie lifted herself from the floor and hobbled to the door. She staggered outside, hesitating a brief moment.

'Yes, you better go before I kill you dead. You been lucky this time. Next time, you better not do the same thing to me.'

She inched away slowly, every second wondering if he'd change his mind and come and finish the job. When she was out of the gate she ran. She rattled the gate outside the Scott house and stumbled to the stairs. She knocked on the door, pushed it slightly ajar and fell to her knees. Someone opened the door, and she began to breathe again.

24

'Oh my God, Junie.'

Philomena knelt on the floor beside her. Junie looked up, eyes rimmed with red. A frail hand clutched at her buttons. There was blood on her hands, on the side of her blouse.

'Help me,' Philomena said and began to lift Junie from the ground. Her body was light, her fragile frame felt as though it could break. Saul took Junie from Philomena's arms, blood transferring from Junie's body to Saul's shirt. Over and over Philomena kept saying to herself, *I'll kill him, I'll kill him.* But she hadn't gone to the house when she'd heard the commotion, seen Gregory's arm rise over and over as he beat the life out of Junie. Instead, she'd cowered in the dark like a frightened animal being hunted as prey. How could she have been so weak, so ineffectual? She would not let this happen again.

Saul put Junie down on the sunken couch in the corner. Mrs Scott fussed around and asked if she had been stabbed.

'I don't know, I don't know,' Philomena panted. 'All that blood. We need to take her to the hospital.'

'We can go and fetch Nurse Charles from down the way. She'll know what to do,' Mrs Scott said, nodding her head as if the matter was settled.

'No,' said Philomena. 'This time I'll deal with it.'

'You not taking my wife nowhere.' They turned to the front door where Gregory stood swaying from side to side. 'Nothing is wrong with her. She just need sleep.'

Philomena marched towards him, hand ready to slam the door in his face. 'She needs more than sleep. How could you do this? You're a monster.' Saul positioned himself behind her. Philomena pointed back at Junie who seemed to have passed out on the couch. 'How could you hit her, treat her like that when she's carrying your child?'

Gregory swallowed, the tension showing in his face when he clenched his teeth.

'She didn't tell you?' said Philomena.

Gregory shook his head.

'You just stand aside. We're driving her to the hospital.' Gregory didn't budge. 'I would tell you to have a heart but I don't know what is beating in your chest.' She stepped forward. 'Nothing more than a cold stone, that's all I can imagine.'

Gregory stepped back, spat on the doorstep and walked away into the darkness.

'Come on,' said Philomena, turning to Saul. 'We've wasted enough time.'

In the back of Saul's car, Philomena sat with her arm around Junie who whimpered at her side, saying she was sorry and didn't want to make trouble. Philomena had not discovered the source of the bleeding, but it seemed to stop as the long journey continued in the pitch black night with only the car's headlights showing their way.

The nurse at the reception got an orderly to wheel Junie to a cubicle but did not allow Philomena to stay with her.

'She's pregnant,' Philomena told the nurse just before the screen was pulled in front of her face.

Philomena insisted that Saul drove home and called the hospital in the morning. She would stay with Junie: she couldn't imagine they would send her home after what looked like a vicious attack. There would be bruises, possible broken bones, maybe a concussion but certainly they would have to heal the bloody wound. Perhaps Junie had been stabbed. The police would be called. Philomena was a witness.

Later, after Junie had been seen by a doctor and transferred to a ward, Philomena was allowed in to see her.

Junie fell asleep in the small room off the main ward where there were three other beds with sleeping patients. Philomena sat beside Junie's bed and took her hand in hers. Junie slept for over an hour, but Philomena beat off the urge to pass out, watching Junie, listening to her breathe, marvelling at how her beautiful face had remained untouched this time. She wanted to kiss her cheek, fix her hair, buy her something equally as beautiful, but she had no idea what. Thinking how ridiculous that sounded in her own head, she laid her head down and looked at her sleeping friend whose breathing was easy and calm.

In a while, Philomena felt something stroke her hand and looked up. Junie was smiling at her. She sat up quickly, wiping the side of her lip. 'Is everything all right? Did they stitch you up? The baby?'

Junie smiled. 'All wonderful. Everything is fine, and I listened to the baby's heartbeat. It's strong. It will all be fine.'

Philomena held her hands to her mouth as she sighed with joy, tears pricking at her eyes but she blinked them away. She needed to be strong for Junie. From now on, she wouldn't leave her side. They spoke into the early hours of the morning, Junie averting the conversation from the beating, talking instead about their Sundays by the river.

'We will get them back, you know?' said Junie with a feeble smile. 'Once he knows about the baby, he'll calm down
and he might let us be friends again.'

'By the time you have your baby, I'll be gone, Junie. If you
have it.'

'What kind of talk is that?'

'I'm scared. I'm worried about what he might do. I just
have this feeling, it swept over me the moment I saw his expression when he heard about the baby.'

'So, you already tell him?' Junie frowned.

'I had to because he didn't want us to bring you here.'

'What he say?'

'I don't think he's too happy about it.'

'I don't believe you. What man doesn't want to see his
child? Raise his children?'

'I grew up without a father. So did Gregory. He might not
have the instincts a father should have. Some men run when
they realise the responsibility of raising a child isn't easy. A
man like Gregory—'

'You don't know how he'll be. I'll start to show soon. He
won't touch me then. I'm certain. And anyway, you didn't
hear me over there last night. You didn't see how I stood up
to him. I can face him now. The baby makes me strong.'

Philomena, exhausted, sat back in the chair. She looked
through the glass partition to the adjoining ward at the clock
and saw it was three in the morning. Then she leaned close
to Junie again.

'And what did he do when you stood up to him?'

'How you mean?'

'What did he say? How did he react?'

Junie looked away. 'Well, he didn't like it, but if I keep it
up, he will get used to it. I will give as good as I get.'

'You are no match for Gregory when he's angry. Drunk and angry, that man could do anything, and I have this feeling…'

'All you want to do is frighten me. You have a feeling, well so do I. I feel things are going to change in a big way.'

'Junie, the man stabbed you.'

'You see, you're wrong. He didn't stab me.' She laughed as if she were talking to an impetuous child. 'I was holding a jar. A broken jar, and the edges cut into me. I can handle myself, and I can look after the baby. You'll see. I'll even write to you in America. Send you a picture.'

'I see.' Philomena nodded her head and sat back. She must find another way to convince Junie and before the next round of violence. And there would be one.

'Phil, stop it. Stop worrying about me. You'll see, tomorrow he will come and collect me. Everything will work out. Just have faith.' Junie squeezed her hand. Philomena smiled back.

25

The sound of movement in the outer ward roused Philomena. Trolleys being wheeled by, footsteps on the linoleum floor, voices, beepers and a telephone ringing and ringing with nobody to pick it up. She detected the smell of disinfectant and looked into the hallway to see a man with skin the colour of mahogany mopping the floor. He moved the mop in a side-to-side motion, making sure no edges were missed and that they were washed several times over. He looked up at Philomena and smiled broadly with long yellow teeth which he continued to show as he carried out his work. She felt the mattress move when Junie woke and sat up.

'You still here, Phil?'

'Of course. I can wait with you until Gregory comes. Are they discharging you today?'

'They tell me I will only be here for the night. But you really don't have to wait.'

'Junie, you have no clothes to leave with. You think Gregory will think about that?'

Junie shrugged her shoulders and looked around the room. 'Where are my things, anyway?'

'I don't know.' Philomena got up and looked in the small cabinet beside her. 'Oh here.' She pulled out the soiled blouse Junie had been wearing the night before. The dried blood stuck one part of the fabric to the other where it had been folded. The skirt was no better. Even her shoes had speckles of dried blood on them. When Philomena looked at her own clothes and her arms, they had traces of blood on them, too.

'Just leave them,' Junie said. 'Gregory will bring something with him.'

Philomena thought back to the time when Gregory's mother had been sick and bedridden. He hadn't exactly been there for her. It was Philomena and her mother who took on the bulk of her care, making sure she had food, and it was Philomena who made sure the prescriptions were filled, not Gregory. He was always off somewhere, away from the house. She suspected he'd spent a lot of time torturing the poor animals in the woods; he had seemed to relish this. She'd seen it in his eyes. There was no sympathy for his sick mother in those eyes.

'You have school today,' said Junie. 'You should go.'

A nurse knocked lightly and entered the room.

'Morning, morning. How is the patient?' She was carrying a chart and a tray from which she produced a thermometer and started to shake it. Before Junie could respond, she popped the thermometer under Junie's tongue and looked at her watch while holding Junie's wrist. She took Junie's blood pressure next and wrote on the chart. She went to leave the room.

'So, is everything okay, nurse?' Philomena asked.

'Yes, all the checks are done, and the doctor will be here soon to discharge you.'

'Thank you,' said Junie. The nurse left and went to start carrying out the same checks on the patients in the outer ward. Someone entered the room with a trolley of hot drinks, and the noise levels on the ward began to rise with chatter.

'Well, then,' said Philomena. 'Should I go?'

Junie nodded and put out her arms to hug her. They embraced for a short moment, Junie's body warm and frail. Philomena left silently, her eyes on the floor as she walked through the now busy ward and into the corridor. Just as she headed for the exit, she saw her mother round the corner, a large cloth bag in her hand. She hurried towards Philomena.

'How is she?' her mother asked sounding out of breath.

'She says she's fine, that everything will be fine. Why are you here?'

'I brought some of Junie's things. I didn't know if she would be staying in or what.'

Philomena guided her mother to a row of chairs along a wall and they sat down. Mrs Scott was perspiring and breathing heavily.

'Gregory let you in to get her clothes?' asked Philomena.

'I didn't sleep all night. I see him making ready to go somewhere this morning so I run on him. I ask if he going to the hospital, he tell me no he have to go to work. I ask him if he work near the hospital and he going and see his wife, he tell me no, at Guadeloupe, he have to go. So I ask if he don't mind I take a few of his wife things to her. He grunt and groan and go back and open the door. He tell me hurry up and take what I need because he have a boat to catch.' Here, Mrs Scott stopped to kiss her teeth and fan her face. 'I tell you, that man … anyway, I look for Junie's clothes. The place in a mess, but he was getting impatient so I just take what I have before he change his mind.'

Philomena puffed her cheeks and exhaled.

'She thought he would come,' she said.

'*Him*! Never.'

'Why does she have such belief in him? She keeps saying he will change, he will change because she's pregnant. I don't know what to do.'

'Phil, I tell you from the beginning that what goes on in a married couple's home is their own business.'

'But, Mum—'

'No, listen to me. Junie knows you leaving soon. Can't you see she's ashamed and embarrassed because of everything she is going through?'

'But she doesn't have to be. She has said herself that Gregory is a monster. From her own lips, Mum, so why doesn't she want to believe it?'

'What you have to understand is that some women feel so hopeless when they find themselves like this. She doesn't feel worthy of you, and she is ashamed to turn to you. Especially as you are doing so much better than she is. Shame. That's what she has. Shame is doing the talking for her.' She put a hand on Philomena's lap. 'All you can do is help her if she asks you.'

'Like last night.'

'Yes, just so. You help her when she asks. You understand?'

Philomena nodded, knowing in her mind that if shame is what drove Junie's actions, then she wasn't thinking straight and that one day she would come to her senses. And what if that didn't happen? Could she really just walk away and leave Junie to fend for herself? It was looking more and more as if she had to.

'I suppose we should take the bag in to her.' Philomena sighed heavily. 'She still thinks he's coming.'

They went to Junie's room. She was sitting up and sipping a cup of black tea.

'Mrs Scott! Thank you for coming to visit me, but did they tell you I'm getting out this morning?'

'Phil just tell me, but I had already arranged to bring some of your things.' She heaved the bag onto the foot of the bed. Junie stared at it and then at Mrs Scott. Her smile faded.

'But where is Gregory?'

'Gregory isn't coming,' Mrs Scott said in a matter-of-fact way. 'He's on his way to Guadeloupe. Said he had work.' She shrugged her shoulders. 'I came up with my cousin, Grady, in his car, and he's waiting to take us back up.'

'Oh.' Junie's voice was but a whisper. The cup she was holding looked about to spill, so Philomena rushed to take it from her. She looked forlornly up at Philomena who tried not to meet her eye. 'He has to work. Of course he does. How else can he take care of a baby?'

'True,' said Philomena. 'Here, finish your tea.'

The doctor was a long time in arriving on the ward. He was a tall St Lucian man with a straight back, who told Junie that she must have as much rest as possible and to come back to the maternity ward for some extra vitamins when she had the money and gave her a small supply to get started with. Junie nodded, Mrs Scott assured him that she'd make sure of it and Philomena sat with her arm around Junie's shoulder.

When the women left the hospital, they found Grady leaning on the bonnet of his car munching on an apple, all the doors wide open for air. The sun was hazy and warm on the skin. The women walked idly, all feeling drained of energy. Once they were seated in his car, Grady sped them off home. No one spoke. Grady turned up his radio and took the mountain road to the sound of a choir singing about praise to the One on high because who else would save their souls when they were lost.

Philomena sat in the passenger seat, the breeze whispering like music of its own as it caressed her cheek. She tilted her head as the song played and closed her eyes. In her own words, she said a prayer for Junie. *Oh Lord, protect my friend. Bring her hope, bring her peace and guide her. Oh Lord, restore the smile you gave her, radiant and white like the orchid. The beauty in her hair, dark and shining as it was before like moonlight dancing off the soft ripples of the river. Let the sun shine from her face again and music soar from her lips like the humming bird's song. And Lord, let us sit beneath the whitewood tree again, her head on my lap while I read to her your good words.*

26

It was a pattern with Gregory. He would laze around the house for days, become restless and drink too much. Somehow, a job would come his way and then he'd vanish for days at a time, sometimes weeks, and then return. On his return, he would treat Junie badly, hurt her either mentally or physically and vanish again as if that would eliminate his involvement in the destruction he left in his wake. Philomena wished he would stay away for good, but as always, there he would be, back in Junie's life and ready to rip open her flesh and take with it just that little bit more of her precious soul. She was fading before Philomena's eyes, and she couldn't do a thing about it.

When they arrived back at the plain, the Scott women accompanied Junie to her house. Inside, they opened up all the windows. Mrs Scott took down the curtains, too, and said she would wash and repair them all for Junie. Junie spoke in faint tones, the few words seeming to wear her out, and her efforts to help them fix up the mess Gregory had made of the house were of little use. She sat on a dining chair as Philomena and her mother cleaned. Philomena took the day off school, but she knew Saul would make excuses for her. He'd probably have to sit in with her class as there was no one else to cover.

'I'll make us something to eat,' said Philomena. 'What would you like, Junie?'

Junie raised her eyes to her and shook her head.

'You have to eat something. You'll waste away. You said there was food in the kitchen; come and show me what you'd like me to cook.'

'I don't think I can eat a thing.' Junie looked down.

'How would you like to come with us to Phil's dress fitting?' asked Mrs Scott. She had her sleeves rolled up, a bucket and brush in her hand after having been kneeling to clean Junie's blood from the floorboards. 'It's tomorrow.'

'No thank you.'

Philomena made a face at her mother to ask why she would suggest that of all things? Wasn't it bad enough that she was going away: did she have to highlight the fact that Junie was losing a friend at such an important time in her life? But Mrs Scott didn't pick up on Philomena's concern for her friend. She had invited half the island, why should she stop there?

'I take it you been invited to the wedding, Junie?' she went on.

Junie looked at Philomena who shrugged and sat at the table opposite Junie.

'I'm sorry, Junie, I didn't think to ask you. I mean, you said before that Gregory didn't want us to have anything to do with each other.'

'Don't mind him,' said Mrs Scott. 'I'll make sure he lets her go. I'll talk to him.'

'Mum, I think it's best if Junie doesn't get him riled up. Don't you?'

'But it's your wedding, and you two girls have been friends for two years. Very good friends. He doesn't have to come.'

'And he would never be welcome,' Philomena said. 'I just have a feeling he wouldn't allow it.'

'And if he did…' Mrs Scott gave her daughter a sideways look. 'If he did, would you like to come, Junie?'

In a soft voice, Junie said, 'It would be nice. But as Phil says, he might be a bit, a bit funny with me if I ask.'

'Then I will do the asking,' said Mrs Scott. 'Let him try to be funny with me. We could go to town and pick you out a dress. Something pretty. A flowery pattern. You are such a lovely looking girl, anything would suit you.'

Junie looked at Philomena with excitement.

Philomena held her tongue. She got up, intending to go to the kitchen to make something healthy for Junie to eat when a truck pulled up outside. With the door and windows wide open, they could see who had arrived. Vincent jumped out of the truck whistling with a trill as he approached the house. Philomena turned to look at Junie who was sitting up, expectantly, and beaming in a way she hadn't done all day.

'Good day, good day,' Vincent exclaimed as he half bowed at all the women before grinning at Junie. He put up his hands. 'It's fine. I know your husband doesn't like you to have callers, but I know for a fact that he was on the carrier to Guadeloupe with a group of labourers today. My little brother was one of them. He knows your husband by the way. And I know that the job they are on starts Monday and finishes Friday. So I just took the liberty to call on you, see if you need anything.' He did a quick sweep of the room. 'I'm on my way to Pa, and I was going to ask if you want a lift to your plot, but I see you busy here.'

Junie rose from her chair and smoothed the front of her dress. She touched her hand to her hair, to the neat cornrow that Mrs Scott had twisted into it, greasing the sides flat when they were waiting on the ward for Junie to be discharged.

'Thank you, Vincent. You are such a kind man.'

Philomena swallowed and stared between both him and Junie. The affection they had for each other was tangible and made Philomena feel uncomfortable.

'Oh, Vincent, these are my neighbours. The Scotts live next door.'

Vincent stepped inside and reached a hand out to Philomena.

'We meet again,' he said.

'You know each other?' Junie's voice lifted in surprise.

'Yes,' Philomena said. 'The day I came looking for you at the river. You remember? Well, I had gone up to your allotment first. Pa was there and Vincent, too.'

'I see,' said Junie. 'And this is Mrs Scott.'

Mrs Scott shook hands with Vincent and sized him up.

'So you know our Junie well, do you?'

'A little,' said Vincent, becoming ill at ease.

'You married?'

'Haven't found the right one.'

'And if the right one already have a baby?'

Vincent looked puzzled. 'Well, it doesn't make her a bad person. I suppose if there is love, the past doesn't matter.' He wiped his upper lip, put his hands in his pockets and immediately removed them.

Philomena went over to where her mother stood right under Vincent's nose and gently pulled her aside.

'You said you're working up at Pa Reynauld's?' said Philomena. He nodded. 'Well, I'm sure you'll see Junie up there when she next comes.' She looked between Junie and Vincent again. They had locked eyes with an unbreakable force. They smiled with their eyes rather than their lips, and she wanted to jump in the middle of them and break apart whatever it was that was passing between them, her mood dampening with each passing second. One visit from him and Junie had brightened up, whereas she had had to beg for Junie to let her help her. Surely she didn't think there would be any future between the two of them. Only this morning, she had declared that the baby had made her a changed woman, that she had the courage to face up to Gregory and somehow turn him into a good father and a loving husband. Junie was a child, inexperienced. She could no more change Gregory than she could run away with this tall and handsome man.

'We were going to have some lunch,' Philomena interjected. 'Do you want to join us as you don't appear to be busy?'

'Oh no,' Vincent said and stepped backwards. 'It was just a quick call. Just to check on Junie, but I'm late going up to Pa, so…'

'You going then?' asked Philomena.

'You don't have to rush away,' said Junie, finding a stronger voice to use now.

'I do,' said Vincent. 'But I look forward to seeing you when you're up there next.' He nodded to the women and turned to leave. Philomena noticed how Junie followed him to the door, waited until he had started his engine and pulled away before turning round again. She was smiling to herself.

'Well, well, well,' said Mrs Scott. 'Somebody has an admirer.' She clucked her tongue and went back to the housework.

'Well, Junie is a pretty girl,' Philomena said. 'But he knows you're married. Does he know about the baby?'

Junie shook her head.

'Well, perhaps you ought to say something and to tell him he needs to be very careful about coming here. You know how jealous Gregory would be if he thought you really did have an admirer.'

'I know only too well.' Junie went back to her chair, resting her chin on her hand, her elbow on the table. The listless look returned to her face.

'I'll cook something,' Philomena said again. When she got no response, she left and went to the kitchen.

27

Philomena woke the next morning with mixed feelings. While she should be happy that her wedding was close and that she'd be starting a new chapter in her life and providing an escape for Junie, she couldn't help feeling that Vincent extending his offer to help somehow diminished her own. It was proving difficult to accept that she was not the only one who was there for Junie and not only that: Junie didn't seem to want to be saved by her.

But she had the last fitting of her wedding dress later, and she'd have to brush these emotions away and look like a happy bride. Junie—in her childish imagining that Gregory would allow her to come to the wedding—was excited about going into town with Philomena and her mother so that she could have a new dress bought for her. They would drive from town up to the country dwelling of Josephine Dennis, the seamstress whom Mrs Scott had sought especially to make her daughter's wedding dress. Josephine came highly recommended, so Philomena had gone along with her mother's choice, though she would have been just as happy to pull out a nice frock from her own wardrobe.

Mrs Scott had the day planned. She was up before day-break—the cock was crowing while she was in the kitchen—cooking a hearty breakfast of roasted breadfruit and fried plantain for the three of them. She called to Philomena and told her to hurry over to Junie's house and bring her round for breakfast. She had arranged a lift with her cousin, Grady, and he'd be arriving soon himself.

Junie was still asleep when Philomena knocked on the door. She let herself in and sensed the calm stillness of the house, the lazy ease at which it sat now that there was no Gregory around. They had washed away the blood he'd spilled, the booze he'd spilled, fixed the furniture he'd up-turned and chased away the rancid smell of nicotine and alcohol with the sweet fragrances of Junie's flowers from the garden. A window had been left open overnight, and the fresh smell of morning air wafted into a room that had un-wittingly transformed into a battlefield just two days ago.

Junie was sprawled across the bed in the half-light, a golden skinned being at rest like something celestial rather than of flesh and blood. She made no sound, but her whole torso moved to the slow rhythm of her breath. Her wild hair had been tamed into a single cornrow, but fronds of sleek black hair had escaped and framed her face. Her pose, seren-ity itself.

'Junie,' Philomena whispered her name as she leaned over her. Junie didn't stir. Philomena shook her shoulder and Ju-nie groaned. Her eyes opened to halfway, taking in a little light. Philomena watched her expressions alter. At first she was startled and looked quickly to her husband's side of the bed, tension in her jaw as she clenched her teeth. At last, her face softened.

Junie yawned and sat up, feet on the floor. She was mo-tionless at first and then stretched both fists overhead. Her limbs were thin, small muscles sculpted into her upper arms, sparse hair in her armpits. She turned around to Philomena.

'Is it late?'

The sun had begun to rise properly by then.

'No, it's early. Mum has got breakfast ready for us. Grady is coming soon. Get up.'

'Of course.' She jumped to standing. 'Your dress fitting, to-day. I can't wait to see it.'

'And you're getting your new dress, don't forget.'

Junie slipped on a cardigan. 'I know and I feel so lucky, Phil. I can't thank Ma Scott enough.'

Philomena turned to leave the bedroom, and Junie trotted after her. Philomena stopped before the front door. 'I just don't want you to build up your hopes about the wedding. Mum might talk fancy about persuading Gregory to let you come, but you know him. You know what he's like.'

Junie looked at her bare feet.

'I am happy for you, Junie. I want you to have nice things, but Gregory has a way of crushing nice things. We just need to be careful.'

A car pulled up. Grady was early.

'Come on.' Philomena took Junie's hand. 'Let's eat.'

When they arrived in town, Mrs Scott gave instructions to Grady to make himself scarce for the next couple of hours and they'd be back at the sea port where he'd parked his car under the shade of a leafy palm tree. The busy bus terminal was very close by, and several cars pulled up to park along-side Grady's in the time it took for them to get out of his car. The town sparked with activity and buzzed with movement and noise. Music played from a café overlooking the sea. People arrived from all over the island for the market stalls and the shops. This was the capital city, Roseau, the place the islanders expected nothing but the best. Saturday was the busiest day.

The three headed to the only department store. A white couple passed them and nodded. Their faces were red, their clothes lightweight and classy. The locals, too, perhaps not in such expensive clothes, dressed well enough for church. Philomena imagined these tourists must be American and that she'd see several women in New York like this one, dressed in narrow calf-length skirts, high-heeled shoes and sunglasses. She would need a whole new wardrobe to fit in. Hers had not caught up with 1950s fashion at all.

Junie fizzed with excitement as she tried on dress after dress, asking of Mrs Scott if she was sure she didn't mind spending so many dollars on her. Philomena had never seen her friend as joyous in a very long time. In the end, Junie chose a light blue dress of raw silk. It had a button-through bodice and a flared skirt. It was short sleeved with a small collar and lapels that were embroidered with small white flowers. There was a thin belt attached to it which exaggerated Junie's tiny waist.

'I love this dress,' said Junie.

'It will be the last time you wear something so tight,' said Mrs Scott, fixing Junie's collar. 'Come on. You need shoes.'

The sandals Mrs Scott bought for Junie were not unlike the ones worn by the American tourist Philomena had seen earlier. Closed at the toes with a strap around the heel. Philomena, despite her trepidation, couldn't help beaming at how beautiful Junie looked and how she was so much more like the glowing young girl she remembered arriving next door two years ago.

Mrs Scott treated them to a cold sliced meat sandwich from one of the street sellers and an ice cream from the parlour near the bay. Grady was smoking a cigarette when they joined him. He looked hot. He stubbed out his cigarette, and Mrs Scott handed him a bottle of root beer.

'Next stop *Paix Bouche*,' he said as he started the engine. He put the car radio on again and drove away from the port. Grady was also going to be Philomena's driver for the wedding. He appeared to be under her mother's commission lately, but there was no other way of travelling distances around the island. It wasn't easy to get transport to and from the country villages and remote hamlets.

Josephine Dennis lived in a small wooden house, painted blue, just on the outskirts of one of the countryside hamlets in the north. She had been newly married herself when Mrs Scott engaged her services and, being pregnant, too, Philomena's was one of her last undertakings before the baby came. Mrs Scott said repeatedly how lucky they had been to get Josephine and that had to be a sign of good luck for Philomena's marriage.

Josephine carried the dress with pride from the far end of the living room to the sofa where Philomena, Mrs Scott and Junie sat.

'You can try it on in the bedroom,' said Josephine, holding out a hand to the room Philomena was already familiar with. When she came out, all of the women inhaled with admiration.

Josephine smoothed and fussed and checked the lengths and seams. The dress was made of ivory satin with a lace bodice. It was panelled and fitted at the waist before falling into a full flare from the hips to Philomena's ankles. Mrs Scott's eyes sparkled with tears as she looked at her daughter.

'So beautiful,' she sighed.

'You look so wonderful, Phil,' said Junie. 'I don't think I've seen another bride like you.'

'Well, don't forget to appreciate Josephine's skill,' Philomena said, looking to the seamstress. 'You have done such a wonderful job. It's no wonder Mum wanted to hire you. Thank you.' She hugged Josephine around her shoulders.

'You are very welcome, and it's very easy to sew for someone with a lovely shape like yours. So, I only need to check you are happy with the length and I'll sew the hem and it's done. I'll give it a good press. And you can pick it up next week.'

'Wonderful, I'll send Grady.' Mrs Scott stood up. 'Now, let's settle up and let you have your afternoon to rest. Mrs Scott patted Josephine's round belly. Junie put her hands to her own. Philomena couldn't help but notice the expression that crossed her face: Junie was having doubts about everything she'd said about Gregory coming round to wanting a baby. Maybe she was wondering about leaving with her. She wished for this to be true.

28

With one glorious week to herself, Junie's spirits were high. She continued to live in hope that when Gregory returned from working in Guadeloupe, he would have had time to think about what he'd done. Now that he knew his baby was on the way, surely he would have had time to adjust to becoming a parent. A spell had been cast over her, it would seem, an impenetrable aura that kept the bad memories out and the hope of better times ahead raising her spirits. She knew Philomena didn't understand her, but there was very little she could do about that. At least Mrs Scott didn't brush aside the idea that Gregory would come around and allow her to go to the wedding. Besides, she had a beautiful dress to wear. It was a lot smarter and elegant than her own wedding day apparel had ever been, and she couldn't help wondering what her mother would make of her, seeing her so dressed up. Would she be pleased for her? Would she admit that she'd been wrong about Gregory? That they were all wrong about him and that he just needed time to be rid of his demons once and for all. This baby was the perfect opportunity for that to happen, the baby would save her marriage.

Junie spent the week keeping the house tidy, keeping her hair neat and her clothes clean. The food Gregory had bought wouldn't last until he came back, and she had wanted to cook him a nice meal on the day he was expected to arrive home. She brought Mrs Scott into her confidence, and she had very kindly told Junie that her kitchen was all hers, and she could help herself to whatever she needed so she could cook something for Gregory. At this, Junie noticed Philomena shake her head, bemused. She wished Philomena had a little more faith. Philomena had, thankfully, stopped trying to lecture her about her marriage, but this meant that whenever Junie dropped by in the evenings for a chat, Philomena said very little at all.

'I just don't want you to have false hope,' Philomena had said and had shrugged her shoulders when Mrs Scott insisted that, if nothing else, Gregory would let her attend the wedding.

Vincent had already told them that his brother was on the same job in Guadeloupe as Gregory and workers were due back on Friday. In anticipation and with Mrs Scott's help, Junie prepared a big meal of meat and dumpling soup. She had been up to her allotment to fetch some limes and had made lime cordial, too. She laid out the table as decoratively as she could, placing a small vase of blush pink roses in the centre, lime cordial in a jug and the dinner service polished and set.

The evening wore on as Junie sat at the table, jumping at any sound from the narrow road, looking through the small window and not seeing a soul arrive. The soup in their bowls grew cold, a skin setting on the top, the consistency beginning to congeal. She poked a spoon into one of them, tried to stir up the liquid part, but it looked unappetising now that it was no longer steaming.

Junie took the bowls to the kitchen and lit the stove, making a *bain-marie* to warm up Gregory's food and keep it warm until he came home.

Junie gave up as midnight arrived. She'd had enough of looking outside and seeing the shadows of trees and letting her imagination convince her that one of them was the out-line of her husband. Or that she could hear the sound of a ve-hicle trundling up the road in the dark when all she could hear were crickets and branches sighing on the night breeze. She covered the soup, which didn't smell as nice as it had when it was fresh, and turned off the stove. She lay on the bed and fell asleep in her day clothes. Before she knew it, light was streaming in onto her face. It felt as if she hadn't slept at all. She was still tired, the sun's rays made her squint and she looked on either side of her for traces of Gregory. There were none. He didn't show his face until late on Sunday afternoon.

He caught Junie unawares. She was on Mrs Scott's veranda, sitting on the step, Philomena and her mother occupying the only chairs. Mrs Scott rocked slowly on her chair, pipe in her hand. She had been good enough to plait Junie's hair again, making small sections with the tail of her comb and working Junie's thick hair into loose braids that hung to her shoulders. She gathered all of them into a ribbon at the back. They'd had a big lunch and were too lazy to do anything else but sit and talk about anything and nothing. Several times Mrs Scott brought the conversation round to the wedding, and each time Philomena directed it away to something else: the preparations for graduation, organising a stage to be built in the school yard, anything but the wedding.

Junie had a strange feeling come over her just before she heard the distant sound of a vehicle making its way up the hill from the village. She realised she hadn't imagined the truck this time because it came to a stop outside her house. She rushed towards the Scott's gate. Leaning over, she saw the driver chatting away to his passenger, a serious-faced Gregory. She rattled nervously at the catch on the gate and ran out just as Gregory jumped out of the cabin. The driver jumped out, too, and was grinning at Junie. Her eyes shifted between this hefty man and Gregory who stood his ground while the other approached her like a wild cat hunting prey.

'Well, little lady, you must be the wife I heard so much about.' He had an accent; maybe he was Jamaican or from Antigua, Junie couldn't be sure. 'When this man tell me he have a beautiful wife, I thought it must be a lie. But here you are.'

She didn't like the way he looked her up and down at all parts of her body like he was weighing her up and about to offer Gregory a price for her. She felt dirty and shot a look at Gregory.

'Say something,' her husband said to her. 'Why you just stand up there?' He looked over at the Scott house.

'Gregory, I…' she faltered. 'Can I make you both something?'

Gregory shook his head and stood next to the gate with one hand on it, the other holding a bulky cloth sack.

'He's not staying.' Gregory looked at his friend who pulled at the seat of his trousers and climbed back into his lorry.

'It was a pleasure,' said the driver. He winked at Gregory and wagged a finger before doing a u-turn on the grassland opposite, running over several wild flowers in his exaggerated effort to leave the plain. He tooted his horn several times before the truck rounded the corner.

Gregory looked long and hard at Junie.

'Where were you just now?'

'I, um, I just paid a visit to Mrs Scott.'

By now, Mrs Scott had left her front garden and made her presence known. 'The wanderer returns,' she said boldly to Gregory. 'I say that because ever since you were a boy, you would go off, here, there and everywhere. You must know this area like the back of your hand. Better than me.'

He didn't respond, only stared at Mrs Scott, waiting for her to finish so he could take his leave.

'Your mother and I used to wonder what you got up to,' Mrs Scott continued, edging closer. 'She said you liked the woods.'

Philomena, who had stayed on the veranda, leaned over it now, just visible to the others assembled in front of the Williams house. Gregory squinted at her.

'I did,' he said, eyes still on Philomena.

'And I really liked your mother,' Mrs Scott went on. 'A wonderful person. You have been blessed, Gregory. A good mother and now a good wife.'

All eyes turned to Junie. She folded one hand over a fisted one and gave a half smile.

'Also, she is a good friend of Phil's as you know,' Mrs Scott continued. 'And Phil has her wedding coming up, and being as the two of them been friends so long, I invited Junie to come and celebrate the special day with us. What you say, Gregory?'

Gregory looked as though he could taste something bitter. He looked at Junie who shrank beneath his gaze. Gregory turned his face slowly back to Mrs Scott.

'You invite my good wife, and you don't invite me?'

'Well, you know, Gregory, as it is, no one really knows your comings and goings. And I know you known Phil a while, but I never really took you two as friends.'

He looked over at Philomena.

'Getting married.' He shook his head. 'Getting married. Interesting isn't it?' No one answered. It wasn't clear what he meant, though he kept his attention on Philomena. When the silence continued, Gregory returned his gaze to Junie.

'Junie. What you saying? You want to go to this woman wedding?'

Junie paused. Swallowed, sniffed. Unfolded her hands and parted her lips.

'Tell me?' His voice lowered in volume, resonating with a cold edge.

'I would like to go, yes,' said Junie. She couldn't make eye contact. She was hoping, praying he would relent, but he just kept looking at her, watering that seed of doubt that was deeply rooted inside her.

'Then go,' he eventually blasted. He raised an arm as if to direct her off to the wedding then and there.

'Thank you,' she said and looked over at Philomena with a grin. 'The wedding is in two weeks.' She directed this to Gregory's back as he opened the gate, let it swing shut behind him and stormed along the path to the front door.

Junie clasped her hands together and tried to contain the urge to jump up and down. Mrs Scott took her hands.

'Now don't bring it up when he's around, you hear me? With any luck, he'll go off on another job somewhere.' She gave Junie's hands a squeeze before going back to her veranda.

Junie hovered on the road between the houses, looking up at Philomena, her hands in prayer as if she had the heavens to thank for Gregory's decision. She could tell that Philomena was distrustful about the whole thing, but Junie rejoiced in the fact that he had said yes. There was going to be a change between them, a shift towards what married life should be.

She watched the Scott women take their places on the front porch chairs, touched both hands to her tummy and rushed indoors to ask Gregory what he'd like to eat.

29

Mrs Scott had been able to secure the large church halfway to town for the ceremony. She couldn't imagine her daughter's wedding being in the run-down wooden church she usually attended on a Sunday. There were holes in the roof near the altar, and birds very often fluttered in to sit in one of these holes and coo and chirp throughout the service. No, that just wouldn't do. Neither would having the reception in the equally dilapidated church hall or in their little house, come to that. She had booked a function room at the hotel by the sea just on the outskirts of town. It was the grandest one on the island, and Mrs Scott was determined to hire it, regardless of the cost. And though the cost would fall to Philomena and Saul, Mrs Scott's imagination and her desires for her daughter to have the best send-off possible was all she cared about.

Despite her previous trepidations, Philomena had allowed the excitement of the occasion to take its hold. She woke before sunrise on her wedding day, overjoyed. She hadn't had much sleep at all. Her mother knocked on her door with a cup of tea and told her to make sure she drank every drop. Breakfast was next, and she needed to eat all of that up, too, because it was going to be a long day and she'd need her strength. But Philomena's insides were tangled into knots, and she couldn't see how she was going to ingest a thing.

Her beautiful dress hung on a padded, fabric hanger on the curtain rail in her bedroom. It was the last thing she saw before she turned off the lamp, and it was the first thing she saw when the sun shone through the window. Mrs Scott carefully opened the curtains so as not to let the dress fall. She looked at it one last time before leaving Philomena's room with strict instructions for her to hurry up.

Philomena looked at the contents of the cup her mother had set down, the tea settling into a calm pool of black once the vibrations of Mrs Scott's busy footfall subsided. It was peaceful now. She closed her eyes to inhale the tranquility. In the living room, she could hear Mrs Scott going backwards and forwards with pails of water to fill the large steel bath tub that she had brought in from the kitchen. Mrs Scott was happy in her bustling, and Philomena fully expected to be bustled and hurried along, too. She was prepared for it. Saul had calmed her down whenever she complained that her mother was spending too much of their money and that it would have been more useful to put those thousands of dollars towards their new life in America. But there had been no stopping Mrs Scott, and Philomena had fallen into step weeks ago.

And now, here she was. The big day, and she smiled once again to herself.

Her mother had placed petals in the water. She washed her daughter's back with a soft sponge, humming as she did and being careful not to get her hair wet. It had been straightened with a hot iron and set in rollers the night before. Mrs Scott helped to pat her daughter dry and sent her back to her bedroom to start oiling her skin. As she was dressing, there was a gentle tap on the front door and she could hear Junie chatting merrily to Mrs Scott.

This was the thing Philomena hadn't expected. That Junie would be at the wedding. At the time he gave his permission, Philomena felt sure Gregory was just trying to shock her and that he'd take it all back and make Junie feel as if she'd imagined it all. He'd change his mind, she'd felt it in her bones. But here Junie was, so she'd been wrong about him. In the last two weeks, he had behaved himself. There had been no shouting or screaming from the Williams house. Junie had been smug one day and whispered, 'I told you so' to Philomena when she passed their house while Junie was gardening and Gregory was smoking from the doorway. Even then she'd thought Gregory was up to something.

Junie knocked on the bedroom door. Philomena was still in her slip and about to take out her rollers.

'Greetings beautiful bride!' Junie exclaimed as she entered. She kissed Philomena on both cheeks. 'Ma Scott said I must hurry up and get dressed and come and help you.'

'I think I can do it.'

'Don't be silly. Sit at the mirror; I'll be back to do your hair.'

Philomena allowed herself to be plumped and preened. She wore her mother's lipstick at her mother's insistence. Philomena never wore makeup, but Mrs Scott said she just had to make an exception today of all days.

When Philomena turned to look at herself in the mirror, she was very happy with what she saw. Junie and her mother said she looked beautiful, and that was exactly how she felt. The three stood silently gazing at their reflection, entranced by their individual dreams. From what seemed like a long distance away, they heard a car horn toot. The second time Grady tooted the car horn, it shook them all into action.

Outside, Grady stood in the hot sun, his suit jacket over the back of the passenger seat, his tie bright and wide. As she got into the car, Philomena saw the door to the Williams house open by a sliver. A cold shiver ran along the length of her spine, but she smiled in spite of it.

There was a light mist of rain as they drove to the church, not enough to spoil their clothes, but thankfully it had stopped by the time they arrived. Philomena's older brother, Pearson, was already there, ready to give her away. She hadn't seen him in a long time but would finally get to know his family after the ceremony, more so once she moved to America. Her brother didn't live in New York but in Washington, which was close enough.

Her mother kept fussing with Philomena's veil as they stood at the narthex. This only made Philomena anxious and Pearson smile.

'Mum,' he whispered. 'She looks beautiful. You go and take your seat. Leave this part to me.'

Junie took Mrs Scott's arm and nodded to the aisle before gently tugging for Mrs Scott to follow. The opening of the second door to the church let out the muted aroma of incense, the dulled voices of guests looking over their shoulders, a bustle of activity rising when they realised it was the bride's mother.

'Are you ready for this?' Pearson smelt of cologne, his suit fashionable and expensive. She had never seen him like this before, and the intensity of the occasion began to build. She swallowed.

'As I'll ever be,' she breathed.

The congregation stood, the organ started up and Pearson offered Philomena the crook of his arm. Nothing had been rehearsed, apart from Mrs Scott telling Philomena innumerable times how she must walk as gracefully as she could. At the altar, Philomena saw Saul's face, the warmth of his smile generating love that had buoyed her for this past year. He followed her every step, seeing only her. Her heart seemed to grow in her chest and halted her breath; she had no idea how she arrived at the altar, looking into the eyes of a tearful Saul through the glassy lens of her own. The last two years had brought her to this moment, a moment that she'd seen as an escape route for Junie and the prospect of a better life. But something within her changed as the priest joined their hands. She knew that Saul's motives had always been fuelled by his love for her, and she loved him back. She loved him dearly, but nothing had prepared her for the realisation of how deeply in love with him she actually was. A tear rolled its way to her chin, she sniffed back an audible sigh of complete joy and saw her future with Saul in a new and elating way.

Philomena had continued to smile, her guests seemingly enveloped in a haze of happiness through the joyful union of the couple. At the reception in the hotel, people shared loving memories, past recollections of wedding days gone by, the food they'd eaten, the clothes they'd worn. Philomena looked around at her guests laughing, sharing jokes, eating and drinking so much she could imagine how lively the dancing would be later on that evening. She herself was already giddy from champagne.

'Oh, Phil,' her Aunt Sylvia said. 'Seems like you have a movie star wedding right here. But I didn't expect anything less.' She cast a knowing look in Mrs Scott's direction. While it was true that Mrs Scott had got very carried away,

Philomena couldn't have imagined a better wedding. She'd forgotten all about her protestations and decided that so much happiness would not have fit into the local church hall and the spread of food never would have tasted so good if they'd relied on her mother's small kitchen. They dined on curried goat, several types of fish and root vegetables, salads, red beans and rice piled high on everyone's plate. A movie star wedding indeed.

Philomena looked over at Junie, who was sitting between two of her male cousins. They were obviously taken by Junie's beauty. She looked very much the movie star in her dress. Her hair lay flat and was scooped into a sophisticated bun at the top. She had borrowed Mrs Scott's pearl earrings and her pearl pendant which lay sweetly at the top of her chest. Her cheeks were flushed as she spoke to both men; she laughed happily at whatever it was they were saying. Then she stopped and looked in Philomena's direction. Their eyes connected, and Junie gave Philomena a warm smile. The smile extended to her large eyes within whose depths Philomena saw a look of love and deep gratitude. Then Junie mouthed the words *Thank You*. She returned her attention to her two admirers as Philomena's gaze lingered on Junie a few seconds more. Saul returned to her side at the table and held her hand.

'Well, my love, here we are Mr and Mrs Mattherson. About to take the world by storm.'

She turned and smiled at him, cupping his face with her palm.

'Mr and Mrs Mattherson. Sounds sophisticated. I like it. Are you happy you married me?'

'What?' He laughed and shook his head. 'What do you mean? It's the one thing I've wanted since the day I met you.'

'I know, but would you love me no matter what? No matter who I was?'

'I'm not sure I understand the question. Are you telling me you're really someone else?' He grinned at her and took another sip of champagne.

'Sometimes, I wonder who I am. What I am.' She stole a quick glance at Junie.

'You're my wife. A beautiful woman and I love you. And I think they are going to clear the tables for some dancing.'

Philomena sighed a laugh. 'I think I'm too full to dance.'

No one was too full to dance. Even if they were, they danced anyway. They danced until they were hot and perspiring, and when that wasn't enough, they sang, too. Someone grabbed Philomena by her hands and danced her around the room, jiggling and whirling and making her dizzy. Her dance partner, whom she recognised only vaguely, swung her around the floor and into several of the guests, and she had to keep apologising. There hadn't been a need, though, because the guests were oblivious, busy bumping into someone else. She saw Saul dancing with Junie; they made a good couple.

When the song finished, Philomena grabbed the opportunity to unclench her dance partner's hands and make her way out of the room. The patio windows were all wide open, a white awning flapping above them. Outside it was dark, but she knew it would be cool and she could take a rest.

Philomena walked into the evening air and continued to walk as far as a low stone wall outside the circle of light from the room. The music was still audible as were the voices chattering above it. She couldn't make out conversations, but every now and then, there was a bark of laughter that put a smile on her face. She sat on the wall and fanned her face with her hand, blowing out a puff of warm air. Her feet ached, and if she could see them clearly enough, she'd find they had swollen. She slipped off her shoes and let out a long satisfied sigh.

'The dancing getting too much for you?'

Philomena snapped her head around when she heard Gregory's voice. Her instinct was to run, but why should she have to leave the comfort of her respite? He hadn't been invited.

'What are you doing here?'

Gregory, who had approached her from out of the shadows, came and sat next to her on the wall. 'Seems to me the wedding is there, not out here. Anyone can sit here.'

Philomena stood up to leave, but he caught hold of her wrist. She shook her arm, but he tightened his grip.

'Woah, woah,' he said. 'Can't a person even wish a person congratulations these days?'

'Let me go.' Philomena looked frantically towards the celebrating guests in the room, but no one could see her from in there.

'I'll scream,' she said, 'shout for someone if you don't let me go.' She was pulling her body from him, but the more she struggled backwards, the more painful his grip felt on her wrist. Her shoulder would come out of its socket if she continued like this. He was not about to let her go.

'What is wrong with you?' She stopped trying to escape and stood her ground as if she wasn't afraid. 'It killed you to let her come here, didn't it? Did you say yes to her so that you could come here and spy on us?'

Gregory rose slowly but didn't release her.

'Did you get jealous because everyone was here having a good time and you were outside, on your own, just like at school? You remember that time?'

He stood, towering above her, his nostrils flaring as he stared down into her eyes.

'You don't know anything about that time.' He spoke through gritted teeth, whisky on his hot breath.

'I do know.' She shook her arm again. 'I do know that I tried to be your friend. I did everything, and you turned your back on everyone. You made yourself an outsider.'

'No,' he shouted. 'No. That was them.' He pointed a finger out into the distance. 'I was a scared little boy. A child, and they laughed at me, people always have. They way my mother did.'

'Your mother was a good woman. She was kind, and you treated her like dirt.'

'You don't know what you're talking about, Miss Philomena. Big, big teacher. Fancy clothes and fancy education. What do you know, anyway?'

Philomena stopped trying to force his fingers off her wrist and looked up at him. The anger was still there, but there was another story being written behind the dark emotion. It was pain she saw. Her own anger quelled for a moment.

'What are you saying, Gregory? You're talking in riddles.' Her voice was level.

'You put on a good show, but did you ever want to know me? Did you ever see me?'

'I don't…'

'You don't see me. Not you, not my mother, not anyone.'

'What I see is a monster. I saw what you did in the woods.'

He pulled her closer, her trapped hand now against his chest. 'I knew it was you,' he hissed. 'Always did.'

Fear swathed Philomena now. Gregory's expression had changed again. *This must be what Junie sees every time he turns on her.*

'But I never told a soul,' she said. 'No one.'

'Thank you for keeping my little secret.'

'Is that what you meant when you said no one saw you? Because you tortured defenceless animals and got away with it? Did you want someone to stop you?'

'I didn't give a damn about those animals because no one gave a damn when it happened to me. Not even that precious mother of mine you loved so much.'

'Who? Who tortured you?' Her voice was a whisper.

'He did.' The words left Gregory's mouth as if they had been large stones trapped in his gullet, choking him, cutting off his air. His eyes, bloodshot from booze became misty. He caught hold of Philomena's second wrist and dragged her several feet further from the hotel, further into the dark. When she looked up at him, she could barely make out his face.

'He?' she said, her voice faltering. 'Your father? He tortured you?'

'You can't do that to a child.' His voice faltered also. 'Not a small boy. It's not right. It's not fair. He hurt me. Not with a stone or a fist. And she, she knew and she let it happen, and now they're both dead.' He let out a laugh. He let go of Philomena's wrists. For a split second, she was motionless but realised this was her chance to escape, so she turned in the direction of the hotel lights and ran. She had gone but three steps away when he caught her again. This time around her waist. He lifted her up. Philomena kicked and screamed, but Gregory forced her back against a tree. He grabbed both her cheeks with his large hand and held her face up to his.

'You kept my secret before. You have to keep this one. You understand?'

She nodded as assuringly as she could though it was hard to even move her head, jammed as it was against the rough bark.

'You keep my secret, or I'll tell everybody yours.'

She squinted up at him, questioningly.

'You think I don't know?' He snorted a laugh and pressed his body up against hers. 'You think I don't see the way you look at my wife? You think I don't understand what goes on in your brain when you watch her naked in the river? Or when you pretend to be drying her body. I sat in the woods and I watched you. The others might not see it. That new big husband you have. Not even your mother. You're disgusting, and people like you don't have a place on this earth.'

He let go of her face but began to grind his body into her.

'There is no place for monsters like you.' Philomena's voice was strained; she tried to force him off her with clenched fists. 'You treat Junie like dirt. Like rubbish. We are not the same. I hate you. I'll kill you.'

'Killing? No, that's my job.' He pulled away, and Philomena lashed out at him. 'I'll kill your little girlfriend one of these days.'

Gregory walked away. She heard his footsteps hasten as he ran off into the dark. Her heart was racing. She leaned forward and held her stomach and began to wretch. She imagined heaving out everything she had consumed in the past few hours but nothing came. Her stomach cramped up, and she began to stagger back to the hotel. The closer she got, she began trying to straighten her hair, her clothes, wipe loose tears from her face, dust her hands off. Instead of returning via the open windows, Philomena darted to the side of the hotel and found another entrance. She scanned the tiled corridor for the nearest bathroom.

'Phil!' She turned quickly when she heard Saul. 'My God. What happened?'

'Me?' She looked down at her dress and saw that it was marked and grubby. 'I—I fell. I needed air. I walked off and couldn't see where I was going and … and I tripped.'

'You tripped?' Saul held her around her waist. He examined Philomena from her face down to her feet. 'Are you badly hurt? Where are your shoes?'

'I had to take them off. I'm fine, Saul. Honestly, I'm fine.' She sounded breathless but tried to find calm from somewhere.

Saul wouldn't let go of her, he held her hand. 'Jesus. Your wrist is bruised.'

'I know, I banged it on a rock.'

'Is it broken? Sprained?'

'Oh Saul, don't fuss. It hardly hurts. I'll be fine. I need to splash my face in the bathroom.'

Junie came out of the hall just then.

'Phil? You—you were gone. What…?'

'She fell outside in the dark,' Saul said. 'Can you go in the bathroom with her?'

'Of course I will.'

They left a concerned Saul in the corridor and entered the bathroom.

'I'll be fine,' said Philomena as she ran the tap. 'I was an idiot, that's all.'

She caught Junie's expression in the mirror. Doubt lingered in her eyes, a question hovered at her lips. Junie was a woman who knew all about covering up the kind of fall that Philomena had just taken. Neither woman said a word as Junie balled up tissues, wet them and wiped Philomena's face and hands. Her movie star wedding ended in silence.

30

How beautiful it had been, how like a dream that she was there to witness her best friend's wedding. Junie remembered her own wedding day, impromptu and quiet as it had been. At Philomena's wedding the day before, Junie thought her face would split wide open if she didn't stop smiling as much as she did. There had been tears, too. Tears of happiness for Philomena and Saul and for the honour of experiencing what a proper celebration of love and commitment should look like. Junie wasn't sure now what it was that had attracted her to Gregory or how she had come to love him. He was brutish and grubby, and he found it hard to maintain eye contact with anyone, especially Junie's mother. But when she was alone with Gregory, he only had eyes for her. He wasn't a man of many words, but he'd found the right ones to convince her that deep down there was good in him and that in his way he did love her too.

She lay on the bed touching the sheet, the space that Gregory should have taken, but he hadn't been there when she arrived home after the wedding. There were times he could be gone for days, not for work, coming home smelling of sweat and grass and goodness knows what else. She couldn't be sure if this was one of those unexplained absences or if he'd gone away to work again. She had questioned him the first time he disappeared to goodness knows where, early on in their marriage, when there hadn't been a job and she could see no reason why a full grown man would leave his young and willing bride alone for so long. Thoughts of an affair had been far from her mind. She had been concerned for his safety, anything could have happened. He hadn't packed a bag. So when he'd reappeared the first time, she'd rushed up to him, worried sick, only having to take a step back because of the repugnant odour that saturated him. She'd asked boldly where on earth he'd been. Gregory had grunted at her, pushed her aside and told her that sometimes a man had to go and do what they'd been called to and she would be sorry if she ever questioned him again. That look behind his eyes, the sign that something troubled him returned. She had seen it before they married, and she'd thought she could look beyond it, hoping that once they were married this look would leave, never to return. At one point, that look seemed to have gone and she believed whatever haunted him must be gone, too. It was only weeks into the marriage before the demon behind his stare resurfaced.

In the early days, she had no idea how the troubled soul within would show itself in the rest of the marriage. Now she knew. The only thing left for her to do was not to torment the beast. She had poked at it, made it rear its ugly head. It became obvious that the only thing that stirred the beast in Gregory was her being there, not anything she said or did. So she learned to weather the beatings, neglect, the feeling of hope fading. When she knew there was a baby, she gave up on the desire to run, instead she would make a home for the baby, with Gregory. At last there had been a glimmer that her hard work had paid off. He had let her go to the wedding. He was becoming a person who could be good, could be kind, and together they would raise their baby.

She touched her tummy now. For the first time, it looked to be swelling. She smiled to herself and formed pictures in her mind of the three of them together, playing in the garden, laughing. As she closed her eyes, another picture came into her head, a glimpse of a familiar figure in the grounds of the hotel when they'd celebrated Pholimena's wedding. As the long net curtains fluttered open and closed by the open windows, she thought she'd seen Gregory's face. It was only a split second, but her heart had skipped a beat. She thought he'd changed his mind and wanted her back home. Of course there was a chance he'd come to escort her home: how was he to know that Mrs Scott had arranged transport for them both. He was just being thoughtful. But then he was gone. Maybe the alcohol had clouded her brain.

Junie sat up. She shook any fears or doubts out of her mind. She would make breakfast for them both, Gregory would return home and everything would be fine.

As she washed her face, she thought of Philomena waking at the hotel, her first morning as a married woman. Philomena had taken a fall and said a very brief goodnight to her guests before going up to her hotel room. At the time, Junie had a strange stirring in her stomach but that was probably the drink again.

When hours went by and there was still no sign of Gregory, Junie paid a visit to Mrs Scott. She was out on her veranda, sweeping, when Junie pushed open the gate.

'Hello, my love,' Mrs Scott called.

'Oh Ma Scott, I came to thank you again for the wonderful opportunity you gave me.'

Mrs Scott batted the thanks away. 'No my dear, it was nothing. Nothing at all.'

'It was everything. It really was. My dress. I love it so much. I wonder if I could wear it for the baby's Christening. You don't think it will be too fancy?'

'I think it will be just right. And it so suits you. As long you don't get too fat with this baby.' Mrs Scott began to laugh loudly and continued when she could control her speech. 'I used to be thin like you. But, two children later, look at me.' She held open her palms and screeched with laughter again.

'I'll try not to overdo it,' said Junie, taking a seat on the porch chair.

'I'll make us a nice tea,' said Mrs Scott. 'Let me just finish up here.'

'Can I help?'

'No, you rest your bones. I've just been so excited since yesterday I can't keep still.'

'It won't be long before Phil and Saul move to America.'

Mrs Scott stopped sweeping and looked sad. 'I know, just over a month. But at least I know she's happy, she married a good man who loves her and will take care of her.'

'Very true. Speaking of husbands, did you see anything of mine this morning? I wondered if he came and went before I was awake.'

'Nobody pass. He gone missing again?'

Junie nodded.

'Work?'

Junie shrugged her shoulders. 'Oh, I'm sure he'll come home soon.'

Mrs Scott put the broom to one side. 'Of course. And you'll see Phil soon, too. She have to come and pack up her things. Decide what she taking and what she leaving behind.'

'And I can help her.'

'Of course. Now let me get that tea.'

31

Philomena woke up happy. Even after she looked at her wedding dress hanging from a silk hanger on the tall wardrobe in her hotel room and saw the brown scuff marks of where she'd been pushed against the tree and had stumbled in her attempt to escape Gregory. She tried to erase the memory with a smile. He hadn't hurt her, not badly, anyway. She had checked her entire body in the bathroom mirror after she'd said goodnight and thank you to her guests. She didn't engage with her mother too much afterwards because her mother was on the verge of asking questions and she didn't want to talk about her encounter with Gregory, not then. Repeatedly, she'd told herself she was fine, she would be fine. She'd hurried up to the room, aware of a few curious gazes from her guests and the hotel staff, thrown off her dress before Saul came up and inspected her skin for bruises. There was only the one on her wrist, throbbing with a purple and blue stain around it. But that wasn't so bad. If anything, Gregory had appeared to be the one in more pain. Mentally if not physically. Not that she excused his behaviour in any way at all. He was a monster, plain and simple in her book, no matter what kind of upbringing he'd had.

Philomena turned to look at Saul, his back, brown, wide and strong as he slept. She thanked goodness for him. Junie had been so unlucky to have fallen for Gregory. Apart from the obvious, he lied, too. Lied about what he'd see in her. That she saw Junie in a particular way. All lies. How could he have known? How could he have seen anything that clearly, hidden like some animal in the woods, spying on her. She hated him even more.

Philomena stroked Saul's back. He had only been sleeping lightly and rolled over at her touch. He'd barely opened his eyes before she sat astride him, pulling off her nightdress, reaching for his hands to hold her breasts while she writhed into his hips until he was deep inside her, her thighs clenched tight against him.

Days after the wedding, Philomena kissed Saul and left for her mother's house. He had taught her how to drive, so she took his car. Her intention was to leave Saul at home, packing, while she went to her mother's house to collect her things and begin the process of deciding what she was shipping to New York. She doubted there'd be much. Mostly books and articles, teaching certificates and letters from Pearson. She would probably discard half her wardrobe.

'You throwing this?' Her mother was at her side picking up every item of her clothing that Philomena threw over her shoulder.

'They're not any good, Mum. You can take what you like.'

'And do what with them? Your skirts wouldn't get up over my knees.' She giggled. 'I'll take them to the church, for the charity box. Maybe Junie would—'

'Have you seen her?' Philomena stopped what she was doing.

'A couple of days ago she was here. I don't know what happen to that husband of hers. He haven't been home.'

'What, since the wedding you mean?'

'Yes, since then. She haven't seen him. Me neither. Good luck to him, that's what I say. But she do look worried all the same.'

Philomena began folding her underwear. She remembered the look on Gregory's face, the last hateful thing he said, that he would kill her friend. This had been her worst fear for Junie. That she would lose her life to that man. How ironic if he'd gone off and got himself killed that very night. Approached the wrong person in the menacing mood he'd left the hotel in. Maybe someone as drunk and as stupid had challenged Gregory, and that's why he wasn't back. It was a terrible way to think, she knew that, but she couldn't stop the images entering and lingering in her mind.

Later, her mother came back to the bedroom to say that dinner was on the table.

'What happen to you, Phil?' her mother asked, stopping at the bedroom door. 'You look like someone pass over your grave.'

Philomena shook her head, forced a smile. 'It's serious work, Mum. All this packing.' She ushered her Mum out of the room holding onto her shoulders as if they were forming a procession. They danced their way to the table to eat. She didn't want to let her mother in on her thought process regarding Gregory.

'You ought to try it,' Philomena said as they sat down.

'Try what?' Mrs Scott poured them both some water from a ceramic jug.

'Packing. You know, when you are packing to come to join me in New York.' She smirked at her mother.

'Never. I'm staying right here.'

Philomena shook her head at her mother's stubbornness.

It became late and Mrs Scott wouldn't allow Philomena to drive home in the dark.

'These mountain roads are dangerous by day; I'm not letting you risk your life attempting all those bends and curves at night. Not at all.'

Philomena had suspected this would happen and had warned Saul not to expect her that evening. Packing had been fairly painless, and she could load everything she needed in the morning and drive back.

Though her eyes had been full of sleep by bedtime, Philomena's night was restless, waking when she thought she'd heard a noise, stirring again when she thought a shadow had passed by her bedroom window. She chastised herself for being so silly. It was probably all the rum she and her mother drank while playing dominoes until it was late.

Philomena's head felt foggy when dawn broke, the moon was still visible and a strange sound stirred her to a semi-conscious state. A stark cry, wailing far into the almost light that rang in Philomena's ears. Not one bird had sung a note yet, probably frightened away by the eerie atmosphere. Had one of their flock fallen? Philomena, coming to her senses, realised that the sound she'd heard was human. She got out of bed, silently leaving her house in her nightdress. She ran along the path to the gate and then into Junie's front garden. Without considering whether Gregory would be there or not, she pushed open the front door.

Junie sat at the dining table, the top half of her body splayed across it, her hair wild and loose. Furniture and ornaments were smashed to the floor, but there was no sign of Gregory. It was then that Philomena saw the blood dripping from the chair Junie sat in. Rich and red it dropped intermittently onto the floor. With one eye half-closed by a dark swelling and the other dry of tears, Junie lifted her head slowly from the table.

'He kill my baby.'

Philomena leapt across the room and scooped Junie up in her arms.

'Where is he?'

'Gone. I don't know.'

'I'm taking you to the hospital.'

'It's too late.'

'No, we must go. There might still be time, and I have no idea what to do.'

Philomena propped Junie against her and scanned the room for something to wrap around her. Anything. But in her panic, she saw nothing but the open door and the sun making its presence clearer by the second. The air was still dawn fresh as they walked into the light. She guided Junie to Saul's car and helped her into the passenger seat.

'The blood, Phil, Saul's car.'

'There's nothing we can do about that.'

Philomena rushed into the house to find the car keys. Her mother was just leaving her bedroom, yawning, her eyes half-opened.

'What the…?'

'Him. He attacked her and he ran. She's bleeding, Mum.'

'Bad?'

'I think she's losing the baby. I'm driving up to the hospi-tal.'

Mrs Scott was rushing with Philomena to the door. 'Hurry but be careful. I'm going to pray.'

With no time to say goodbye, Philomena ran to the car, started the engine and drove away as quickly as she could.

Junie didn't move in her seat apart from the times momentum took her body sideways as Philomena swerved around the many turns in the road. It was still early, and she hadn't come across a single car. The residents and shop keepers in the village were only just spilling out of their houses and stores as the village idly woke from its slumber. Philomena looked around thinking she'd see Gregory skulking around in a dark corner somewhere, but her guess was that he'd slid off into the woods and would be hiding out until he thought the storm he'd created had passed.

When they finally arrived at the hospital, Philomena parked awkwardly across the main entrance. A man in overalls came running out of reception crying, 'No, no. Absolutely no parking.'

Philomena threw the car keys at him. 'Here, you park it. This is an emergency.'

The duty receptionist had just come off the phone and looked over the desk at Junie shuffling along, being held up by Philomena. She called along the corridor for help, and a nurse came running to attendance.

'Wait one moment while I get a wheelchair.'

'Thank you,' Philomena whispered to the nurse's retreating back. In seconds, the nurse was wheeling Junie to the emergency room where she spoke to a doctor.

'Cubicle three,' she said to the nurse who then pushed Junie to a bed. It looked as if someone had vacated just seconds ago as the sheet was messy and, as yet, unchanged.

'Can I have you on the bed, please?' said the doctor and put on her glasses as the nurse helped Junie out of the wheelchair.

'Could I come in with her?' asked Philomena.

'You can come back in a minute,' the doctor said. 'I just need to examine the patient, and I will call you in.'

The nurse ushered Philomena away and closed the curtain around the cubicle. As Philomena walked heavily out of the treatment room, she heard the doctor say, 'Name?' in a strict voice. She stopped and rested her body against the wall in the corridor and began to cry. She covered her face with her hands and sniffed, trying to compose herself so she could be of use to Junie or the doctor if she came to question her. A patient on crutches walked by and stared at Philomena who realised she must look like a patient herself. Bare feet and a nightdress. The man on crutches must think the doctor had given her bad news. She sniffed again and looked up at the ceiling. She imagined her mother praying with all her might back at home, so she offered her prayer. The same one she thought up the last time she was here with Junie.

32

After what seemed like the longest of times, the doctor emerged from the emergency ward. She looked over the top of her glasses at Philomena as she clicked her pen shut and tucked it into the top pocket of her white coat. Her eyes swept up and down Philomena's scant attire. Philomena crossed her arms over her chest.

'How is she, doctor?'

'She'll be okay. There was a lot of bleeding, but she is quite stable now. I don't think she knows where she is, and she wasn't very responsive.'

'Has she lost the baby?' Philomena lowered her voice.

'And you are?'

'We are neighbours, I'm the only one looking out for her.'

The doctor inspected Philomena's flimsy nightdress again. 'And the husband?'

'He did this and then he ran.'

'I see. Well, I'm afraid the pregnancy is no longer viable.'

Philomena stepped back and bent over almost double.

'Are you going to be sick?' the doctor asked, looking from side to side.

'No. No, I'll be fine. Could I go in and see her?'

'They took her out the other way on a trolley. You'll find her on St Joseph's Ward where she will get some rest.'

'But I can go and see her?'

'It isn't visiting hours.'

Philomena rolled her eyes. This doctor must be the strictest in the hospital, but despite her attitude, Philomena was determined to see her friend right away.

'Aren't you cold?' asked the doctor. 'You could go home and dress. Come back at visiting?'

'I'm not leaving. It's too far to go.'

'Fine.' The doctor called a nurse and asked if she would be so kind as to find a gown for Philomena. 'You can make your way to the ward. Tell them Doctor Stevens said it was fine for you to visit.'

'Thank you, doctor.'

The nurse quickly supplied Philomena with a gown and led her through the emergency room and then on to St Joseph's Ward.

'I believe your friend was here not so long ago?' the nurse asked as she hurried along the white corridors.

'That's right. Did you treat her?'

'Not me, but the nurses were talking about her. Mind you get her away from whoever did this to her. She's too fragile that one. She can't take another trauma like this.'

Philomena knew this all too well. Gregory had said he would kill her, but he hadn't succeeded this time. It was time for Junie to leave him for good. Her ship to America was not due to leave for another three weeks. She hoped she could protect Junie until then.

The nurse led Philomena all the way to Junie's bed. She was awake and smiled with the half of her face she could move. The nurse touched Philomena's arm and left the two women alone.

The eight other patients on the ward were sitting up and having breakfast. There was a tray with a bowl of porridge on the side table next to Junie. Philomena asked if she wanted to eat anything, offering to feed Junie.

'No thank you. I told them to take it away, but they said I might feel like it in a minute. I won't though.'

Philomena sat on the chair by the bed. 'It's fine. I'm sure they will find something for you later. Or I'll fetch something from home.'

'Home? I don't know where that is.' She looked earnestly at Philomena. 'I'm not going back there. Not for him to kill me.'

'You have no idea how happy I am to hear you say that at last. I can take you to Saul's. As soon as you're out.'

Junie touched Philomena's hand.

'Thank you, Phil. I don't think your husband is going to like the way you started your marriage. Away from him already.'

'He understands.'

They sat in pensive silence. Philomena was weighing up the situation, wondering how she was going to get Junie abroad with her. She wondered if three weeks was enough time to sort out all the paperwork. She knew only too well that anything official took an eternity to happen in Dominica. The wheels turned slowly, and the American government moved equally as slow as the rules on immigration were being tightened one minute and slackened the next. But she would start the process. Perhaps the people buying Saul's house wouldn't mind delaying so that Junie would have somewhere to hide until she'd organised everything. Her head spun from all the planning, rethinking, the changing of plans and pondering the alternatives. It wasn't going to be easy.

Junie fell asleep as Philomena's mind whirred. She took the opportunity to find her car and drive over to see Saul as his house was closer than going straight home. She asked the nurse if she could let Junie know that she would return as soon as she could.

She drove back to Saul, explained everything, changed and set off again. This time with Saul driving her over to the Scott house. Mrs Scott came running out when she heard the car.

'She lost the baby, Mum.' Philomena slammed the car door. Mrs Scott shook her head. 'But she says she won't go back to him. Saul said she could stay for a while, but the house is being sold and the new owners have a contract, so I don't know where she'll go after that.'

'We'll find a way,' said Mrs Scott.

The women went into Junie's house to pack some of her clothes and personal items. A tornado had passed though the small space. Philomena couldn't understand how she'd not heard Junie crying out or the furniture being tipped over. They picked up the scattered furniture, put away fallen pictures, swept away the broken ornaments. They fixed everything they could and cleaned the whole house before Saul drove Philomena back to the hospital.

Philomena ran quickly to St Joseph's ward carrying some clothes for Junie in a bag.

'Saul is in the car. He's very happy to have you stay with us. You don't need to worry about anything now, Junie. I will take care of you.'

'You are both too kind.'

Junie was weak, her eyes hollow, her skin slack and grey. Philomena walked Junie slowly to the entrance and left her to wait while she went to ask Saul to bring the car round.

'I'll be very quick.'

As she and Saul returned to the entrance, Philomena saw Junie having an intense conversation with a woman she couldn't see clearly. The woman handed Junie a piece of paper and walked away just as Philomena jumped out of Saul's car.

'Who was that?' asked Philomena.

'A friend,' said Junie. 'You know her. She's your seamstress, Josephine Dennis.'

'And you two are already friends? I thought you'd only met her once.'

'She was here visiting earlier. We started talking.'

'What did she just give you?'

Junie didn't answer as Philomena helped her into the back seat of the car.

'Thank you for coming, Saul,' Junie said.

'Not at all, it's my pleasure. Ready?'

Junie nodded. Philomena stared at her, waiting for an answer to her earlier question.

'Josephine's baby is due soon,' Junie sighed.

'I'm sorry, Junie.' Philomena's eyes glistened. 'Really sorry.'

Junie shook her head and lowered her gaze.

Saul whisked them away from the hospital.

33

The days went by slowly, and each day Philomena would check on Junie's progress. The drive back to Saul's house seemed to have sapped Junie of all her energy. She had looked pale since Philomena collected her, the spark gone from her eyes. Her appetite was cut, and she left her hair in a messy pile at the top of her head and put Philomena off every time she offered to wash it and style it nicely.

'What is the point?' she kept saying, and Philomena tried to persuade her that it would lift her mood.

It had been on the tip of her tongue for days to ask Junie about the mysterious note that Josephine Dennis had slipped into Junie's hand, and Philomena, short of searching Junie's pockets, couldn't see where her friend had put it. It was obviously something secret. A message between her and her new friend.

Saul had seemed agitated and restless, and after a week of hanging around the house doing odd jobs and keeping himself to himself, he took a drive over to his parents' house for the day. Philomena seized the opportunity to encourage Junie to talk about future steps. In her mind there was only one clear path. The one thing she hadn't established was where Junie would hide away until Philomena could send for her to come to New York.

'What will you do, Junie? You haven't talked about where you plan to go if you're not going back to him. Isn't it time you made decisions?' Philomena and Junie sat drinking cold coffee at the table. The windows were wide open, the warmth of the early evening sun soothing their bare arms as it floated inside, red and gold in the distance, getting ready to set.

'I don't want to think, Phil.' Junie had her hands around the small tin cup.

'But Junie, Gregory has been gone for over a week. You really should…' Philomena stopped. Junie was shaking her head. 'What?'

'I know what you're thinking, Phil. It's been written on your face since this happened. You want me to come to America with you, even after I said it wasn't a good idea.'

'But things are different. Before, you said you were going to try to make things work with him. You thought the baby would change him. But now…'

'Now, I don't have a baby. I don't have a husband, and soon I won't have you.'

'Stop saying that. I'm here. Always have been. Even when it didn't feel like it to you.'

'Look, this isn't a decision you can make without Saul. You want this to happen, but I don't think he does. Be honest.'

'He's a kind man.'

'I know that. He is wonderful, and you are a very lucky woman. I wish I could have been, but I have to deal with what God grant me.'

'Junie, we have choices.' Philomena turned to the open window and watched a busy lizard sneak up onto the sill, turn itself around in a complete circle and trail the path of its entrance before slithering out to the outer wall. She sighed, calming the stirring motion of her frustration. With Junie, with Saul, with herself. Why was this so difficult? She wondered if it was fear of the unknown that kept Junie rooted here.

'So,' she said, turning back to the table and the last dregs of her coffee. 'If you don't come with me, what will you do?'

'I have to leave.' Junie stood up as if she was about to walk away that very second.

'And where will you go?' Philomena asked, standing too.

'Back to my mother's house.'

'Your mother? But you said…'

'He would never believe I would go there. It would give me some time. Gregory told me he would kill me, and I believe him.'

'I'll make him see sense, make him see that losing your baby was punishment enough.'

'You of all people know that man have no reason. No. I will go and beg my father for money, my brother, anyone who can help. If they know I desperate, they will give me something. I'll get on a ship. I'll go anywhere.'

'But not with me?' They both paused for breath. 'Junie…'

'Yes, Phil—I know what you going to say.'

'You don't. It's not about America. I was going to say, I have money. Saved up. No one knows about it. Not even Saul.'

'And you will lend me some?'

'I will give you all I've got, Junie, but…'

'But what?'

'I want us to go away together.'

'Together? What are you saying? You have a ticket to board a ship. You have a new husband, a new life.' Junie shook her head, incredulous.

'They are nothing to me, Junie.' Philomena surprised herself with this outburst as though a stranger had spoken. But a wave of desperation had forced this statement, from her stomach, from her heart. Gregory had been right; she knew it deep down: she felt for Junie the way she should for her husband. She could not give her up. She couldn't lose Junie.

'You don't mean that, Phil.' Junie began to pace to and from the bedroom door, her hands on her hips trying to process the situation.

'No, Junie. Listen. What I mean is—nothing is anything without you.'

'I don't understand your poetry way of talking, Philomena.' Junie laughed. She looked uncomfortable and stared down at Philomena's hand when it clasped her upper arm.

'Junie.' Philomena released her grip. 'I love you.'

'I love you too, Phil. You are my sister and my friend.'

'No, Junie—I mean, I love you.' Philomena held Junie's face very softly between her hands. She leaned towards her and kissed her mouth. Junie allowed herself to be kissed. Encouraged by the response and with her heart pounding within her chest, Philomena put her arms around Junie and kissed her more passionately, their tongues caressing, their breath heavy. Philomena sighed, her thoughts on nothing but this kiss. If she was being truthful, she'd pictured this on more than one occasion; she had never imagined Junie would kiss her back. Then, out of nowhere, Junie broke away. She wiped her lips with the back of her wrist. She looked ashamed. Horrified.

'We shouldn't have done that,' she said taking several steps away from Philomena. 'I shouldn't have let it happen. I don't … I don't want to talk about this.'

'Junie.'

The sound of Saul's car approaching the house put an end to the conversation. Each of the women walked back to the table and sat with their coffees in front of them.

'Good evening, ladies. I'm back early, I'm afraid.'

'Don't say that,' said Junie, springing up out of her chair. 'I don't want you to feel like I pushing you out of your own home, Saul. Anyway, thank you for your hospitality but I'm going in the morning.'

'Really?' Saul looked from one to the other.

'Yes,' said Junie. 'If it's all the same with you, could Phil drive me to the house to collect a few things?'

'No need to ask,' said Saul. 'You two go right ahead.'

Junie squeezed his arm as she headed outside. 'I'm just going out for a little walk before it gets dark. See you soon.'

Philomena said nothing and stared at the door as it closed.

'All right, Phil?' Saul said casually.

'I'm fine,' she replied without looking up.

34

It was a quiet drive back up to the plain. The women hadn't said very much to each other since yesterday. Since the kiss. Junie had been bubbly and chatted inanely about anything and absolutely nothing at all to Saul. He chuckled at her thoughts on the weather and how different the coffee tasted at breakfast, even though it was the same brand and Saul added the exact number of spoons to the coffee pot as all the other days she'd been there. She kissed Saul on the cheek and said this was goodbye for good and wished him lots of luck in America.

Saul waved the women off, and they began the long drive with sullen faces, the smiles fading the second Saul could no longer see them. A yellow bird had fluttered onto the roof of the veranda, and Philomena had watched the jerky movements of its head as Junie skipped merrily to the car after waving to Saul. The bird flew away when Philomena started the engine.

She drove slowly, the car bumping from side to side as it always did on the rough terrain down from Saul's house. The tall peaks of the mountains reached for the fluffs of white that sat still against the brilliant blue of the sky. Birds swooped in flocks, gliding systematically past the clouds and away over the mountain tops. The silence in the car grew unbearable, and as if Junie could read Philomena's mind, she reached down and turned on the radio.

It was a Dominican news channel; a well-spoken man with an English accent announced another call for West Indians to come to Britain, back to the Motherland, to work. The jobs were plentiful and their country needed them to put Britain back on its feet. Junie changed the station settling on one that played music for a quadrille. She rested both hands on her lap, one tapping the other in time to the music, her face turned away from Philomena. A vast array of vibrant greens from the forest and the tiny houses spreading around the mountains kept her transfixed.

Philomena eventually leaned over to turn the music down. The song had changed several times, and in between, a woman with a strong Dominican accent read the local news and made announcements about who had died, at what age and who they'd left behind before giving a time check and playing another lively song. The music had been grating on her nerves, and now, quite close to the village near home, she had had enough.

Junie turned to look at her for the first time.

'You don't mind, do you?' Philomena asked.

'Oh no. I don't mind.' Junie went back to looking out of the window.

As they began the journey up to the plain, Philomena turned off the radio.

'We need to look out for him. If he's there, it's going to be difficult to get your things and go. Maybe you should stay down so he doesn't know you're here. I can go and test the water.'

Junie slid as far down into the seat as she could and kept her head clear of the open window. Mrs Scott came out to greet Philomena. She hugged her mother and asked if Gregory was next door.

'Oh, he's long gone. Back for two minutes and off on another job. Trinidad this time, and as far as I know, he'll be gone another day or two.'

'Good, because Junie's in the car. She's leaving him.' She opened the door for Junie, and Mrs Scott grabbed her in a hug.

Mrs Scott asked for details as the young women followed her up to the house and was surprised to hear about Junie's decision to return to her family for help.

'Well, she is your mother, I suppose. I only hope she has an open heart. After all, you're her daughter and you've been through a hell of a lot with that man.'

Once they were inside, Mrs Scott began to fuss around Junie.

'Now, before you pack, I need to make you a tea. You look pale, and how would that be if you show up at your mother house looking like that?'

'It might make her more sympathetic,' Philomena mumbled to herself, but aloud she said, 'I don't think her mother is going to mind how she looks, Mum.' Philomena slumped into a chair.

'And what get into you?' Her mother put her hands on her hips. 'Now Junie, I'll go out and find a good nettle to make you a tea. It will give you strength. You have a long way to go. Phil, driving you all that way?'

The young women looked at each other. They hadn't discussed the intricacies of Junie's journey back to her mother.

'Er, no, Mrs Scott,' said Junie. 'I can get there on my own, if I can get a transport from town.'

'I'll drop her in town, then,' said Philomena. 'On my way home.'

'Well, she can't leave before I comb all that hair of hers and she pack and I make us all something to eat.'

'Really, Mrs Scott, I can just go and get my things.'

'Nonsense.' Mrs Scott pushed Junie aside and picked up her cotton bag from the hook on the front door. 'I'll get the nettle and anything I think you might need, and I'll brew you up a nice tea before I tackle that mess you calling hair.'

She was out of the door leaving Philomena and Junie in the uncomfortable atmosphere they had created and that neither Saul nor Mrs Scott had been aware of. Time ticked slowly by, and they waited patiently for Mrs Scott to return just to have someone upset the stillness in the house. Eventually Philomena jumped up from her seat.

'I'll make coffee.'

She left the house and took her time brewing coffee when she should have been boiling water for her mother's bush tea. Philomena brought back two cups of coffee and placed them, steaming, on the dining table.

'I've got some things in my room I'm not taking with me when I go to New York,' she said. 'Would you like to see if there is anything you might want?'

'Yes, please.' Junie followed Philomena, who opened the bedroom door for Junie to enter.

'Have a look through the things on the bed. I'm not taking any of those.'

'Thank you, Phil.'

'Look, Junie.' There was exasperation in Philomena's voice. 'We haven't spoken about it since yesterday. Are you trying to make me suffer?'

'Philomena, we did a wrong thing…'

'It's not wrong. We're not wrong. We can't deny what happened, Junie.' Philomena walked over to the bed where Junie stood with folded arms, her back to her, staring out of the window over to the dark mountain leading to Pa Reynauld's. Philomena waited patiently until Junie formed her answer. Finally, she turned around.

'Philomena, I never loved anyone the way I love you. But not in the way you love me. That way is for a man and his wife. We are friends…'

'Junie—'

'Very good friends.' She took Philomena's hand. 'We've come to the end now. It has been the best friendship I have ever had in my whole life, Phil. Why should we spoil it now?' Junie leaned in close, smiling so that Philomena would do the same. Philomena kept her eyes turned down, moved her face away before shaking off Junie's hand and returning to the living room. She flopped into the window seat and stared out at the oleander. Junie followed her in and gently turned Philomena's cheek up to face her.

Just then, Philomena thought she heard the sound of rustling coming from the other side of the oleander bush. She got up, abruptly, and peered out of the window. Outside, she saw a dog sniffing around in Junie's garden. A big brown dog. A cross-breed like many of the dogs on the island. Tall and thin, wearing a collar.

'But what the hell is that dog doing in your yard?'

'What dog?' Junie bent to look outside. 'I've never seen a dog come up here unless it's with someone. I wonder who own it.'

'Look how he's pulling up your flowers. I'll go and shoo him away.'

Junie caught Philomena by her arm before she could leave and whispered, 'Don't.'

'Why? What is it?'

'Look,' Junie pointed out of the window. Her hand trembled as she took a deep breath. Philomena stared out again, and this time she saw him. Gregory stood by the front door. He scooped water out of the barrel by the side of the house into a bowl and whistled to the dog. The dog bounded over to Gregory. It jumped in a circle, yelping, before stooping over the bowl of water and lapping away at it with a long pink tongue, nearly sending the bowl across the yard.

Gregory put his hands in his pockets, looked up and yawned. He stood watching as the dog drank. Very slowly, he turned his head towards Philomena's window and smiled. The women stepped away. Junie lunged back so far she fell against the table, their coffee cups sloshing dark liquid up the inside of the cups. Just then, Mrs Scott walked into the house.

'You see who come?' she gasped.

All three women were speechless. Mrs Scott led Junie and Philomena by the hand to the couch and sat them down before tiptoeing to the window. Keeping a distance, she peered out. Philomena placed her arm around Junie. Junie's body shook, her eyes pinned to the window.

'He's going inside,' Mrs Scott announced. 'Let me go and make you that tea. We just act calm. He doesn't know you're here. Just be still, all right?'

Junie nodded. Philomena watched out of the window as Mrs Scott went to the kitchen. Gregory nodded up at Mrs Scott from his doorway.

'He has the nerve of the devil.' She turned around to look at Junie who sat hugging her knees. Tears rolled down her face. She rocked back and forth, her eyes squeezed shut. Philomena went back to the couch and put her arm around Junie's shoulder.

'He know I'm here. He know. He been waiting for me.'

'No, no,' Philomena whispered. She pulled Junie's head to rest on her shoulder. 'He doesn't know. He sees Saul's car, but he won't think you're here. For all he knows, Saul is here and he won't try anything.'

The door opened and both women sat up. Mrs Scott brought a cup of tea over to Junie.

'Here, this will help you steady your nerves. Don't you worry, nothing is going to happen to you, nothing at all.' She placed the cup between Junie's trembling hands, but there was a quiver in Mrs Scott's voice.

From the window, Mrs Scott looked back at Philomena who was awaiting her mother's reaction. The look on her face said it all. He was still there and probably there for the night.

The evening drew close. The women stayed indoors and said very little. Philomena had tried to persuade Junie to leave everything for another day. They could jump into the car quickly and drive away before he even realised they were in the car. Junie refused to move.

'He'll know. He'll get to me before you even start the engine. You don't know him like I do.'

Philomena stayed silent. There were a lot of things Junie didn't know about the man she married.

In the quiet of the living room, Mrs Scott combed and cornrowed Junie's hair while Philomena sat at the window seat, keeping a check on Gregory's movements and observing the tension in Junie's shoulders.

In staccato movements, Philomena began to prepare for the evening while Junie sat without stirring or saying a single word. Philomena could only imagine the thoughts going round in her friend's mind. She thought they could wait until Gregory was asleep and then put it to Junie that they drive away then. So far, Gregory had only gone into his house once or twice, remaining outside smoking and drinking and calling to the dog. As though he were watching the house, taunting them.

'It's getting late,' Mrs Scott said. 'I'll need to go out and cook some dinner. He'll wonder why I'm not.'

'It's true, Mum,' Philomena sighed and moved away from the window. 'Should I come and help?'

'Stay with her. She needs you.'

Mrs Scott went out to the kitchen. Philomena heard her singing a hymn at the top of her lungs. She heard the kitchen utensils she was using, and when she couldn't sing any louder, she whistled. Anything was better than the stony atmosphere in the living room and that damn dog barking relentlessly as Gregory sent it after a stick. The dog trampled back and forth over Junie's flowers.

'Here we go, Phil.' Mrs Scott came into the house, carefully carrying a pot of chicken soup, watching it as though it were a child walking on a cliff edge. She kept her eyes on the pot until she was sure nothing would spill and it was safely placed on the table.

'Well, come on,' she clapped her hands together. 'Plates, bread, juice—in the kitchen. Go.'

'Yes, Mum.' Philomena rushed outside to fetch the remainder of the meal to the table. The evening air felt like dipping into the cool river compared to the heated tension in the house. Outside, the dog continued to bound across the garden. It seemed to have endless energy but its owner's head had sagged to one side. Gregory was asleep on his chair. She quickly gathered the jug of juice and the plate of bread, eager to tell the others that this could be the perfect opportunity to run, but she heard Gregory whistle to the dog, and her feelings of hope were quickly dashed.

Neither Philomena nor Junie spoke during the meal. They left that to Mrs Scott who spoke for three people, as nervous as that appeared to make Junie feel. She chatted as though this was a nice visit from their neighbour and that Gregory sitting like a sentry beyond the oleander was just an illusion. A dream.

Philomena kept one eye on the window, listening for Gregory to go in and close the door, waiting for him to switch out the lights in the house and then they'd be gone. It would mean her having to drive in the dark, but she would do it if it meant Junie was safe. She would also have to drive Junie all the way to her mother's house because there would be no other form of transport this late. But she would do it.

Anger crashed at Philomena's heart. She hadn't wanted their farewell to be like this. She realised that after kissing Junie things would never be the same, that the slightest chance of persuading Junie to come away with her might be lost. But it was a chance she had been willing to take. She had to kiss her, even though it would mean losing Saul. Losing his love for her, turning her back on her love for him. She had wanted to sacrifice it all for Junie. But now, Junie was going for good, running off in the night, stealing a quick goodbye as she left her in the uncertain future she faced.

Philomena took her troubled conscience with her outside as she cleared away the supper plates. She decided to wash the dishes, keeping an ear out for what was happening next door. Still Gregory remained at the front door. He stood as Philomena returned to the house and stretched his arms up.

He let out a loud yawn and went inside, scratching his back-side as he did. He closed the door and left the dog rustling around in the dark.

'I think he's going to bed,' Philomena said in a hushed voice when she went inside. Mrs Scott went to the window seat and sat down. She squinted through the glass.

'Wait,' she said. 'The door opened. He's out there again.'

Philomena felt her shoulders slump and turned to see Junie huddled on the couch as before.

'Ah,' Mrs Scott whispered. 'He turn out the lights. Yes, he close the door. He taking the dog. He going.'

'You sure, Mum?' Philomena looked outside, too. In the dimness of evening, she saw Gregory walking down the hill, the dog barking and bounding around his legs as he fol-lowed. Gregory had no bags with him, his hands in his pock-ets.

'Junie?' Philomena turned to find her looking up at her with unblinking eyes. 'We can go now. Say something, make a decision.'

Junie stood, robotically. 'I'm going next door to pack,' Ju-nie said.

'No,' said Phil. 'We can't hang around. He's far enough away for us to get in the car. You can crouch. I'll drive and you'll be free.'

'But I have things in there, personal things. I can't just turn up with my hands swinging at my mother's house. My father gave me a bible. My aunt gave me her rosary. I'll be quick. And you know Gregory, the only reason he will go down to the village is because he run out of booze. For all we know, he might not even come back tonight.'

'But Junie…'

'Phil. You said I must make a decision, and here you go making it for me. Again.'

'You're right. I'm sorry,' said Philomena. 'Of course. You go. I'll wait for you here.'

'You don't want to come and help?'

'You know what you need in there. Just come back when you're ready to go. I'll be here.'

Junie left and quickly ran along the path, disappearing from sight into the indigo shadows. Philomena watched as a lamp went on in Junie's house and the feeling that everything was about to change couldn't weigh any more heavily on her heart.

35

Junie lit the lamp, noticing the slight tremble of her fingers, the shiver on her skin as she looked around the house. Considering Gregory was back, the place was reasonably clean. She knew that the Scotts had set to work on it while she was in the hospital and felt a tug at her heart when it sank in— just that little bit more—that her decision to go home would mean the loss of kindness and friendship she had only known since moving to the second house on the plain. She would miss the women terribly, and she would miss the closeness she had developed in her relationship to Phil. She didn't want Phil to think she was leaving because of the kiss. She couldn't understand why she had let it happen. She did kiss Philomena back but only to reciprocate the fondness she had for her friend. Nothing more than that. Junie knew straight after saying to Philomena that what they'd done was wrong, would break her heart, but she couldn't express, in that moment, that her feelings of love for her friend got messed up in her head, in her heart and tangled with the grief of losing a baby she had fallen so deeply in love with, too. Not one of them had talked about the baby and what it meant for her to have this loss weighing her down. They didn't want to upset her, so they carried on as if it had been nothing. The baby had been everything, and she wanted to talk about missing the child. One day, when she could write about her feelings, she would put it in a letter to Philomena and they could be friends again, even if miles and miles away.

In the bedroom, she dragged her large bag out from under the bed. Her bible was still in it, along with her rosary. Even when she had learned to read, she hadn't looked at a single page of the leather-bound bible. She flicked through it now and something fell from the pages. A dollar note. Her father must have put it there for emergencies. If only she had known about the money those times when Gregory had left her alone for days, no indication of when he'd be back and she had run out of food. She shook her head. Too late for that now. She must pack. And fast.

She began to fill her bag with as many of her clothes and personal possessions as were clean and still worth keeping. It didn't take very long. She left behind her work dungarees and the boys trousers Gregory had picked up for her from somewhere on his travels and the old dress that had worn thin with age.

She sat on the bed and gave herself five seconds to look around and think. Was there anything she had forgotten? Yes, the lovely blue dress she'd worn to the wedding, and the shoes. She had asked Mrs Scott to hold on to those for her; she was probably folding those away now. It was time to leave. As she stood, Junie heard the front door open. Philomena must have changed her mind about helping or she had come to hurry her up.

Running out of the bedroom, already grinning, she froze when she saw it was Gregory. The smile on her face remained like a photograph of a happier Junie.

'Well, Junie. You look like you pleased to see me.' Junie did not speak. 'Well? Nothing to say to your husband after not seeing him for so long?'

'I thought. I thought you not coming back yet.'

'So you made other plans? Whose clothes are you wearing? You dress like you going somewhere? You going somewhere, Junie?'

'No.'

'You sure?'

'I sure.'

Gregory sauntered up to Junie. As she knew, from sitting and waiting all day for him to leave, he had been drinking. She knew he had also smoked a great deal of marijuana and his eyes were pink and watery. He bumped into a chair as he approached her and put his finger to his lips to shush the chair as it scratched along the wooden floor, coming off two of its feet but not falling. Gregory leaned close to Junie and laughed for no reason. He continued to smile as he danced around her in a tight circle, looking her up and down, sniffing her hair and brushing imaginary dust from her shoulders.

'Yes, man. You looking good. Good like you going somewhere.'

'No, Gregory. To bed I going. Is getting late.'

Gregory stopped circling and stood behind her, bending his head to speak softly into her ear.

'Is not so late, Junie. If is bed you want to go, maybe I can —what shall we say—accompany you?' Junie pulled away and walked quickly towards the dining table where she righted the chair that Gregory had knocked askew. Before she knew it, he was beside her again. Leaning against her back, talking into her ear, his breath hot and sickly. He reeked of alcohol, and as if from nowhere, he produced the remainder of a quarter bottle of whisky and slammed it onto the table in front of her. Where on earth had that come from?

He hadn't been gone long enough to get to the village, buy more alcohol and get back when he did.

'Drink with me,' he said.

'I not … I don't want a drink. Is late.' Junie leaned forward to escape his stench. Gregory had most of his weight on her, and she was trapped between his sweaty body and the table.

'Is never too late for a drink,' he cried aloud. Gregory picked up the whisky bottle and danced around the room singing, 'Is never too late to drink, my Junie, is never too late to drink.'

Junie wondered what had become of the dog and if she tried to run now, would the dog jump at her, trained by Gregory to keep her inside? It had happened too quickly. One moment, she was about to escape into freedom, and the next, her jailer had appeared, and she was weak with fear and helplessness. And though her heart raced in the middle of her chest, she tried to remain composed on the outside. A wrong word, a wrong look and he would smash that bottle in her face, she knew he would.

'You have a new dog, Greg?'

'Yes—but he's not out there now.' He went to the door. 'Do you want to see where he get to?'

'Not now. In the morning,' she stuttered. 'We have time.' She sat down at the table and rested her palms on it. Her hands shook so much she tried to hold them still, placing one on top of the other. Gregory grabbed two glasses from the side dresser, pulled up the chair opposite Junie and unscrewed the bottle top. He filled a glass to almost overflowing and passed it across the table to Junie. He tried to fill his glass but the contents of the bottle had all gone into Junie's. He sat shaking the bottle over his glass. He did that for a few seconds before understanding that it was empty. Just to be sure, he put the bottle to his lips and sucked in air, viewing his wife with one eye closed.

'You not drinking?' he spluttered as he struck the table with the empty bottle. Junie straightened her back sharply at the sound of it, sitting upright, hoping he didn't notice her flinch.

'It's not too late for you to take a walk, meet my new dog. I should introduce you.' Gregory belched and rubbed his chest with a fist. He looked over at the door.

'It's dark. And anyway … I don't want to meet him right now,' Junie said and got up quickly, making her way back to the bedroom.

'You rude girl,' he called after her.

Seeing her packed bag, Junie backed out of the bedroom: she didn't want him following her in there. Instead, she picked up the full glass of whisky he'd poured for her.

'You have this, Gregory. I think I might go and trouble Mrs Scott for some of her nice lemonade and come back to join you. Your drink no good for me. It make me feel sick sometime.' As she went to walk away, Gregory grabbed her wrist.

'No,' he said.

'No?'

'No, you not going anywhere. When I finish my drink, we going in the bedroom. I need comfort. I been working hard.'

'Gregory, not tonight. I so tired as you see me there.'

'A wife cannot be tired for her husband, I tell you that before.' He stood, pushing the chair back with his heel. It crashed to the floor. Junie was backing away from Gregory, but he still had hold of her wrist. His grip became tighter and tighter. Junie's eyes darted to the window, but from inside, she couldn't see the Scotts. Philomena was waiting for her;

she wished she could signal to her. She noticed that Gregory's eyes drooped to almost closed. The second he fell asleep, she'd run. Leave everything, her packed bag, even give up the blue dress if she could only escape.

'You see that stupid dog?' His words were slurred. 'All he needed was a good kick to make him mind me.' Gregory knocked back the contents of Junie's glass, spilling most of it as he grabbed it up and drank every drop. 'Everyone needs to mind me.' He began to laugh, releasing his grip on Junie who eyed the door. Gregory started dancing again, singing something nonsensical to himself.

'Dance with me, nuh?'

'I, I don't want to dance, Gregory. Not now,' Junie stuttered, trying to edge her way to the door.

'I say dance. So dance.'

'Gregory, you dance. I tired. I will watch you.'

'All right,' he said. 'Watch me dance.' He began to prance around the room. 'You see how good your husband can dance?'

For a split second, Gregory turned his back, and in that moment, Junie bolted for the door. A few strides onto the path, that was all she'd taken, glancing towards her neighbours' house, before Gregory flew out of the door, diving towards her and bringing her down onto the croton bushes lining the pathway. She hit her head on the gravel and let out a cry. Immediately, she heard someone on the veranda steps next door and saw Gregory staggering towards the oleander, undoing his trousers.

Another opportunity. Junie made a run for the gate and saw Philomena fiddling in the dark with the latch. Gregory rushed at Junie, caught hold of her hair and dragged her screaming along the path, and in seconds, she was back inside the house. She heard Philomena shout, 'Junie, I'm coming' just as Gregory tossed her into the living room like a sack of rubbish. She rolled across the floor and landed in the corner next to the heavy dresser. Gregory swayed above her, his fists clenched.

'Leave her alone!' Philomena cried. She stood at the front door pointing at Gregory then towards Junie.

'Who the hell are you to tell me what to do? You—get out my house!'

'Yes, I'm going, but I'm taking her with me,' Philomena said. She puffed out her chest and took a tentative step towards Junie.

Gregory rounded on her, a fist up at his chest. 'Just one more step. You understand me?'

'Philomena,' Junie cried. 'Please go. Just go.'

'You heard her, Philomena. Now, get out.' Gregory stumbled across the room. He grabbed hold of the edges of the dining table as though he were on a ship that was rocking on a rough sea.

'Please Phil.' Junie was frantic. 'I beg of you.'

'Junie. What are you saying? You know I can't leave you here like this.'

Gregory chuckled and mocked Philomena's voice. 'Can't leave my pretty little friend.' He collapsed into manic laughter.

'Phil.' Junie stared hard at her. 'Look at me. Trust my decision. I want you to go. Now.'

Philomena turned reluctantly to Gregory who was looking around the room as though he'd lost something. He saw the drink bottle and began peering through the brown glass for another shot.

'Okay, Junie. I'm going.' Philomena looked questioningly at her friend who gave her a deep nod. 'You know where I am.'

'Yes,' said Junie. 'I know.'

Philomena closed the door behind her, and Gregory began to laugh.

'You know you can't trust that one, don't you? All fancy and fake. All lies, just like the rest of them.'

'I know,' said Junie. 'That's why I tell her to go.' She sat up with her back against the wall, her shoulder pressed to the dresser. 'I think I want to see that dance now. Can you show me how?' Junie's voice trembled, but she knew that in his current state, Gregory wouldn't notice. She knew it wasn't long before he passed out. Running had been a mistake, had only made him angry, but she would wait now. That's all she could do. She couldn't outrun him, but she could hope to wear him out.

Gregory picked himself up and began to totter around. He looked ridiculous. As her fear began to abate and her waiting game began, a hot fury started to rise in her stomach. *Two years*, she thought. *Two years of my life*. Gregory danced close to her, circling and knocking a side table off balance. *And I lost my baby*, she thought. *My baby*. Gregory shuffled his feet and wound his hips, moving closer still. She could see that he'd urinated in his trousers. *I hate you*. The second Gregory was near enough, she raised her feet so that they caught up in Gregory's legs. He lost his footing and began to fall. He was falling towards her and would crush her in the next moment. In a flash, Junie rolled aside and Gregory's full weight came crashing down. His head hit against the dresser with a hacking sound, his neck bending awkwardly before he collapsed in a heap beside her.

Silence filled the room. No laughter, no prancing like a fool. He lay still on the floor. Hate burned within her, anger at herself for thinking this stinking lump could ever make a good father. A good husband. Eventually, her pulse began to settle. She looked at his body, drunk, foul, unable to move an inch. She could walk away, and he couldn't catch her if he managed to wake. If he could wake.

'Gregory? Gregory?' She knelt beside him and touched his thick upper arm. She shook him; he was a motionless mass of clammy flesh. She saw that there was a shallow ticking on his neck. He was still alive. By now, she knew that when he drank himself unconscious, he could sleep through a hurricane. He wouldn't know anything until the morning.

Junie got to her feet. With her hands on her hips, she looked down at Gregory and spat on his face. She then rolled up her sleeves and grabbed hold of him by his ankles. She pulled him with all her might until she was finally able to drag him as far as the door. She opened the door wide and continued to drag Gregory out of the house. Philomena stood hovering by the front gate.

'What are you doing?' she whispered. 'Let's go. Junie, let's go.'

'Is Ma Scott inside?' Junie looked over her shoulder at Philomena as she puffed and wheezed after dragging Gregory's weight that far. It was as if the bulk had not mattered. Something else was driving her on to something she had to do.

'She's inside praying,' Philomena said urgently. 'What are you waiting for? You can get your bag. He won't wake up. Where you going with him?' She opened the gate.

'No Phil. You go away. Go home. *I* have to do this.'

'Do what? Where you going?' Philomena halted at Junie's command for just a breath before running down the path and grabbing one of Gregory's ankles. Then she helped Junie pull Gregory up to the toilet outhouse.

'You leaving him there to sleep it off?' Philomena asked.

'No, he going and use the toilet.' Junie opened the door.

'But Junie, he's passed out, he doesn't need…'

'Quiet.' Junie bent down to undo the front of Gregory's trousers and pulled them down to his thighs. 'Help me turn him over,' she whispered to Philomena.

'What?'

'Help if you're helping or go back home.'

By now, Gregory's body felt heavy to Junie and she knew she couldn't manage this on her own and she wished Philomena would just stop asking questions. They rolled Gregory face down and pulled him up from under his arms until his head and shoulders slumped on the toilet.

'Now go,' she told Philomena.

'Junie—I don't like this.'

'So go. Now.'

Philomena backed away but did not leave. Junie grabbed a handful of Gregory's thick hair in her fist. Unwittingly, Junie's face contorted into the expression she'd seen on Gregory's face the countless times he held her in a corner, trapped her, beat her until she was out cold. Then, with all the strength within her slight frame, fuelled with all the anger and remorse of the last two years, Junie slammed Gregory's head down onto the toilet bowl.

They both heard bone break and saw the toilet bowl fracture as blood spilled down its sides and out of the motionless Gregory.

'You think he dead?' Junie asked, but before Philomena could answer, Junie pulled Gregory up again by the hair, his neck limp as she brought his head down as heavily as she could. 'I think he dead now.'

Junie stood over Gregory and watched the blood, dark and shiny, leak from his body the way it had leaked from hers, every time he broke her skin. The time he punched her lower abdomen with all his might when she was pregnant and kicked her until he was satisfied the baby inside her would not survive. She had watched the blood spill then.

'Junie.' She thought she heard Philomena's voice. She wasn't sure. She didn't know anything else but to get his blood off her.

She stepped away without expression and walked with purpose back to the house. She pulled off everything she was wearing. Every item splattered with blood. She changed quickly into the old dress she had planned to leave behind and wrapped her bloody clothing in an old towel. She went outside to the barrel of water by the front door and scooped handfuls out to wash her face and hands. She was aware of Philomena, standing at her side, watching in silence. She covered the barrel with its lid.

'Get rid of these for me. I going now.' Junie looked down at the clothes bundled in the towel.

'Wait.' Philomena's voice was level, calm.

'I can't Phil—you see, I have to go.'

'Not yet. If you do, they will come after you. The police. They'll need to ask you questions. Ask us questions.' She pointed to her house. They'll come because it's their job, and they'll ask what happened and why you didn't call them. And you need to have an answer for them that you won't be ready for in a few days. When you realise what happened here tonight.'

'Phil, how can I stay? I—'

'No.' Philomena looked deep into Junie's eyes. 'I have an idea.'

36

Philomena ran back to her garden and into her house carrying the bundle of bloody clothes. Her mother's hands were held open in expectation of an explanation. Then she noticed what Philomena was holding.

'Take these and hide them well,' Philomena said, shoving the towel into her mother's hands. 'When I go, you go and fetch Junie and bring her here. Just sit here and wait for me to come back. Just do as I say and everything will be fine, Mum. Do you understand?'

Her mother nodded. 'But Phil, what happened in there? This is blood. Junie?'

'It's not hers.'

'You mean … him?'

Philomena blinked her eyes, once, slowly. 'And now I'm going to go to the police station.'

'What? No.'

'Mum, it's a crime scene. This is our story, and you must tell Junie to repeat this. He came back drunk. Junie was terrified, afraid to get in the car so we waited. He staggered out to go to the toilet but didn't come back to the house. I went out to check on him. Understand?'

'Yes, yes. But you need to wash up. You have blood on you.'

Philomena looked down at her clothes. Her cream blouse was dyed a pinkish colour. Blood had dripped onto her white tennis shoes. She changed all of her clothes. Her hands trembling, she washed them thoroughly and went to start the car. As the engine turned over, she saw Junie standing in her garden looking out across the plain as if she could see something. She drove down to the police station as fast as she could.

There was no one in the station, so Philomena stayed in her car and waited until first light. Walking idly along the narrow village street where she'd parked but had not slept all night, she saw a fat sergeant, a bunch of jangling keys in his hands as he approached the station door. He was eating a roll filled with ham.

'Teacher Scott? Is that you? You look like you sleep in your car.' He unlocked the door and invited her inside as he switched on the lights.

'Good morning Sergeant David. It's been a long night.' She let out a small laugh on a sigh. 'I didn't know you closed at night. I came here to report a death, and there was no one here.'

'A death?' The sergeant's eyes bulged, and he put his half-eaten roll on the counter. 'Not Mrs Scott? You should have gone to your doctor.'

'It's not Mum. It's my neighbour. Gregory Williams. He was drunk last night and…'

He picked up the roll and took another bite. 'I see, I see. Him again. You know he spent quite a few nights sleeping off the booze in here. Especially when he lose at gambling.'

'I wouldn't know. I only know I should come here to report it. His wife is all alone up there, and somebody needs to…'

'Yes, yes. I'll send someone as soon as I have an officer available.'

'Thank you, Sergeant'

'Of course. And thank you for doing your duty.'

Philomena gave a thin smile and a nod as she backed away to the door.

'We'll miss people like you and Head Teacher Mattherson when you go in America.' He had been at the wedding. Philomena had danced with Sergeant David. He was a good friend of Mrs Scott's from church. He winked at her before picking up the telephone.

Out in the morning air, Philomena could finally breathe. All night, her mind moved in circles as she wondered over and over if this could have been avoided, if right at the beginning she could have prevented this outcome. Gregory or Junie. She'd always had the feeling that it was going to be one of them, so why hadn't she been pro-active? Last night, even when Junie begged her to leave her alone with Gregory, she could have refused. Gregory was so drunk, what if she'd waited, bided her time just outside the door and seized a chance to help Junie to safety? Now Junie was going to have to live with his death over her head for the rest of her life.

Her hands began to shake again at the realisation that she was going to have a murder on her conscience, too. She looked at her hands, trying to will some calm into them so that she could start the car. In the crease between her forefinger and thumb was a tiny stain from Gregory's blood.

37

Philomena drove back to the houses on the plain, sighing long breaths, trying to settle her agitated heartbeat. If nothing else, she had to remain calm and indifferent when the police arrived. Gregory hadn't been anyone's favourite person, apart from the men he gambled with or drank with in the village. But then they were either after his money or just as bad natured as him to care how he treated his wife. It was his wife whom Philomena cared about now. She had to see this thing to the end, for Junie.

Philomena checked her rear view mirror. The police weren't racing along after her to get to the scene. The sergeant would rather finish his breakfast than get a forensics team up to the house for Gregory Williams. On that note, she didn't think the local police would be equipped to carry out a serious investigation and the details of last night might easily be seen as an unfortunate accident. That's what Junie had planned. She had planned it, Philomena thought. She'd probably thought this up a long time ago. A crime of passion or pre-meditated murder. Her analysing brain drummed loudly in her head. How would she explain to Saul that she was right there at the scene of the crime and that she didn't stop Junie? She would have to act nonchalant when he wanted to discuss it, keep from telling him the truth because that would only implicate him. The last thing she would tell him, as they sat trying to discuss the details over a pot of coffee, was how she helped drag an unconscious Gregory in the dark across the garden and into the toilet. She was just as guilty as Junie.

As she got closer to the house, she saw her mother standing outside. She was pacing, her arms folded.

'Why aren't you with Junie?' Philomena stepped out of the car and looked at the house. 'She is inside, isn't she?'

'Yes, but I can't get her to calm down. She keeps saying she must escape before it's too late. I don't know what to do with her.'

Philomena slowly mounted the veranda steps. Junie came rushing out.

'What did they say? Is someone coming?'

Philomena rubbed Junie's arms.

'Shh, shh. It's okay. I told you, everything will be fine. Running only makes you look guilty.'

'I am guilty. Do you know what I did?'

'You defended yourself, Junie. That's what you did. You saved yourself.'

'It's not my place to take a man's life because he did something bad. I could have just gone. You could have just drive me away, and I wouldn't have to see him any more.'

'What you did, you had to do, Junie. He drove you to this. He's the one to blame.'

'No, no, no, no, no.' Junie shook her head from side to side and paced the veranda up and down.

'Junie, you can't do this now,' Philomena pleaded and followed her to the other end of the veranda. 'Not now that I have the police coming.'

'I had hours to get away.'

'They would come looking for you. Listen to me, can't you see how it would look if you were suddenly not here? Believe me, it will be better this way.'

They turned to lean on the rail when they heard voices and footsteps coming along the road. They saw a number of locals walking up the hill, talking loudly and seeming to argue with each other.

Mrs Scott, touched Philomena's arm. 'The news is out, and they want to come and see for themselves. Can you believe that? Who else you tell?'

'Only the sergeant.' Philomena ran to Junie's gate and stood in front of it.

Seven of the village folk stood before her. This was news that didn't take long to spread in the village. It would be the talking point for months to come. Nothing could be more enticing than this. Death was the biggest story of all.

'Can I help you?' said Philomena.

'Oh, Teacher Scott, good morning,' one of the women said, grinning. She had no front teeth in her smile. 'I hear something unfortunate happen last night.'

'Yes, something did, and the police are on their way. You should get back home and wait until the official report of the accident.'

'An accident?' one man said from the back of the crowd. 'I hear he owe someone money, and they come up and kill him.'

The crowd erupted into outbursts of speculation, jostling and pushing each other to try to see over Philomena's shoulder. The body was well hidden from view. Philomena turned her attention to her veranda where both her mother and Junie leaned out to view the crowd. She raised both arms, clearing her throat as if she was at the front of the classroom.

'It's very good of you to come and pay your respects to Mr Williams' widow, but she is very upset, as you can imagine, and out of respect, I must ask that you go back to your homes and let the police come and do their job.'

As she said that, she heard the wheels of a car. The sergeant was being driven by a constable who looked far less interested than the crowd and who aggressively pushed people aside for the sergeant to get to the gate.

'Teacher Scott, you here again?' the sergeant asked.

'I was trying to keep them out.'

'I see, but don't worry, we're here now.' He looked at her for a second before Philomena realised that he wanted her to move aside.

As he entered, the group of people walked into the garden, too, and a few more had come up from the village and gathered at the front gate. Philomena watched as Sergeant David and his constable walked into the open doorway to Junie's house. They came out seconds later, Sergeant David's chubby hands swaying at his sides. He crooked a finger and beckoned Philomena over to the door.

'And where is the body? Also, where is the wife?'

'Oh, she was very upset, and I left her with my mother.'

'Please tell me where I can find him and go and call Mrs Williams, if you would.'

Philomena nodded. 'He's in the lavatory. He collapsed there, I think.' She turned and tried to make her way through the crowd of onlookers, whom she believed had doubled in numbers.

Junie stood at the front door of Philomena's house, mouthing the word, No, over and over.

Philomena whispered in her ear. 'You can do it, Junie. Think about how calm you were last night when you told me to leave you with him. Do that again. It's so important that you do. Come with me now.' She held Junie's hand and led her back through the people who cleared a path, staring at her, shaking their heads. *Poor thing, poor girl*, they said. They had certainly changed their attitudes. All they ever did was talk about her behind her back, thought Philomena, judge her and discuss her bruises. Not one of them had ever offered her a hand of friendship.

Philomena was still holding Junie's hand when they approached Sergeant David who was inside the small toilet, looking over the body. Mrs Scott wasn't far behind. The constable nodded when he saw the women. Junie placed her head onto Philomena's shoulder when the body of her husband came into view. Sergeant David walked the women back into the garden where the crowd had moved in even closer to the scene, some walking up to the front door and peering into the upturned living room.

'So, Mrs Williams. You spend the night next door at your neighbour?'

'Yes, Sir.'

'And Teacher Scott, you can verify this?' The sergeant was writing in his notebook.

'Yes, Sir. I don't know if you know, but Junie has been staying with me since coming out of hospital. You know she lost the child she was carrying?' Sergeant David coughed, he looked under his brow at Junie and then back at the notebook. 'Well, we came back yesterday, and Junie came in to say her goodbyes to Mum, collect her things. We had no idea what had become of Gregory, but we saw he wasn't home, so it was a good opportunity to leave.'

'I see,' he said, scribbling further.

'But Gregory came back, and Junie was trapped inside the house with us.'

'I was afraid, Sir.' Junie glanced up at David, her eyes doleful.

'Of course you were. So, how did you come across the body if you were too afraid to come out of the house? How did you know he'd fallen if you were at the Scott's? I don't believe you can see much in the dark from over that side.' He screwed his brow, and the women all looked at each other.

'We were all just waiting—I suppose,' said Mrs Scott. 'Waiting for him to fall asleep so that Phil could take Junie away.' She pointed to his notebook so that he could write it down.

'It was noisy next door, I think I heard something fall in the house. A chair or a table maybe,' said Philomena. 'Then he came out, falling around the yard. I can only assume it was to get to the toilet, and I suppose he must have fallen. Banged his head. You see, we waited and waited to see what he would do, but there was nothing. At first, I thought he'd fallen asleep there, and then I couldn't help myself, I thought something had happened to him, so I came out to see if he was all right.'

'So you were the one who found the body, Teacher Scott?'

'Yes, I think I said that when I came into the station.' All three women looked at his notebook. He screwed his brow, clicked his pen off and then on, and jotted something down.

'Look, Mrs Williams,' said Sergeant David. 'You go back by Teacher Scott, and we will take care of this. I need to try and get these people out. They ruining your garden. I'm sorry.'

Getting rid of the evidence. That's what the crowd was, un-wittingly, managing to do. Some had walked into the house before the police could stop them. Some had walked through the yard to the back where Gregory lay and gasped with their hands over their faces. But none of them, not even the police, had noticed the tracks his body had left when Gregory was being dragged out of the door, past the kitchen, along the side of the house and up to the toilet in the night. With their meddling, they had disguised any evidence that a crime had ever occurred. No matter how much they speculated over the events leading up to Gregory's death, they would never stumble upon the truth. The police seemed convinced this was an accident; all that was left to do was get a doctor to write a certificate and the whole tragic mess would be over.

Philomena squeezed Junie's shoulder as she walked her through the crowd. She spotted a truck had stopped outside the house. It was Vincent's truck, and she scouted the faces for him.

'Junie!' He stood in front of her and went to take her hands.

'We need to get her inside,' said Philomena. 'She's in shock.'

Vincent followed the women to the veranda. Junie kept looking over her shoulder at him as Philomena tried to usher her inside.

'Wait,' said Junie at the door. 'Could Vincent come in?'

'Of course,' said Mrs Scott.

Inside the house, Junie ran into Vincent's arms.

'What are all these people doing here? I was on my way to Pa's, and I saw the crowd. I was worried about you.' He rubbed her back.

'No need to worry, Vincent,' Philomena said. 'It was Gregory. Fell in the toilet, drunk, smashed his head open and ... and died.'

Vincent gasped and looked down at Junie.

'Were you hurt? Did he hurt you?'

'No, I was fine. I had Phil and Mrs Scott.'

'So he's really…? He's dead?' Vincent looked at the women one by one for confirmation. They all nodded, solemnly.

'And what are you going to do?' he asked Junie. Junie shrugged her shoulders. 'Do you need somewhere to stay for a while?' asked Vincent.

'She can stay here,' said Philomena.

'Phil, do you mind if I just go out and talk to Vincent for a moment?' Junie said in a small voice.

'Why should she?' said Mrs Scott. 'You go ahead, my dear. You must feel terrible.'

Philomena watched them leave the house. She noticed the protective way Vincent guided Junie with a hand at the small of her back and the demure way she looked up at him. They went out to the veranda at first, but as the police had successfully moved the villagers on, Junie led Vincent to the opposite side of the plain, across the dusty road to the grassland opposite. At the window, Philomena stood with her arms folded. Junie and Vincent were talking, their heads together. Furtive, she thought.

'What do you think they have to talk about?' Mrs Scott said. 'They make a nice couple, anyway.'

'Mum.' Philomena sounded exasperated. 'She just lost her husband.'

'She just killed her husband.' Mrs Scott's voice was dry and clipped. She sat on the couch and took out some knitting. 'My heart can't take this excitement. Phil, can you go and make us some tea?'

'Yes, Mum.' She gladly left the house but couldn't hear anything of what Junie was saying to Vincent. She appeared to be doing most of the talking.

'I'll come back up here with the doctor and arrange to have the body taken away.' Sergeant David's voice made Philomena jump.

'Sorry,' he said from outside Junie's gate. 'Didn't mean to startle you.' He looked over at Junie and Vincent. 'At least she has friends around her,' he said before getting into the car.

Eventually, Junie returned to the house and Vincent drove on to Pa Reynauld's. Philomena offered her tea, but she refused.

'What happens now?' asked Junie.

'You might need to sign something before they take the body,' Philomena replied. 'Do you want me to do it?'

'I can write my name,' said Junie wistfully. 'Pa taught me.'

'Oh?' said Philomena. 'That was good of him. So, what will you do after you've signed the papers, Junie?'

'I'm still leaving but maybe not quite yet.'

'Would you like me to drive you to your mother's? The offer is still there.'

'Thank you, Phil. That would be lovely. At the weekend? Saturday?'

'Of course,' said Phil. 'I'll get myself back to Saul's. He must be wondering where I am.' She took Junie's hands. 'I'll be back on Saturday morning, then. It's done now, Junie. You can get on with your life.'

Philomena wanted to say more. She wanted to make another attempt at persuading Junie to follow her and Saul out to New York, but this was the wrong time. She suspected Junie was still reeling, then on glancing at her before leaving for home, Philomena noted that Junie looked pleased with herself, content somehow. She wished she knew what she was thinking.

38

Philomena was exhausted. It felt as if her whole life had been lived out in the space of two days. Nothing that came before could have prepared her for the events of the last forty-eight hours. She couldn't tell if she'd lived them or dreamt them. But she was awake now and far from recovered.

She opened the windows in both the driver and passenger seats so that gusts of wind would whirl around her face, through her hair. She hoped the breeze would carry off the heaviness she felt in her mind and in her body, too. It was hard to make sense of what had happened, how she'd lied and how she would live a lie for always. She thought back on the individual minutes of those forty-eight hours and tried to find the slightest second within one of them when she had the power to turn things around.

She remembered Gregory's dog barking in the night, still yapping and echoing in her head. Was it trapped somewhere, waiting for Gregory to put it out of its misery? She hoped it was resting in peace, like Gregory. It wasn't that she liked Gregory or would ever miss him, but that he died was a step further than even her hate for him allowed. Her stomach churned, her thoughts weighed her down.

Philomena pulled over at the side of the country road, rushed across it and began to throw up into the long grass. The yellow petals of the wild flowers bent away from the sound of her heaving stomach, a clear fluid hurling itself

260

from her body. She stood with her hands on her knees, look-ing at how her deep sense of guilt had fouled something so beautiful as those flowers and the pale green reeds of grass. How cruel it seemed.

Slowly, she walked back to the car. She had left the door wide open; anyone could have driven into it, but no one came along the road. If someone had stopped, she might have been tempted to tell a perfect stranger what she'd been a party to. But then Junie would end up in prison, both she and her mother had helped in some way. She more than Mrs Scott, but she couldn't let her mother take any blame for this.

Philomena shivered as she got back to the car. Goose pim-ples formed on her skin, though she was sweating. She rubbed her arms and then looked at her face in the rear view mirror. She looked atrocious. Her breath must smell, too. She wished she had some water to drink. How would she cover this up when Saul asked her what the hell had hap-pened to her? She didn't relish having to brush him off with another lie, like the day of her wedding after her confronta-tion with Gregory when she'd told Saul she'd tripped in the dark, fallen and sullied her dress. The stains were still there. The worst things in life are the most indelible.

Continuing the long drive home, Philomena's mind turned to Junie. If she felt this bad for being complicit, then how must Junie feel? She'd watched closely the rainbow of emo-tional changes she'd witnessed in her friend. From fear to anger, from aggressor to nervous wreck. Lastly, she appeared serene. Rested, though neither had had any sleep. Junie had begun to smile right after speaking to Vincent. She had been ready to run before that. Make herself look guilty and try to escape. Philomena thought she'd made a good job of calming her down, but when Vincent spoke to her, she was like a new person.

The car juddered up the hill to Saul's house. She looked at the dials on the dashboard. They were nearly out of petrol; she could easily have been stranded, but she hadn't thought about anything but the murder. Just saying the word in her mind, murder, made her want to throw up all over again.

She switched off the car engine in a dreamlike state and stepped out of the car. She heard the front door open and footsteps approaching her.

'Phil?' The concern in Saul's voice made her weak, lose her balance. Her feet stuttered before her mind could control them to take a step forward, away from the car, to the house. She toppled into Saul who wrapped his arms around her and helped her walk. Her legs were not hers any more, she wasn't herself any more and she fell against him, crying hopelessly, clinging to the front of his shirt. He shushed her the way one would a restless baby, in the end lifting her off her feet and carrying her inside.

'The bath I ran for you must be cold now.' Saul sat in a chair at the side of the bed. He was smiling. He placed his hand on Philomena's arm and held tight.

'How long have you been sitting there?' Philomena asked. 'How long have I been asleep?'

It was growing dark outside. It must have been late afternoon, early evening.

Saul looked at his watch. 'It's almost six. So about five hours, I would say. But have you had enough sleep?'

Philomena nodded. She was still in her clothes. She had cried and cried, that she remembered. But she couldn't remember falling asleep or feeling Saul remove her shoes and cover her with a blanket.

'You know you talk in your sleep?' Saul leaned over the bed and smiled down at her.

Philomena crossed her brow. 'What did I say?'

'Nothing that I could understand. I thought you said my name. Which was nice. Given that I thought you'd run away from me. I was expecting you home yesterday. I've been worried.'

'Saul, I'm so sorry. It was Junie.'

Saul sat back in the chair and placed his hands in prayer between his thighs which were wide in the chair.

'Well,' said Philomena, easing herself up to sitting. 'It was Gregory. She couldn't get her things from the house because he was there and she was too frightened of him chasing after her that she couldn't leave the house. And when he … no, that wasn't it.' She had said this in a robotic way, but this was not the story they had given to the police.

'So, what is it? I mean, she up at her mother's house now?'

'Actually, no.'

'What? After all this time?'

'Saul, you don't understand. Gregory died last night. He staggered home drunk when we were planning to leave and must have, well, he fell and banged into the toilet bowl and … and then he died.'

Saul stood and rubbed a hand over the smooth curls of his hair. He turned to rest his hands on the back of the chair.

'So, she's not going by her mother?'

'She is, on Saturday, and … I offered to take her. Is it all right?'

'Yes, but I'm coming with you.'
'You don't have—'
'I said I'll come.'
'We need gas. It's almost empty.'

Saul left the room. She could sense his frustration. He never got angry, not with her. She'd never seen him cross with the children at school or raise his voice at anyone. Not even when a student was getting on his last nerve. He remained calm. Kept a clear head. She imagined he'd left the room because yet again there had been a drama and a situation that involved Junie. He held his tongue when Philomena talked about her, sat and planned Junie's life on her behalf, wished she could be a better friend to her. She had told Saul that she loved Junie as a sister and searched his expression for signs of jealousy. There had been none. Only a slight coolness in the way he'd got up, went to the dresser and asked if she'd like a shot of rum before dinner.

She heard him tinkering about in the next room. Most of their things had been shipped to New York. Not that there had been much to send. Just a large wooden crate of wedding presents, all their clothes and a small quantity of household goods. They had a small suitcase each to take on the boat to Antigua and then the ship from there to the American mainland. Philomena searched around for something to change into. She was aware of the smell of vomit oozing from her and the cloudiness of her brain, all of which she hoped to wash away in the shower.

When she walked into the living room after a long time in the bathroom, wearing fresh clothes and a towel wrapped around her hair like a turban, Saul had made dinner. She was starving but wasn't sure she could eat, or if she did, hold it down.

Saul touched her hand as it rested on the dining table.

'I'll be glad when we leave this place once and for all.' He smiled.

'A new start. A new life.' She smiled back then picked up her knife and fork, turned to her plate and slowly began to eat.

39

Saul stopped for petrol in town before setting off on the drive to collect Junie to drop her home to her mother. His and Philomena's journey to New York was scheduled for next week. Saul was giving the car to his brother who would be taking them on the first leg of their trip. There was a dinner planned for the couple: a farewell party at his in-laws. Philomena's mother would be there and her aunt. She had said most of her goodbyes to everyone who counted in her life. She anticipated a huge scene when she finally said goodbye to her mother. She had vowed, though, that she would not give up trying to get her mother to come out to live with them. She hoped that persuading her would only take a matter of time.

As they approached the two houses on the plain, Philomena noticed that there was a car parked on the side of the road and three men were stood beside it, deep in discussion. She recognised Sergeant David and the doctor from town, but she didn't know the third man. His police uniform was from the station in the capital, Roseau.

Saul jumped out of the car and nodded to the men before walking around to get the door for Philomena. 'I wonder what this is,' Saul whispered to her.

Philomena shook her head and stared at the men as she got out of the car. It was clear that Sergeant David wanted her to join them. There was no sign of Mrs Scott who would ordinarily have run out of the house on hearing Saul's car.

Philomena and Saul walked over to the men positioned outside Junie's house. Philomena glanced quickly at Junie's closed door. Why hadn't she come out, either?

'Sergeant,' said Philomena with a grave nod.

'Morning, Teacher Scott, Head Teacher Mattherson.' Sergeant David reached to shake Saul's hand.

'No need to be so formal,' said Saul. 'Please call me by my first name, we're no longer teachers here now. Soon off to America.' He chuckled. 'Besides, Phil is a Mattherson now, too.'

'Of course,' nodded the sergeant. 'You know Doctor Benoit, and this is Inspector Lake from the Roseau Constabulary. We had a bit of a problem winding up this case, Teacher … Mrs Mattherson.' He pointed his thumb at Junie's front door.

'Please just call me Philomena.'

'Well, Philomena,' David began as he pushed his peaked cap up off his brow and scratched his head, 'since I spoke to you last, a few questions have been raised and headquarters can't simply file this case away until we get some answers.' He took a quick sideways look at Inspector Lake.

'Of course,' said Philomena, crossing her arms and looking up at Saul who stood so close beside her she could feel his body breathing. His breaths were slow and measured, unlike her own. She looked at the inspector next. His face was stern, looking directly at her.

'You see,' David went on. 'When I came back up with the doctor, he was concerned about where Gregory's body lay. He didn't think the position of the body was consistent with a fall. Not even for a drunk man. The way his trousers were undone, another bruise on the side of his head, the bruising on his forehead where it supposedly hit the latrine.' He rubbed his head again and fixed his cap down further. He hadn't worn the cap when he'd come to investigate before. Now he spoke in English instead of patois, and his way of speaking had changed. 'And you say Junie was waiting to pack her things when you noticed Mr Williams came back drunk?'

'That's right. She was with us.'

'And she didn't leave the house without you noticing? Perhaps you and mother had gone to bed?'

The inspector cleared his throat.

'You see,' said Sergeant David. 'The constable who came up with me did notice a packed bag in the bedroom. It would indicate that Junie must have packed at some stage in the day. Was it before or after Gregory had his fall?'

Philomena looked up at Saul. She shrugged her shoulders with her arms still crossed. 'I don't remember her packing. I mean, Gregory might already have packed her things while she was at the hospital without her knowledge. Maybe he didn't expect her back.'

'Hmm,' said Sergeant David and rested his chin in his hand.

Inspector Lake cleared his throat again. 'We need someone who could spread some light on the situation. You see, there are inconsistencies in your story.'

'It's not a story. It's true. Everything I told you. I told you everything I know.'

Saul put his arm around Philomena. 'I hope you're not accusing my wife of lying, sir?'

'I'm not accusing anyone of anything. We just have to be sure that Mr Williams falling as you described is all there is to it.'

'Do you need a written statement?'asked Saul. 'Have you got one from Junie?'

'We would have taken her in to question her,' said Inspector Lake, 'but she appears to have left. Along with the packed bag.'

'What?' Philomena looked at the house again. She thought she'd sensed that the house was empty since Junie hadn't come to the gate to greet her. Her gaze dropped; a deep sense that those four walls would remain empty for a very long while made her shiver.

'And you haven't seen Junie?' asked David.

'No Sergeant. I have no idea where she is. We came to drive her to her mother's place.'

They all looked from one to the other.

'Could you give me the address?' Sergeant David asked.

'I don't know it. She was going to direct me.'

'Where did she live before?'

'Coulibistre, I believe, or was it Colihaut? I'm sorry, I really don't know exactly. I'm at a loss myself.'

It was true. She was at a loss. Philomena unravelled her crossed arms and immediately wrapped them across her chest again. They fell limply to her sides when she felt the inspector's eyes on her. Again, she looked up at Saul.

'Is there anything else we can help you with?' Saul asked the men.

'Well, if you're sure that's all you know,' said Inspector Lake, 'then I don't think there is much else we can do here.'

There was an uncomfortable round of nodding heads, half attempts to shake hands with the other before the three men retreated, climbed back into the car they'd arrived in and drove back down to the village.

Philomena turned to Saul. He was straight-faced. Out of the corner of her eye, Philomena could see her mother emerging from her house.

'I don't suppose you have anything else you want to tell me about this?' Saul looked into her eyes as though he were searching for something deep within her. In her soul, it felt. He didn't blink once. Philomena held his gaze then slowly shook her head.

'Nothing. Nothing else. We just need to find Junie.'

Saul spluttered the word, What, in disbelief. Philomena rushed to her mother.

'Is she here? Is Junie inside?'

'No, of course not. The girl gone. I didn't even see her go. We were talking yesterday, the next thing I know the police are knocking on my door asking when last I see her.'

'And what did you say?'

'I tell them the truth. Just like I tell you. Now, are you coming in?'

Philomena reluctantly went inside, Saul following behind. Philomena couldn't sit down, though her mother had invited them to have some tea and cake.

'No, Mum. I need to find Junie. I don't understand why she just took off when she knew I was going to drive her to her mother's.'

'Because she's a grown woman who has a mind of her own?' Saul barely looked up at Philomena who was pacing the living room.

'I know she has.'

'Well, stop trying to control her life.' There was agitation in Saul's voice. 'She's in some sort of trouble, Phil. You'll be gone from this in a week. Let it be. Just let her sort out her own mess, and don't implicate yourself.'

'I am implicated. I said I'd help her, and I will. I need your car.'

Saul stood up. 'Where are you going? Wherever it is, I'm going as well.'

'I don't think you should, Saul.'

'And I don't' think *you* should, but you're doing it anyway, aren't you?'

She bowed her head. Turning to her mother, she said, 'Mum, I'm sorry but I have to go.'

'But where?'

'First, up the way to Pa Reynauld's. Maybe Vincent knows something. They were talking a lot the day the police came. So maybe…'

'Take care of my daughter,' Mrs Scott said as they left the house.

Saul turned on the car radio on the short drive up to Pa's. Philomena had him slow down when they got as far as the allotments just so she could check to see if Pa or Junie were there. Surely the police would have been up and checked already. As she suspected, there was no sign of Junie. She directed Saul up the narrow road that became a path as it approached Pa's old house. She was relieved to see Vincent's truck parked in the front.

Philomena climbed out of the car and went to knock on Pa's door. Vincent opened it. He stood back, looking surprised to see Philomena and Saul standing there.

'Morning,' he said brightly. 'You come to visit Pa?'

'Good morning, I'm sorry to just drop by.'

'Hello!' Pa called with a cheery voice from inside. 'I never mind a visit from any woman brave enough to come up into the mountain. Come in, come in.'

Vincent stepped aside for them, opening his palm to welcome them inside.

'Pa, I'm so sorry to trouble you, but I actually came to ask after Junie.'

'Junie? What happen to my precious girl? It seems like a long time since I see her. Is she well?'

Philomena looked anxiously between Pa and Vincent. He had his eyes fixed on Pa and didn't acknowledge Philomena.

'As far as I know, she is. I saw her a few days ago. You know her husband died?'

'The boy did tell me, yes. I won't be shedding any tears. Don't suppose anyone will, mind you. All the same, it was her husband, though.'

'Yes, that's right,' Philomena said. 'But the police have been asking questions. They want to talk to Junie, but no one has seen her.' She was breathless. She turned to Vincent who shook his head and rested his gaze on the floor.

'I was supposed to take her back to her mother's house,' she said, eyes still on Vincent.

'Are you going to look for her there?' Pa asked.

'Possibly. But I know she used to visit here, so I just thought… '

'And she gone? She didn't leave a letter or something?' Pa eased himself forward in his chair and shook his head.

'I didn't check the house, but Junie could barely write.'

'She could write a little,' said Vincent.

Philomena snapped her head towards him. 'Oh?'

'Pa taught her.'

'And did she say anything to you about going anywhere?' Philomena moved towards Vincent.

'Not to me.'

'Nothing, then?'

'He already told you.' Saul stepped closer to her. 'Maybe we should allow these gentlemen to get on with their day.'

They made to leave the house, Vincent following and holding the door open.

'If you see her,' Pa said, raising his hand, 'tell my precious girl I would love to see her soon.'

'I will,' said Philomena and then followed Saul to the car. He started the engine without a word and turned the car in the small front drive before heading back down the bumpy lane to join the main road.

'He's lying,' said Philomena. 'Holding something back, I can tell.'

'Who?' said Saul. 'Pa? You heard him say he hadn't seen her. Why would he lie?'

'Not him. Vincent. I could see in his eyes that he knew something.' She turned to Saul. 'Why wouldn't she trust me? Why did she plan to leave and not let me know? We'll have to check the house. Maybe she did leave me a message. Now I know she can write.' She folded her arms and sat back in the seat. The unsteady movement of the car on rocky terrain made her body bump and roll from side to side.

'You sound annoyed that Junie can write,' Saul said as they approached the two houses. 'I thought you wanted her to improve herself.'

'I do.'

'Well, it sounds like she's done more than that.' He stopped the car.

Mrs Scott was on the veranda, calling. 'Any news?'

Philomena shook her head and went straight to Junie's house. With Saul behind her, she shoved open the unlocked door and went inside. Just inside the door, she looked around for evidence of a note from Junie.

'Should we be entering a crime scene?' Saul asked, also looking around the house.

'It's not a crime scene. It was an accident. Help me find a letter.'

Junie had tidied the house, put the fallen furniture back in place, just the way she would do after one of Gregory's outbursts of violence. Philomena could remember the state of the house since that night, how it looked through the open door when Junie was dragging Gregory out. She hadn't been back inside the house since Junie told her to leave and that she would deal with Gregory. A shiver ran down her spine as she remembered thinking that night, after closing the door behind her, that she might never see her friend alive again.

'There's nothing here, Phil. No letter. She's taken her things and gone.'

'Well, someone must have helped her. She couldn't have carried all her things on her back to her mother's. Vincent was a part of her plan. I'm sure.'

'Are you sure Vincent is the only person she knows with transport?'

Philomena thought for a moment. The most obvious person to have helped Junie leave had been Vincent. He could have driven Junie to her mother's house. Driven her anywhere, in fact. She only wished she knew where. She at least wanted to know Junie was safe before she left for New York. Then something came back to her. A quick flash of memory from the day she and Saul picked Junie up from the hospital. The pregnant woman, Josephine. The seamstress who made Philomena's wedding dress. She had slipped a piece of paper to Junie, and Junie hadn't mentioned anything about it to Philomena. She wished now that she'd quizzed her, but the fact that Junie never brought it up again meant that she wanted to hide something from her. Was Josephine Dennis Junie's secret accomplice?

She laughed at how ridiculous she sounded in her own mind. As Saul said, Junie was a grown woman. She could come and go as she pleased. Yet, still. Philomena could not let this mystery go. She had to know. She had to find Junie. See her one last time.

40

Philomena had met Josephine Dennis' husband once before. It was the day she had her measurements taken for her dress. James had been out working on the front garden as he was when Philomena and Saul approached the blue wooden house that the Dennis' owned. They parked their car on the grassy verge just along from the house. James straightened up when he saw them.

'Afternoon,' James said with a smile.

'Hello, Mr Dennis. I don't know if you remember me. Your wife made my wedding dress, and I just wanted to ask her a question.'

'You getting married again?' James joked.

Philomena laughed. 'This is my husband, Saul, and no, just the one husband will do for me.' The men shook hands. 'Is she home?'

'She will be very soon. She was at my mother's house.'

It was just seconds later that Josephine arrived, her stomach bulging, her pace heavy.

'Oh,' Josephine exclaimed and waved at the couple in her front garden. 'Nice to see you again.'

'Good afternoon, Josephine. I'm so sorry to bother you, but I'm looking for my friend. You know her. Junie?'

Josephine's broad smile closed. She looked furtively, or so Philomena thought, at her husband, James, who carried on with his labouring in the yard, this time a little way away from the group.

'Junie?' Josephine repeated.

'Yes, I was up at her house to take her up to her mother and found she'd gone. No one knows where. I'm really worried, you see? She just lost her husband, and she's probably in a fragile way. I just wanted to know she's all right so I can stop worrying.'

'Why you think she not all right?' Josephine's eyes darted to the front window of the house. Philomena's eyes followed hers.

'Well, it was a shock, her husband's accident. And some people don't cope very well. I'm sorry Josephine, but could I trouble you for some water? It's a long drive up here.'

'Of course. Excuse me. I'm coming just now.' Josephine walked as quickly as she could to the house, rubbing her back. Philomena hesitated, wondering if she should follow Josephine inside, but Saul signalled for her not to. In a few seconds, Philomena became restless and walked towards the front door. Just as she stretched out her hand to push the door, Josephine appeared with a tall glass of water.

'Here,' she said. Philomena drank slowly, her eyes on the small opening of the door. She couldn't see anyone inside, but if Junie was in there, she might be hiding.

'Thank you,' said Philomena, handing Josephine the empty glass.

'You're welcome. And how was the wedding?'

'Oh, we had a wonderful day, thank you. It was perfect, just like the dress.'

They exchanged smiles. Josephine held onto the glass.

'So then, you haven't seen her since the hospital?' Philomena asked.

'The hospital?'

'Yes, I saw you there, talking to Junie. You looked as if you were up to something.' Philomena chuckled and tapped Josephine's hand.

'To be honest, I never really knew Junie.' Josephine fiddled with the small gold crucifix around her neck. 'I saw a girl in trouble. A girl with sadness in her eyes, and I offered to pray with her one day. I hope wherever she is she finds God in her life. Especially now.'

'Now?'

'Yes, she's a young widow. She has to start her life all over again.'

Philomena nodded. 'Well, I won't waste more of your time. Thank you, Josephine.'

They waved to James as they left the gate. Philomena gave one last look over her shoulder and saw Josephine entering the house and closing the door.

'Don't tell me. You think she's lying, too,' Saul said playfully as they walked back to the car.

'Not lying exactly. Protecting perhaps.'

'Protecting Junie? From what?'

'Whatever she thinks Junie needs protecting from. You know what these religious women are like.'

'No, I don't. I only know I'm starving and I want to go home. Are we finished now?'

Philomena turned to him, her eyes pleading. 'One more place, Saul. Just one and then I'll give up.'

'Just one.'

They drove all the way to La Plaine without stopping. Saul's back was soaked through, and he kept wiping sweat from his brow. He hadn't said very much but kept the radio on. The music, the crackling reception when they were out of range of the main radio station helped to fill the enduring lack of conversation.

When they arrived in La Plaine, Philomena couldn't remember if Junie ever told her what her maiden name was. She felt foolish, now, with Saul looking at the side of her face, waiting for her to tell him what they were going to do next. She stared through the windscreen, not really observing the village in front of her, instead she was listening to a little voice in her head that was telling her that this was a mistake. That if Junie came back at her mother's house by herself, then perhaps that's the way she'd wanted things. Doing everything for herself, without Philomena, finding her independence. But Junie had clearly taken Vincent and Josephine into her confidence. Why not her? Was it because of the kiss? Philomena was tying herself up in knots. She couldn't second-guess Junie's actions or her motives. She just needed the truth, and only Junie could give her that. Philomena stepped out of the car. Saul, who already had his door open to get some air, stepped out and slammed the door shut.

'Do you mind telling me where we're going?' he said, following her as she walked along a wooden walkway outside a small row of battered shops. There was music coming from one of them, the smell of salt fish drifting out of another.

'I already told you,' said Philomena. 'Her mother's house.'

'But you don't know where that is, do you?'

Philomena shook her head.

'Then wait.' Saul pulled her by her arm and drew her to face him. 'Why don't you ask someone, or were you just planning on knocking on every door in the entire village?'

'No, of course not. No, I...' She looked helplessly up and down the street. 'I was going to ask in here.' Philomena walked back to the shop smelling of salt fish, straight up to the counter.

'Good afternoon. Good afternoon, Madam.'

A woman who sat on a dining room chair behind the counter of the grocery store put down the large fan in her hand and looked at Philomena. An electric fan was on right beside her. It was enormous and whirred loudly, making the corners of the paper carrier bags in a pile on the counter flutter. She returned Philomena's greeting, but it was barely audible. Philomena moved along the counter to speak to the shop owner who was clearly not going to budge. Philomena noticed that the woman's dress was partly unzipped at the back. Her upper arms seemed too heavy for the lower parts, rolls of fat hanging from her elbows. Her face was bloated, her eyes milky and it was hard to determine her age.

'I'm sorry if this sounds funny…' Philomena searched the woman's face for a response. 'But I'm looking for a friend of mine who used to live here a couple of years ago. Her name is Junie, and her married name is Williams. A young girl, pretty. Do you know the one I mean?' Philomena's grin hurt her face. The woman raised her eyebrows and chin simultaneously. Philomena took that to mean yes. 'And by any chance, is she back here? I was trying to find her mother's house. Would you happen to know where that is?' She could feel Saul stepping from one foot to the other, and she wished he would stop. The woman might become suspicious and not give her the information.

'You know the river up there?' The woman laboured to lift her arm. Philomena looked in the direction she was pointing. 'Just follow it.'

'Oh, okay. Should I walk, or should I take the car?'

'Your car cannot pass there. Is best you walk.' She picked up her fan, waved it back and forth in front of her face and continued to stare out of the shop window as if she were in a daze.

Philomena took Saul's hand and hurried him up the road, hoping to find the river the woman had pointed towards. There was a turning not far up from the wooden walkway. A grassy path with trees whose branches grew over it in an arch seemed to point the way to the river. They walked along the overgrown path until they were beside a green river. It was narrow and smelt of leaves or some kind of tea, something her mother would brew. A little further along, Philomena spotted a house. It was ramshackle with sections of it looking as if they had been built on as an afterthought. Corrugated iron along most of the roof.

'Do you think this is Junie's house?'

Saul shrugged. A pair of small dogs came yapping up to them, making so much noise as they jumped and danced around their ankles to disturb the tranquillity of the setting.

'Tad and Bebe, warn yourself!' A woman's angry voice rang into the throng of barks and yelps. 'I tired of telling you.' Just then, a woman with light brown skin came into view, appearing from the side of the house. She clapped her hands at the dogs, and they ran towards her. 'Mash!' she yelled at them, and they obediently quietened down and ran off through an opening in a nearby hedge.

'What you want?' the woman asked, tilting her chin at Philomena. 'Why you don't use the front door?'

'I'm so sorry.' Philomena approached her. 'The lady at the shop sent us this way.'

The woman tutted as though this wasn't the first time it had happened. 'Well?' She looked further annoyed.

Philomena stared at the woman for a second or two longer. She could see Junie's large eyes in this woman's face, though hers looked tired and heavy-lidded. She had the same heart-shaped lips as Junie, though chapped and unsmiling.

'You want me to stand up here whole day?' The woman was about to turn away.

'I'm looking for Junie.'

The woman stopped in her tracks. 'What for?'

'Not for anything, I was just paying a visit. She's my friend.'

'That worthless girl has friends?' She looked Philomena up and down and then Saul in turn. 'Friends who have money, fancy clothes and nice shoes?'

'Junie lives, lived next door to me. She came there with her husband, Gregory.'

The woman kissed her teeth. 'That son of a… She not here. I told her not to ever come back if she take up with that crook. That criminal.'

'So, she didn't come by here in the last few days?'

'What would she want to do that for?' The dogs came back, running through the hedge, barking as loudly as before, chasing each other. 'I said *mash*!' This time Junie's mother swung a foot and hit one of the small dogs square in its jaw. Both dogs scampered past Philomena and Saul and ran up the river. 'Look, lady. I haven't seen that girl or that man since their so-called wedding. I haven't got time for her, and she haven't got time for me. Simple as that. Anything else?' She rested her fists on her hips.

'No, no, that's all. But thank you. Good day.'

'And good day to you.' She turned her back but had second thoughts. 'So why you looking for her? She steal something? She do something?'

'No, Junie didn't do anything. You have a very lovely daughter. She's a good person.' Philomena turned as did Saul, and she followed him back along the river path they'd just come from. They could hear the dogs barking from somewhere among the river bank foliage even after they'd joined the road and were walking back to the car.

Saul didn't start the car straight away. The two of them sat, deflated and pensive.

'Well, I suppose that's it.' Philomena sighed, her eyes warm with tears. 'Junie's gone. And I don't know where.'

Finally, Saul started the car. 'I'm sorry, Phil.'

'Saul, thank you for doing this. It means a lot. I'm sorry.' She sniffed and rubbed the rims of her eyes. 'Should we go home?'

'Ours or your mum's?'

'I suppose we ought to let her know what happened.'

'Come on.'

It was with low spirits that Philomena sat and ate with her mother and reported back their findings. Or lack of them. Mrs Scott speculated that the girl was having a secret affair with Vincent and didn't want people to know as it was so soon after her husband died. People might think Vincent had something to do with it. Philomena supposed it was a possibility but why the need to hide that from her?

They set off for home after an early dinner. They had gone but a few minutes along the road before Philomena asked Saul if he could pull over one last time.

'What is it?'

'I want to say goodbye to the river. We won't be back here before we go. I just wanted one last look.'

'For Junie?'

'No, not for Junie, I accept that she's gone.'

The sun would be setting soon. There was just enough light left to see their way to the river. They walked to the rock where Philomena sat and read to Junie. Where they laid out their clothes to dry while Philomena combed Junie's unruly hair. Where they told each other their dreams, and from where Philomena looked at Junie swimming in the river, wishing that they could have a different kind of life. The whitewood tree looked down on them, and they sat quietly tracing the gentle ripples in the water. They listened to the whistle of tiny birds who fluttered through the many branches and heard the rushing of waves far down the river where it ran fast and wild and out to a distant blue sea.

Philomena squeezed Saul's hand. She smiled at him; he returned a smile with ease, folding his hand around hers.

'You still don't understand, do you?' he said in a soft tone.

'Understand what?'

'Why Junie went and didn't tell you.'

'I'll never understand. I thought we were friends. Best friends.'

'And you are. That's why she couldn't tell you. You know too much already. More than I know you will ever tell me. The police came back because there is a lot of suspicion over Gregory's death. More than either of you told them. She knew; she worked out that they would have more questions and so she had to go. And she didn't tell you because if they asked you, you would tell them the truth, and that is that you don't know where Junie is. All you need to know is that she is somewhere they won't find her. If you can't find her then neither can they, and that's the best outcome for your friend.'

'But Saul…'

He shook his head. 'I know you're hurt. But that will pass. You'll learn to live without her in your life, just as she will you.' He put his arms around her and drew her close. Philomena sobbed into his shoulder. She felt the energy drain from her. She felt Junie walk away from her and knew she would never see her again. She had left Philomena with just these memories: the ones by the river. The good times when their friendship was the happiest it could be. When Junie sang and splashed in the river, when Philomena laughed and taught her to read.

She put her hand on her heart as though she could fix her memories there. She looked into Saul's eyes and told him, without words, that it was time to go home. With a man who loved her. The man she would cherish for the rest of her life. And she loved him all the more.

After

Winter was an assault on my body for more years than I cared to imagine. I begged Saul to find a job somewhere south. Florida. Texas. Anywhere where the sun always shone, the way it did at home. I never thought I'd ever adjust, but I have. A blanket of white covers the entirety of Central Park as I carefully walk through trying to keep my balance while my hands are wedged deeply into my pockets.

I've just finished tutoring Tommy Fitzpatrick. His parents are rich, and they can afford the extra tuition after school. Tommy is slow, very slow when it comes to English Literature, but I've helped him a lot. He doesn't appreciate it, though. He'd much prefer to be out playing football with his friends. But he'll never get to college with his current grades, and all the Fitzpatrick children have gone to Harvard, like their father.

It's not far to go now, nearly dark. I'm used to the streets by the apartment. I used to find them loud and wild. The Puerto Ricans blared boleros and mambo music from their bodegas, the black boys bellowed conversations at each other and looked me up and down because of the way I dressed back then. Now the young boys on the street step aside and call me Ma'am. I suppose at fifty-five I look like a Ma'am to them. Though I still feel like the young teacher in her twenties who embarked on a new life across the sea. I have learnt so much about life since then.

When I turn the key, I hear Martha and Sam arguing about something. Sam is back from college and will be off to London to study a PhD. He separated from the girl he met in college. Amanda. A white girl. Who would have thought? I will miss him. I think that's why he moved back, albeit temporarily, so I could have him close until it's time for him to leave. I'm sure Saul engineered that in some way. But all Sam ever does is annoy his younger sister.

Martha kisses me as I walk into the hallway. She helps me off with my rucksack and my coat.

'I hate your son,' she says.

'You'll miss him when he's gone.'

I slip my boots off and Mum comes out of the kitchen.

'Food's on the table. You look tired.'

'Thanks Mum,' I say and tut. Mum still speaks patois, much to the children's annoyance. Mum moved here after I'd found her a small apartment of her own, ten years ago. She finally realised that old age and that walk up from the village to a lonely house was more than she could handle, and here she is. A beautiful hot meal on the table, just as Saul comes home, too.

Saul had been right about me learning to live without Junie in time, but I still think about her. Hoping that wherever she went she's as happy as I am.

Time changes many things. But it could never change my time with Junie, all the days we had as friends, everything we shared together. It was a long time ago, and yet, I remember Junie as though we had just had lunch together that afternoon or bathed in the river that same morning. I hear her voice as clearly as I hear my own children's, and I see her face every time I look into a clear blue sky.

Saul wonders what I dream about when I disappear into my own thoughts once in a while, or stare out across the city towards Central Park. But if he really thought about it, he'd know that I could never forget her completely. He thinks that the poems I write, or at least some of them, are about him. Maybe some of them are. But mostly—in my poems—I'm remembering my friend. Junie Williams.

29 Years Earlier

Vincent parked his truck where he'd promised he would, just before the bend in the road, just before anything or anyone coming up the hill from the village could be seen by anyone on the plain. At that time of night, it was so still and quiet, an engine might be heard, and Junie had to take a chance that Mrs Scott would be fast asleep. She'd spent most of the day with Ma Scott, listening to her talk about what Junie's life could be now that she didn't have that man dragging her down.

That man, whom Junie would have preferred not to have to talk about, was gone now. She had seen his hand when they took him away. A large, dusty and bloody fist that slipped out from under the plastic sheet covering his body as they lifted it out of the toilet and carried it away on a stretcher. Someone had asked if she'd wanted to say anything before they took him, and she'd shaken her head in such a way that they must have thought her desperately upset by her loss, so they'd hurried out of the yard, and that's when his hand flew out. One last angry gesture, aimed at her, as if she could ever forget any of them.

She closed the door like a whisper, looking up at the Scott house before leaving her gate. She'd made sure the bolt wasn't on since coming back from visiting Ma Scott earlier. It was all she could do to stop herself hugging that kind and warm woman, who had been more like a mother to her than her own had ever been. It was Ma Scott who had gone to her wardrobe to retrieve Junie's lovely blue silk dress and the shoes she'd worn to Phil's wedding, saying, 'Here, no need to hide these here now.' Junie had wondered how to ask for the dress without revealing her plan to pack everything she had and run away before the police returned with more questions. Before leaving the house, she'd contemplated wearing the dress for when she met Vincent, but it was a dress for celebrating in, and she was sure that one day she would have something wonderful to celebrate.

'I didn't hear the truck,' Junie said as she handed Vincent her bag and jumped into the passenger seat.

'I did my best.' Vincent squinted into the night through the windscreen. 'You sure Mrs Scott will be asleep?'

'Positive. She's a very sound sleeper, and we had a little rum after dinner.'

Vincent started the engine and turned the truck in the narrow road and drove back towards the village.

Dark shadows floated past the truck, a soft whisper of breeze brushing Junie's brow through the open window and the silence of the night making her feel drowsy. Junie looked at Vincent who turned and smiled at her.

'Thank you,' she said. It wasn't the first time she'd thanked him for what he was doing. They'd talked about it, the morning after the murder, after the police had been called, after half the village had ended up in her garden, trampling what was left of her beautiful flowers. Vincent had helped her forget about the state of the garden as he discussed finding her a safe haven where she could lie low until the circumstances surrounding Gregory's death had died down. He'd known, straight away, that they would see through Philomena's story. It wasn't sound enough, they were bound to ask more questions. Junie couldn't plead self-defence, and Philomena would be in trouble, too. It had all made sense to her. She knew, without Vincent having to spell it out, that they would be back to interrogate her. And he'd been right.

She had agreed that it was best to run as soon as she realised that her friend might be arrested. Philomena had done too much for her; she loved her too much to allow that to happen.

'Promise me,' Junie had said that day on the plain. 'Promise not to even say a word to Pa. Just tell him I love him and I will always remember his kindness. I wish I could say goodbye myself. I wish I could tell her...'

Vincent parked his truck at the back of his house. He carried Junie's bag, and she followed him inside. There were two other houses built close to the hillside Vincent's large house was built on. In the daytime, she would have to be very careful not to use the back rooms and to stay inside because his house could be seen, though from quite a distance, by at least one of the other houses. In a few days, the sum of money that Vincent was to withdraw for Junie would be available and the plan for her to leave Dominica would be set in order.

It was lonely in Vincent's house when he was out at work. He couldn't afford not to go, and Junie wouldn't hear of it because she knew it was important to keep up the facade. On the Saturday evening, Vincent looked worried when he came home.

'What is it?' she said. Junie's smile sank when she saw his face.

'It's your friend, Philomena. She was looking for you.'

'You didn't say anything.'

'Of course not. I never would. But she knows I have something to do with it, that I know where you are.'

'Phil is smart. Very smart. What if she comes here?'

'I hope not. It's harder to lie than I thought, but one thing is for sure, the police have closed the case. You're free, Junie. They won't be looking for you.'

'Then it's time.'

Vincent held both her hands, tightly. They stood just inside the front door, hearts beating intensely. There was no need for words, but Vincent couldn't hold his in.

'I want you to stay. Stay with me. I love you, Junie.'

'I know.' Junie pulled away and threw herself onto the sofa by the open window. The sky was fading to indigo, and crickets had begun to hum outside. With heavy feet, Vincent followed her, sat beside her. His eyes never leaving hers. This time she took his hand. 'But I need this. I need to go, and I need to start my life again. I can't just carry on here. Carry on as if nothing before mattered, that it didn't happen. I need a new start. I don't know who I am, Vincent. A daughter, a wife, a liar, a killer? How will I ever know?'

'But so far away. You're going so far away. All alone.'

'I won't be alone. I have the address Josephine gave me. I know where to go and what to do. You taught me everything I need to know. One day, I'll send back every dollar I borrowed from you.'

Vincent shook his head.

'I will. I am going to. And Vincent.' She tilted his chin upwards. 'I will never forget you. And I love you, too. Always.'

Junie was glad she had taken Josephine's advice about what to wear on the ship. It wasn't the occasion for the blue dress, there was still time for that, still time for a celebration, she hoped. The journey lasted days, all of them blending into the other like an interminable dream of blue turning into grey turning into white. Of waves and waves of water, never ending, never relenting and never becoming calm, like the knots in her stomach. Until one afternoon, she saw dark rocks in the distance, the images of grey and brick and steel and the unfamiliar getting closer and closer. Fear overwhelmed her. She hadn't known what to expect, and she wasn't sure if this was the right place. But it had to be.

Junie's feet took her to the viewing deck, along with several other of the passengers. The ship hooted loudly and another from the mainland was returned.

'Is this the place?' she said in a whisper.

'This is it, love,' came a voice. 'This is England.'

Thank you for choosing

A Prayer For Junie

I really hope you enjoyed it. Your thoughts mean the world to me, and I'd love to hear what you think. If you have a moment, please consider leaving a review—it makes such a difference in helping new readers discover the book.

You can share your review at your preferred retailer.

I also love connecting with readers on social media, so please do follow my journey and say hello on Instagram and TikTok. @franclarkauthor

Thanks so much for your support!

Fran x

Now read the next book in the Island Secrets Series: *The Long Way Home*

Connect: Hop onto my ***website*** for links & info!
franclarkauthor.co.uk

And: Join my ***mailing list*** for a Free Read! And be ahead of all my offers, news and updates!

Also by Fran Clark

Lovers

Other books in The Island Secrets series:

Holding Paradise

The Long Way Home

When Skies Are Grey

The Hope series:

Wherever You Will Go

However Far We Fall

About the author

Fran Clark is an author of emotive women's fiction, whose stories are deeply rooted in the connection between London and the Caribbean. Born to Dominican parents and raised in West London, her work explores themes of identity, resilience, and the strength of women—often inspired by the vibrant storytelling of her mother.

Her first novel, *Holding Paradise*, was published in 2014 and later reimagined as the first in the *Island Secrets Series*. Fran holds an MA in Creative Writing from Brunel University and lives in the English countryside, where she teaches vocals and leads a local choir.

She also writes contemporary fiction under the pen name Rosa Temple.